Sophie Gravia grew up in a town just outside Glasgow and has always had a love for the English language. At a young age, she found herself writing funny stories or poems to friends and family for special occasions, and after high school she undertook a performing arts diploma, flourishing in her creative writing class. Sophie now works full time as a nurse in a busy city hospital.

In 2020, Sophie started writing again as a distraction from the ongoing pandemic, cheered on by fans of her hilarious blog, 'Sex in the Glasgow City'. *A Glasgow Kiss*, her debut novel, shot straight to number one in the erotic charts and has been a word-of-mouth sensation ever since.

SOPHIE GRAVIA

Meet Me in Milan

x

ORION

First published in Great Britain in 2023 by Orion Books,
an imprint of The Orion Publishing Group Ltd
Carmelite House, 50 Victoria Embankment
London EC4Y 0DZ

An Hachette UK Company

3 5 7 9 10 8 6 4 2

A CIP catalogue record for this book is
available from the British Library.

ISBN (Mass Market Paperback) 978 1 3987 1569 1
ISBN (eBook) 978 1 3987 1570 7

Typeset by Born Group
Printed and bound in Great Britain by Clays Ltd, Elcograf S.p.A.

MIX
Paper from
responsible sources
FSC® C104740

www.orionbooks.co.uk

When writing my third instalment of Zara's escapades, it occurred to me that my books may be less about trying to find love, and more about the unwavering bond of friendship. Love is love, and a life without a man is most certainly manageable. A life without a friend is just unthinkable.

This book is dedicated to all my friends,
I love you all,
Sophie x

Chapter One

Twenty glorious weeks, two fantastic days, and nearly twelve perfect hours have passed since Andy and I became official, and things are, well . . . pretty incredible. Who'd have thought that me, Zara Smith, would bag herself one of the most handsome, funny, sexy, down-to-earth guys in the city? Our whirlwind never seems to cease – it's an endless string of late-night sexy texts, romantic walks, weekend trips, compliments, and family dinners together. But my God, whoever said being baw deep in a relationship was easy is talking absolute shite. I had to make some severe sacrifices to get where we are today, like purchasing more razors than Sweeney Todd, changing my bedding far more regularly than I like to just in case my fake tan silhouette is being judged, and I have even had to swap my go-to discoloured-crotch cotton comfies for lacy, glittery thongs, which basically signed the fucking prescription for a guaranteed yeast infection and a bad bout of bacterial vaginosis.

But it's not just the sacrifices, it's also the sheer amount of time you need to invest in the fuckers. I mean, surely I'm not the only one who finds it challenging to stay on top of their own personal hygiene after factoring in everything else? There's housework, actual work, date nights, getting ready for date nights, as well as finding time to have a social life and exercise. I am now continuously on high alert *just in case* my sweet boyfriend decides to pop by. Never mind dealing with the impossible task of watching my weight whilst I'm getting carted off to cinema dates, drinks and dinner in town, pancakes for breakfast or *Harry Potter* marathons with a Bargain Bucket and dip. It's a downright impossible task that I think only men have figured out so far. For now, I'm pretty confident Andy will see a few extra pounds as some extra cushion for the pushin' and not bat an eye. And as romantic and exciting as the first couple of months of a relationship are, I'm looking forward to the onesie, top knot, curry-stained Oodie and granny-pants phase to commence and for my anxiety levels to simmer down.

After years of obsessing and borderline stalking any man that so much as gestured for me to cross in front of their car on a busy road – wondering in bed at night if they were trying to flirt or just save me from being knocked down by an angry Uber driver – I finally seem to have found the one and with not a hint of a red flag in sight. I mean, don't get me wrong, there have certainly been some things I've had to adapt to, like the way Andy chews his food so loudly that my fists clench and rattle with resentment. Or the way he sings, like proper tries to serenade me, all the while staring into my eyes for admiration. I pretend to smile but inside

I'm desperately trying to keep down my spicy chicken wings. Oh, and there is, of course, the teeny tiny issue I have in that I'm highly allergic to his dog, Tyson.

Despite this, a few months ago, any one of these minor matters would have resulted in me running for the Campsies. Still, with a pocket laced with antihistamines and a new drug habit developing with weekly visits to the chemist because of his furry friend, I've learned not only to cope with his quirks but find them kind of cute.

My best friend Ashley has thoroughly kissed and made up with her lovely boyfriend, Dave. Since reuniting, she moved back into their flat, and they seem happier than ever. She's still my right-hand woman at the clinic and marketing the life out of my brand. As a result, Individualise is booming. I have a waiting list of clients, and my concept of individualising aesthetics has taken off all over the city. I've been teaching the basics to other clinics and have even taken on two new practitioners from Botox Boxx, Lisa and Olivia. The girls bring a young, hip, trendy vibe to the clinic, specialising in piercings, microblading and laser hair removal. My ex, Tom, is still working hard here too. He's embracing his new teaching role with the new starts, and, as always, the clients treasure his charming, handsome self. He seems genuinely happy for Andy and me, checking in and engaging in some form of bromance with him since Raj left, and to be honest our friendship is great. We have a great laugh together and I treasure our platonic set-up, no more analysing his smirks and flirty behaviour, just friendly patter and lots of work talk. Tom and Raj are getting on better than ever, although I can tell they are both missing one another as Raj continues to live it up in Dubai. Huge things are happening with pop-up aesthetic shops over there. His face is becoming very recognisable in aesthetics and other cosmetic surgeries, which is his speciality. I find us talking more now than we did when he was at home – he's constantly checking that I've paid the clinic bills and the staff wages and completed the mound of admin work I now have to oversee. Deep down, I think he misses the banter and bustle of the clinic, but the Middle Eastern lifestyle has ultimately won him and his family over.

All in all, my life seems to be *finally* following the stereotypical course of action. Knowing I have the job, the friends and now a handsome, trustworthy man by my side, I don't know what more I could possibly ask for. Just finding that one man to have in my corner, someone supportive to chat to, who wants to be with *me* is a welcome relief. I don't have that dreaded anxiety whenever Andy's phone pings that he might be messaging someone else or crazily wondering if he'd rather be with strangers walking past us in the street. He is the confidence boost I needed. Even if his fucking dog is killing me slowly and the medication is causing me to sleep ninety per cent of the day away when I'm with him, I am simply head over heels, and every single thing in my life is going exactly to plan.

Ping.

I glanced down at the new Apple Watch I'd purchased on a whim to get healthy.

Reminder: Lunch with Jason at 1 p.m.

Shit, I almost forgot about that today. I hadn't seen my friend Jason for months, although I tried to keep in regular contact with him since qualifying as a nurse. Jason was my final mentor, and if it weren't for his persistent pushing and wake-up calls, I probably would've still been in a dark dungeon weeping over Tom. He'd recently crept into my DMs demanding a lunch date, and of course I jumped at the chance to catch up.

I walked out of the treatment room to the shop floor and immediately spotted the new starts looking flustered as they caught my eye. They seemed to still be working me out and could be a little uneasy at times, curious about how rigid I was as a boss.

'Hey, you two OK?' I asked, grinning at the pair.

Lisa bobbed shyly. She was the tallest of the two girls, twenty-five and our official laser hair removal specialist. Since moving to us, she was slowly coming out of her shell, and I could tell her work ethic was strong. She has a two-year-old son called James and is entirely focused on building up her clientele and growing her branding for his sake, which I completely admire.

'We're fine, just finding the best lighting for some Insta stories,' Olivia gushed back cheerily. Olivia was only nineteen but the sweetest little powerhouse. She has bright red hair, and I don't think I'd seen her repeat a hairstyle yet; from space buns to plaits to curls, she'd done it all. Olivia specialises in microblading and piercings, bringing a whole new range of quirky clients through the door. Her needlework is precise, and she is entirely fearless. Her presence on social media is vast, with thousands of TikTok followers watching her piercing videos every day.

'Try the corner at the front door. The lighting's great there,' I replied.

'Thanks, Zara,' Lisa said, smiling as Olivia bounced over to the corner.

I walked over to the desk and joined Ashley, who was engrossed in the booking system.

'I forgot I have lunch today with Jason. Will you make sure I'm free between one and two?' I asked, admiring her latest set of black-and-white dog-tooth acrylics as they hit the keyboard.

'Good job I didn't forget, isn't it?' She snickered and we giggled. 'I linked everyone's phone calendars and things to the booking system, so I literally know where you all are at all times.'

'Ash, that's probably illegal.'

'No, it definitely is.' She shrugged. 'For instance . . .' She popped her finger in the air and began pressing keys again before smirking. 'Today, Tom is receiving a parcel from Amazon consisting of some classic moccasin slippers. I've always seen him as a slider kind of guy.'

I chuckled, shaking my head. 'Well, he does do long shifts,' I said. My voice squeaked as I found myself defending him.

Ashley's face screwed up for a brief second before her thoughts jumped ship again. 'Please, can I come to lunch with you, Zara? I hate when you have other friends and I need to eat alone!' She lowered her head and pouted. 'Pleeeeease!'

'Eh, no way. That's awkward. I only see Jason once in a blue moon. *Plus*, I need you to stay here; the girls have quite a busy afternoon of clients.'

Ashley stomped her black stiletto on the tiled floor, then sassily flicked her hair back as another train of thought came over her. 'Is Andy coming in for product day tomorrow?'

I nodded, still breaking into a proud smirk whenever my boyfriend's name was mentioned.

'Like, why don't you just discuss it at home? It frees up an entire morning or afternoon of clients for everyone else.'

I shrugged. 'It's a team meeting, though. I want all of you to be involved. Plus, I thought you loved product day?'

Ashley's head swayed. 'I do; it's a complete skive. I was thinking for the financial aspect, though. You could mix business with . . .' Her voice deepened into some form of a Russian accent as she turned sharply to my face. 'Pleasure, you know!'

I laughed loudly, pushing her face away from mine as she invaded my personal space.

'Stop being so creepy, man! I'm not mixing anything, it's all' – I tried my hardest to imitate the vaguely European voice – 'pleasure, pleasure, pleasure with him!'

Ashley giggled back. 'And I suppose if the meeting got cancelled, drinks afterwards would be too and that's my favourite part of the ritual.'

Our after-meeting work drinks had started recently as a celebration of exceptional sales figures one month, and had quickly become a regular occasion on the calendar.

'Right, I'm going to head, shouldn't be too long,' I called out, waving to the girls still selfie-ing from the corner of the room.

Outside, George Square was fresh and lovely. I took a deep breath and began the short stroll towards La Vita Spuntini. It was the middle of July. Although the weather was cloudy, it was a mild day in Glasgow, just another Monday afternoon, and most of the people who laced the streets were businesslike until I hit the bustle of shoppers on Buchanan Street.

I was looking forward to meeting up with Jason. I hadn't managed to pick up any shifts in the hospital for almost a year, so I was eager to hear all about the latest dramas in the ward I'd trained in. He always had a great story to tell, and I missed his uplifting energy.

As I turned the corner, I saw Jason waving at me with an enormous grin on his face.

'Hi!' he screeched from a distance, and I hurried my walk a little, feeling slightly out of breath from the five-minute stroll. 'Aww, you are a full wee businesswoman! Look at you!' He held my shoulders, darting his gaze at my black jeans and blazer combo. 'I've been so excited to see you, Zara!' he added as we walked into the restaurant.

'Me too! How are you? What's been happening?'

8

He was glowing and his infectious welcome made my heart burst as I realised how much I'd missed him. He was wearing skinny grey jeans and a black leather aviator jacket, although it must have only been for fashion purposes as it was pretty clammy in Glasgow.

'I'm good. Proper fucked from three twelve-hour shifts, but hey! You probably can't recall what that feels like, though, Miss Zara,' he said jokingly, rolling his dark eyes at me.

I smiled as a tall Italian-looking waiter approached us. 'Table for Smith, please.'

'Follow me, please.'

He led us to a cosy seat in the corner and Jason and I sat down.

'And just so you know, I am still very familiar with twelve-hour days,' I said. 'My friend Ashley books the life out of me at times. She gets ragin' if I need a bathroom break!'

Jason giggled, grabbing his menu. 'So, how *is* the business going then? Do you love it?' I watched his bright eyes skim down the menu.

'Yes, absolutely. It's growing well. We've got a couple of new treatments. A new piercer too, actually, so if you want anything pierced, however discreet it may be, it's on the house!' I winked.

Jason's jaw dropped. 'Aw naw, no way! I couldn't. Do guys seriously come in to get their boabies pierced?'

I had forgotten how loud Jason's voice was as he held his chest in disgust. I ushered him to *shhh*, but I couldn't stop belly laughing at his reaction.

'She can do them, but she's not done any at Individualise yet. Maybe you should be her model for the Gram?' I laughed as he gaped in horror.

'Oh my God, I thought that was an eighties thing too.'

The waiter approached the table hesitantly, not knowing if Jason was ready to discuss the menu.

'Can I have a Diet Coke and the penne amatriciana?' I asked, returning my menu.

'Ehh . . . Awk, I'll have the same. Sorry, she's got me all flustered.' Jason laughed dramatically as the waiter walked back to the bar.

'So, how's the love life?' I asked Jason, and his face screwed up a little.

'Hmm . . . I'm getting some, put it that way. Met up with a porter from work the other night on Grindr, had no idea he worked in the hospital and now I see him every day. Mortifying!' We both giggled. 'But how is yours, more to the point? I seen the sexy photo on your Instagram the other day – that just-woke-up pose. Meaning "we just had sex"!'

I blushed slightly, recalling the exact photo Jason was talking about and feeling slightly proud as that was the exact angle I hoped would come across and of course we absolutely had just had sex. 'It's good. I have like a proper boyfriend, *finally*!' I felt a small surge of happiness in my stomach thinking about Andy.

'Yes, finally!' he repeated. 'Nah, I'm so happy for you, babe, you deserve it! Especially with the whole Dr Adams carry on.' He pursed his lips and made a small tutting sound.

I nodded my head, agreeing with Jason. I still felt embarrassed about some of the antics I got into when I was mad for Tom. The image of my very public humiliation running from Tom's flat dressed in a fuckin' pick 'n' mix played across my mind. I shuddered at the thought.

'You know he's never been the same since it all. Dr Adams, I mean.'

The waiter approached the table with our drinks. I popped out a paper straw and immediately began sucking down my Diet Coke as I stared at Jason for more information.

'What do you mean?'

Jason let out a sigh. 'Well, you know how he was. Always very flirtatious, like every second word was an innuendo. He's just so blah now. Like, hmm . . .' He paused, considering his words. 'He's so serious now or something. Boring bastard almost.'

'Really?' I was puzzled. I could feel my face tightening up. *Were we discussing the same guy?* I hadn't seen any change in Tom recently. He was always bubbly and full of his charming masculine energy at Individualise. 'He's totally fine in the clinic with all of us. But he's going for his consultancy this year in the hospital. Maybe he's trying to stay more professional?'

'Wait, he still works at the clinic? What the hell!' Jason let out a choking sound, as if his drink had gone down the wrong way. When he recovered, he screeched with laughter.

'It sounds weird, but it's fine, it's . . .' I thought about the dynamics of the clinic and broke into a smile.

'It's good, actually. We're all just like best buddies.'

'Aye, fuck buddies more like!' Jason winked. 'No, no, I'm joking. Wow, Zara. It's cool of you and nice how you've moved on, and karma has well and truly made him still single!'

My heart felt a bit achy for Tom. I wanted him to be happy. The thought of him not being his fun, charismatic self in the wards since the humiliating drama of me versus Harriette made me wonder what was going through his head and how it all affected him.

'Well, anyway, tell me about work. I want to hear it all!' I clasped my hands excitedly, keen to take the spotlight off myself.

'It's been wild. Like, on Monday we had this patient admitted overnight, presented with abdo pain. She was scanned – a bowel blockage.' Jason shrugged, unimpressed, as he encountered this scenario frequently. 'The surgeons said it was small and would resolve on its own, so no surgical intervention needed.'

At that moment the waiter returned with our food. 'Your lunch,' he said, setting our plates down on the table. 'Can I get you anything else?'

I shook my head quickly at him with a rushed smile, eager for the rest of Jason's story.

'So, they held off overnight,' he continued once the waiter had gone. 'The usual situation, slowly deteriorating the following day. Then that afternoon became septic, then of course peri-arrest most of the fuckin' day until – boom. Full-blown cardiac arrest, and we're rushing her into Theatre.'

I was on the edge of my seat, ploughing through my pasta. 'They got her back, mind you, but it was *ooh* . . .' he added, munching away, shaking his head.

'Fucking hell. That's bad. The poor woman.' I sat back on my seat and paused for a moment. 'But I'm weirdly jealous! Honestly, I miss that so much, Jason. All of that.' I thought back to my days on the ward and that adrenaline rush you experienced when a patient got so sick and you snapped into action, doing absolutely anything you could to keep them alive. To leave the hospital so physically exhausted but unbelievably fulfilled that your decisions that day had participated in saving someone's life is a buzz I don't think many people can encounter unless you work in that field.

He laughed. 'I mean I had fuckin' skiddies that shift but, still, that feeling when you see them get better, it's what it's all about. You need to come back, do a couple of extra shifts a week, even. We are always short-staffed; you know what it's like.'

I sighed, feeling that my days in the wards were a lifetime ago. 'I don't know if I'd have the time, honestly. Plus, would I even remember what to do in that situation?'

'Eh . . . aye! Because you were my fucking student and I taught you exactly what to do.' His eyes gave me a warning scowl across the table. 'It doesn't leave you, Zara. A couple of shifts, and it'll be like you never left!'

I smiled back at my friend. I'd always loved my training days at the hospital and if it weren't for my friendships with Ashley and Raj, I would probably still be there now. That relationship and wanting to help people was exactly why I'd wanted to go into nursing in the first place.

'Anyway, aside from that drama, I've been studying for an interview.' Jason blushed, suddenly becoming unusually vulnerable. 'I don't like telling anyone, because the chances are I won't get it. But there are ten positions so I hope to fucking God I have a shot at one!'

'Oh, amazing, good for you! What's the job?' I asked.

He was full of excitement again as he began to explain. 'Basically, they're building a team of acute surgical Advanced Nurse Practitioners. They'll be helping scrub in Theatre, perform minor ops, help out with the trauma at the front door of the hospital, and there's even chat about helping out at big incidents. Like major road traffics, stabbings and stuff, we are in the toon after all! So aye, mainly stabbings!'

I gasped. 'Honestly, *wow*. You would be amazing at that! It sounds like the dream job. Like *Holby City* shit.' I laughed.

'*Holby*? Hun, this is *Grey's* shit. Just find me McDreamy! But, you know, I'm pitching it for you too. Think about it. If you are still into the acute side of nursing and not just a big hot-shot aesthetics nurse. There are ten jobs, Zara, not one. Of course, there's a hell of a lot of interest but . . . the dream team could be back together.'

'It sounds unreal, but I've been out too long now.' I shrugged, feeling disappointed.

Jason shook his head. 'My arse! They train you up!

And I'm sure Anne would give you a glowing reference.'

I could feel my palms get sweaty at the thought. It was the type of job that I'd once dreamed of – that adrenaline rush, the patients, the making a difference.

'Do a couple of shifts, see if you still miss us,' Jason said. 'The closing date isn't for another few weeks, so you've got time to study and apply. That's if you really want it, and personally I think you'd shine.'

Despite the conflict and doubt I was feeling, I beamed at him. 'I have a lot of catching up to do before I could even set foot in the wards again!' I laughed.

It felt great to talk to someone about real nursing again. I hadn't realised how much I missed that side of my life until now.

Soon, we finished up and split the bill. After lunch, I headed back to the clinic and completed my afternoon of aesthetic procedures, the conversation and possibilities I'd discussed with Jason rolling over and over in my head.

Chapter Two

Later that night, I headed round to Andy's. It was my new favourite place to go after work, especially late at night. He usually finished a few hours earlier than me, and tonight he'd promised me dinner upon arrival. After locking up the clinic, I caught a taxi and made the short trip to Clyde Street. Andy rented one of the trendy new blocks of flats overlooking the river. I pressed the button for the lift, my legs unable to contemplate the three flights of stairs it would take me to walk up.

As the lift doors opened, I noticed Andy's front door was wedged open slightly.

'Hey!' I called out as I walked in, closing it behind me.

'Come through, I've made you fajitas,' he said proudly. Andy was standing over the hob grinning in my direction. I noticed he had shaved his head a few days earlier as it wasn't as dark and spikey. His body stood tall and I admired his perfect smile and dimpled cheeks. I couldn't help but copy his infectious grin. As I entered the open-plan living and kitchen area, the smell of spicy Mexican food made my stomach rumble even though I hadn't long indulged in my pasta lunch with Jason.

'*Ooft,* this smells delicious!' I said, approaching him by leaning over the worktop and greeting my handsome boyfriend with a kiss on the cheek.

'No Tyson tonight?'

'Nope, don't get him back till tomorrow.'

Jackpot! I thought. It was the only thing I appreciated about Andy's ex-relationship, the fact they still shared custody of the pooch. 'And . . .' He leaned back over to kiss my lips. 'I made the chicken mild for me and extra spicy for you.'

Great. I instantly regretted exaggerating my love for spicy food at the beginning of our relationship in a bid to appear more cultured, and now my head began prepping a midnight-hour plan for the toilet when I knew the fajitas would be fleeing from me and I'd have an arse like the Japanese flag.

'*Mmmm* . . . Thank you!' I smiled back. I took off my coat and walked back towards the living area, laid my coat down across the couch, then approached the dinner table. 'How was your day?'

'Good, babe. I was on a few conference calls. *Oh,* I was chatting to Raj for a bit too,' Andy added, as he finished dishing out the food while I sat down.

'Oh yeah, what was he saying? I missed a call from him earlier, but I was with a client.' I reached for a tortilla wrap, which was already laid out on the table with some dips, and started to fill it as Andy dished the chicken onto the table.

'*Ooft*, no, I'll let him tell you.' Andy grinned as he took a seat opposite me, spooning his plain chicken onto his own wrap.

'Don't leave me hanging. He'll tell me anyway!' I replied, gasping at my boyfriend's suss behaviour.

'I know he will, but it's his business to tell.' Andy shrugged. He was always so laidback and chill. He didn't seem to get involved in the drama of the aesthetics world, and I loved that about him, but there was something undeniably curious about his smile.

'For God's sake. Is it good or bad?' I asked.

'Good. It's all I'm saying.' There was a brief silence in the room. Andy paused and placed his wrap down and sighed.

'What?' He giggled.

'You are going to make me FaceTime him just now and ruin my dinner, do you realise this?' I threatened him playfully, and he laughed as I wiped down my hands ready to find my phone.

'OK, OK, keep eating.' Andy took a sip of water. 'Juju has secured a HUGE spot in Dubai Mall for a pop-up aesthetics show. Raj will be mic'd up and performing on a stage in the middle of the mall with really well-known big-time models.' Andy's eyes popped with excitement.

'Shut up!' I squealed.

'No, it's going to be *massive*. Nothing has been done like this in Dubai ever. Fuck, you couldn't practise injectables over there till a couple of years ago. Plus, it's obviously the biggest mall in the fuckin' world.' I thought back to my time in Dubai and wished I'd spent less time chasing cock and actually ventured out of the hotel room and witnessed some of the famous sights it has to offer.

I sat back in my chair, feeling an overwhelming amount of pride. 'He's seriously killing it over there!'

Andy nodded his head eagerly, half a wrap stuck to his face and with chicken falling off it. 'Yes, he is!'

'Who secured the deal?' I asked.

Andy's teeth glimmered back slightly shyly and he patted his chest with his hand. I gasped, pushing back my seat and leaping over to him. Andy pulled me over his lap, and I kissed and kissed and kissed him.

'I'm so fucking proud of you! Is your boss buzzing?' I asked.

Andy was blushing. 'He said it's the biggest deal the company's had so far. So, you could say that, aye.'

'*Aww* . . . Come here!' I kissed him hard on the lips again.

He panted, tugging on my bottom lip with his teeth. I could feel the mood suddenly turn sultry in that single action. He pushed his chair back, giving me slightly more room to explore his body. I giggled, understanding his guy language almost immediately.

'I'm so . . . so . . . proud.' I kissed his neck and then his chest and gazed upwards, watching his reaction as his body flinched at how close we were.

'*Mmm* . . . Show me how proud, darlin',' Andy mumbled, pulling down his zip and assuming his head-back blowjob position in an instant.

Well, as much as I can't be arsed with the locked jaw, I suppose he has earned a little sook, I thought, letting out a discreet puff as I could still hear the delicious fajita sizzle in the background.

I slowly slid down his legs, kissing his shirt until I got to his jeans.

'Will I show you, baby?' I reached into Andy's zip and then the boxer slit, exposing his semi-erect penis with a bit of manoeuvring. It was already aroused from the little roleplay, so I continued to kiss it gently. 'Who's a good boy?' I asked, moving my way up towards the tip of his penis. It was growing harder and extending with each touch.

'*Ohhh yes . . .*' Andy inhaled through gritted teeth in anticipation.

Finally, I ran my tongue right up the centre of his now rock-hard dick. I felt my saliva drizzle down it and paused for a brief moment to ensure I had full control over him, then began sucking and gagging, spitting on the tip the way he usually liked. I was twisting and turning his foreskin, re-enacting the latest wholly educational Pornhub video I'd watched recently called 'The Blowjob Bitch'. I'd noticed Andy enjoyed a certain wrist action and I began tugging while licking the tip of his penis. 'Aww, Za. That is so fucking good,' I nodded, pretending to enjoy it just as much as him. His eyes met mine briefly and I could feel his dick push further into my mouth. 'Mmmm . . . yes, baby!' He yelled. I opened right up and began really going for the deep throat when Andy's moans suddenly halted.

'Zara, *Zara*.' He sat up rigid, abruptly prying my mouth off his penis by pushing my forehead in a rush.

'What?' I asked, swiping the excess saliva from my mouth.

'Holy fuck. Get aff me!' Andy scrambled off the seat and bolted towards the bathroom.

What the hell just happened?

'Andy, are you OK?' I followed him to the bathroom, but he had closed the door. I began chapping loudly. 'Andy? Babe? What's up?' My stomach suddenly dropped. *Had I gone in with too much teeth? Did I twist it too hard?* Shit, had I snapped his banjo? I hadn't done that in years.

'Finish your dinner. I'll be a couple of minutes,' he called back in a high-pitched tone. I heard the sprinkling of water as the shower turned on.

Jesus. What the fuck's going on? I wondered.

I stood still at the door waiting for a few minutes, but could only hear the shower water running and the odd pant from Andy. Reluctantly, I made my way back to the dining table. *What the hell is up with him?* Distracted, I reached over to pick up the remains of my wrap as the smell of Mexican food wafted past me. The spice hit the back of my throat, making me cough slightly. I reached for my glass of water. Then it clicked.

Shit. The extra-hot fajitas!

He had a fajita-spiced phallus. I gasped. *Ouch!*

I stood up and slowly walked towards the bathroom door again. I could hear him yelp from the shower as I chapped on the door.

'I'm sorry!' I murmured.

'Five minutes, please, babe. Five minutes,' he replied.

I hesitantly returned to the dining room not knowing if he was ragin' at me or the situation.

Another ten minutes passed before Andy finally reappeared from the bathroom. He had a towel wrapped around his waist and another hanging off his shoulders. We glared at one another in silence, then burst into laughter together.

'Zara, that was not funny,' he said, still laughing and shaking his wet head.

I was in hysterics. 'You were the one who' – I cleared my throat and imitated his deep voice from earlier – '*made them extra hot for you, babe!*'

We continued laughing loudly together while Andy tried to grab my waist to stop. I stood up from the chair, turned to him and kissed him.

'I'm sorry, seriously. I didn't even think. I was really trying hard with that blowjob too.' I gazed into his bright blue eyes, running my hands over his damp shoulders.

'I know, darlin'. It's OK. It was fuckin' stingy, though.' He smirked and I bit my lip, still trying to remain composed as tears of laughter filled my eyes. 'I think my dick will be out of action for the night now. It's so red.'

'Surely not!' I was shocked. The man had been walking around with a hard-on since the moment I met him.

He nodded, looking very serious. 'I think I'll need a night to recover. The big man is rid raw and throbbin', darlin'. So, I'm afraid you know what that means, right?'

My heart suddenly fell slightly in my chest. *Oh shit, does he want me to leave?* Surely our relationship could withstand one night of abstinence. 'Oh, erm, what's that?' I asked nervously.

'Tonight . . . is all about Zara Smith!' Andy let out a wicked laugh and pulled my vibrator from under his towel. 'Ta da!' He gave me a wink and I laughed out loud. 'Get into bed then,' he said, and I jumped in excitement.

'OK, give me two minutes, I'm just going to the bathroom.' I leaned over and pecked his lips. 'Get it all wet for me coming through.'

I walked through to the toilet and squeezed out a pee before lifting one leg up on the bath panel to give my fanny a quick wash from working hard all day. I lathered up the soap, rinsed, and briefly wafted the air to my face. *Fresh as a fucking daisy.* I pulled my knickers back on and walked through to the bedroom where Andy was waiting.

'Andy?'

There, on the bed, was my beautiful, handsome boyfriend overly analysing my Rampant Rabbit.

'What are you doing?'

Andy looked up at me.

'Zara, I feel kind of intimidated by the size of this thing! It's huge!' His eyes expanded widely and I blushed, remembering paying the extra £9.99 for maximum length and girth.

'It's just a normal dildo size.' I shrugged, lying out of my teeth.

'It's not a normal dick size, that's for sure.' He chuckled, still turning the rubber cock and examining every ribbed edge.

'Stop! Give it back.' I giggled, conscious of the juicy cum streaks because I couldn't remember the last time I'd washed the fucker. There was no way I was paying £6.99 for dildo wipes when a quick rub down the bed sheets was sufficient.

'I just want to look!' He said, teasingly, bringing it closer to his face.

Oh, God. Please don't sniff it. I panicked.

'It's not as good as yours, you know.' I leapt towards him, trying my best to distract yet reassure him at the same time.

Andy laughed and reached forward, grabbing hold of me. 'Well. OK, then, that's all I need to know! Come here, you!'

He threw me down on the bed with the biggest grin on his face.

And I spent the rest of the night getting vibrated all the way to heaven.

Chapter Three

The following day Andy woke early to sift through his emails while I scampered around his flat gathering my scattered belongings. I could smell fresh toast and the aroma of coffee brewing around us and, compared to me, Andy seemed utterly relaxed.

'Will you calm it for five? I've made you breakfast,' he said, peering over his laptop screen from the dining table.

I turned to say something but got distracted by the pile of Lurpak-slathered toast and the cup of coffee sitting on the worktop waiting for me. I smiled gratefully, but I couldn't risk eating this early on and adding strain to my already bloated stomach. The fajita farts were crowning my anus and my muscles were holding on by a fucking thread. I wasn't prepared to let them go along with my relationship. Instead, I waddled uncomfortably through his apartment.

'I'm sorry. All my things are everywhere. I don't want to be late.'

Andy laughed. 'You could always like . . . have a drawer here or something? You live out of bags. No wonder you can't find anything.'

I paused and felt my eyes widen. *Wow, a drawer?* Next, I'd be moving in, having babies and booking the Old Fruit Market for my wedding venue. *OK, Zara, are you ready for this?*

I wanted to react but I stood still, not knowing how I felt about this sudden level of commitment. I had never had someone so open to settle down before but I knew I loved Andy and this felt like how the appropriate next stage of a relationship should be.

'Erm, yeah. Coolio. I mean, sure, a drawer would be cool.'

I mean, I did spend half of my time there, and I loved Andy's flat. It was new and modern, compared to my old tenement building, and was still situated in the centre of town, but I also loved my own space for nights I could completely slob out make-up free and enjoy the clutter and chaos of my place.

Andy's face screwed up a little. *Shit, maybe that was too cool,* I thought.

'If that's too weird then it's fine. I'm just thinking for practicality reasons. You humfing bags to work and leaving things between houses must be annoying for you, babe.'

I stopped in my tracks, placed my earrings on the table, and shuffled up to him. I could feel my heart quicken.

'No, no. Absolutely. A drawer sounds great,' I said, then smiled and pecked his coffee-tasting lips.

'Good, now have breakfast, and I'll drive you to work.' Andy winked sexily, stood up and slapped my arse.

'Agh!' I clenched in utter surprise, *just* managing to hold my wind as the silly cunt almost blew his fucking hand off.

I darted my eyes around the open-plan space as he made his way out of the room towards the bathroom, I was looking for somewhere, anywhere I could expel my farts. The kitchen diner and living room all flowed nicely together. Not the best when you had an odour to ditch. My stomach cramped. *Shit, shit.* Then I suddenly spotted the small balcony out of the corner of my eye. *Fucking perfect.* I hurried over to the doors, feeling a cold sweat begin to perspire off me as I fiddled with the lock. *C'mon, c'mon.* Finally, the door burst open, and I stuck my arse out on the balcony, lifting my dress upwards just in the nick of time.

BRRAAAAPPPP. Relief, finally relief.

'Jesus, really? Come on, girl.'

Hearing a cockney voice, I turned to the right. Andy's neighbour was standing on his balcony, ferociously wafting my gas while he smoked his morning cigarette. Unfortunately, the poor bastard was standing downwind.

'Morning!' I called out, cringing, and vaulted back into the flat, pulling the doors shut behind me.

'You set?' Andy asked, returning to the living room with his suit jacket on, absolutely none the wiser and looking unbelievably shaggable.

'Yep, almost.' I leapt towards the kitchen counter and took a few bites of breakfast, finally feeling brave enough to get it down me. I slurped a large gulp of coffee and felt the most relief I had all morning. 'Let's go!'

I grabbed my bag, and we headed down to Andy's parking bay to make the short journey to Individualise.

'How was your lunch with your mate yesterday?' he asked as he began driving through town.

My face lit up thinking of Jason. 'It was really good to see him. Honestly, you will love Jason.'

Andy was concentrating on the road but grinning as I chatted away.

'He's applying for this incredible new job that's coming up. Like, a whole new role in the hospital.'

'Cool, doing what?'

'Well, it's hard to explain, but basically being a lead surgical ANP.'

'A what?' Andy squinted at my abbreviation.

'Advanced nurse practitioner.' I giggled at the tongue twister. 'He'll be trained to do procedures doctors normally do. He even said there's chat about assisting at emergencies, like road traffic collisions and things. *Oh*, and in Theatre and stuff, lots of trauma. He'd be shoving in chest drains, central lines and keeping people alive. Like proper medicine.' I started to feel a ripple of excitement again as I gabbed about nursing.

Andy was shrieking with horror at the thought.

'What!' I teased and jokingly slapped his bicep.

'You get excited over the weirdest things, Zara. That's my idea of hell,' he replied, shaking off the images I'd planted in his mind.

'That's why I went into nursing in the first place, you know, to be part of the madness. I always loved a bit of *Scrubs* or *Casualty* when I was younger. And to help people, obviously. So, meeting him kind of made me miss it a bit,' I admitted.

There was a brief silence.

'He did also sort of say that ten positions are coming up,' I continued. 'They want an entire team of staff doing this new role. Jason actually said I should do a few shifts a week again in the wards to like get my skills back up, and to see if I fancied trying out for the interview too. I know I probably wouldn't get it, but it's good to have interview experience as well.'

Andy seemed taken aback. '*Woah*, slow down sweetheart. You'd honestly go back to the NHS?' He glanced across at me. My face must have displayed the confusion I was feeling, because he continued, 'I'm sorry, hen, but I have no idea why someone who has *just* managed to get out of the wards would want back in?' He seemed flabbergasted.

'I'm not sure what you want me to say.' I paused, thinking. 'I erm . . . I like it, I suppose. It's actual nursing,' I replied shyly, feeling embarrassed by his judgement.

'And you seriously think you could do all of that stuff? Go to road traffic accidents? Put in drains and act like a doctor but get paid as a nurse? I personally think you'd be off your head.'

My eyes widened as I felt a rush of shock push through me at Andy's strong opinion on my career.

'Well, I'd be trained to do it all. Plus, I'd get paid higher, obviously, for doing the role,' I murmured, suddenly feeling hot and panicky at the interrogation. Andy stopped the car at the traffic lights and turned to me.

'Oh, *really*? More than you do running a private clinic?' he questioned.

'Erm . . . I'm not sure? I've not looked into it that much.' I shrugged.

'Surely you won't be as well paid working for the NHS? Even if you worked between the hospital and the clinic, financially, you'd take a massive hit.'

I sank back into my seat as he began driving once more. 'Yeah, I suppose. I didn't even ask about the salary. But it was only an idea. Nothing's set in stone. Jason said I'd be good at it and to be honest, I didn't give the pay a second thought. Financially I get by at the clinic, yes, but it was only a passing thought I suppose.' I felt a little taken aback by his reaction and wasn't sure how to respond without any conflict.

Andy indicated left and eased his car into a space just outside the clinic. He paused for a moment then huffed slightly.

'You need to think about pay. You're an adult now, Zara. You have a good thing going with the clinic here, and personally I don't know why you would take a step backwards just because your pal thinks you'd be good at it. You've just got the clinic back up and running. You're dealing with accountants and brands and big fuckin' companies, hen.'

But I wasn't nursing.

'Listen, your future is my future too. Financially we have to look at the big picture. Seems mental to think

30

about going for something you haven't done in years, for shit pay and long hours. Just be realistic, we have to make decisions like this together.'

I shrugged and attempted a tiny smile, suddenly feeling brought back down to earth.

'I suppose I just loved the wards, Andy. It's always been something I was passionate about. But I know what you're saying. I love the clinic work too. I do realise I have a good thing here, I'm not daft.' I paused for a moment, realising that I had never had someone who wanted to build a future with me before. 'Thanks for the lift. I'll catch you in a bit.' I opened the car door and stepped onto the bustling street.

'I know you're not daft, Zara.' He smiled warmly towards me. 'I'll see you at two for our meeting, OK?' he added.

With a nod I waved Andy off as his grey Mercedes zoomed down the street, trying to ignore the heaviness on my chest.

Inside the clinic I found Ashley and Tom chit-chatting at the desk.

I hitched a smile onto my face. 'Morning!'

'Afternoon,' Ashley said under her breath, noticing I was five minutes late.

'How is Zara today?' Tom asked. He was already dressed in his dark blue scrubs, his hair swept back from his chiselled, slightly stubbly face.

I nodded as I took off my coat. 'Can't complain. Although, I do have *another* boring morning sorting the books for the accountant, but then we have our sales meeting this afternoon. I'd much rather be seeing clients and getting some Glasgow gossip!'

'I remember when a sales meeting with Andy was the highlight of her month! Remember, Tom?' Ashley teased.

'Hmm . . . indeed! What's happened, Zara? Tell your old Uncle Tom.' He winked in my direction.

'That's the creepiest thing you have ever said,' Ashley muttered, her face twisting in disgust. 'And you say *a lot* of creepy things, Thomas.'

Tom smirked, seeming proud of the insult. They both turned to me, awaiting a reply.

'Nothing is wrong, fuck sake!' I said defensively.

The pair continued to stare me out.

'It's just that I went for lunch yesterday with Jason, and he was telling me about a new job coming up and—'

'Ah, yes! The surgical ANP roles,' Tom cut in. 'They've just received funding for an entire team of them apparently.'

'Yeah, that's the one. So, I was telling Andy, and I said it sounded amazing. It's why I originally went into nursing. It's like my dream job—'

Just then, the door opened, and a young woman walked up to the desk, calling a halt to our conversation.

'Hi, good morning. Do you have an appointment?' Ashley asked.

'She does indeed. Linda, how are you, darling? Let's take you through to the clinic room.' Tom led his client away.

I waited until he'd shut the treatment room door before continuing. 'So, I said it was my dream job and that I was thinking of doing one or two shifts a week in the wards again, and maybe one day I'd have the skills to go for a job like that.'

Ashley leaned forward curiously. 'And what did Andy say?'

'He said it would be a step backwards. Like went into a full lecture about how it's not as much money, and I need to think like an adult.' I raised my eyebrows at my best friend, who looked like she was pondering. 'What do you think?'

'OK, so, brutally honest: he has a point. Could he have said it nicer? Fuck *yes*. But why work twelve-hour shifts for practically no money when you could work here with *me*, and get paid the big bucks.' Ashley swooshed her long blonde hair to the side, having lost my attention as she diverted it back to the computer screen.

'I don't even know if I would go back. It was just an idea,' I muttered.

With that, I turned on my heels and headed to my treatment room. Alone, I sat down at my desk, letting out a slight gust of boredom as I loaded up the spreadsheets for the accountant.

The morning perished slowly, and my eyes often glazed over, sinking through the screen. My mind drifted back to what Andy had said. *You're an adult now, Zara.* Who the fuck did he think he was? I mean, he wasn't my dad, despite the occasional Daddy patter he enjoyed during roleplay, but that was the only time he got to boss me around. Surely I could do a few shifts in the wards again. I didn't want to leave the clinic, I was only considering a few shifts per month to keep my nursing skills up. I'd only been qualified in nursing for a few years and didn't want to lose everything I had just learned slaving through university to be in the same job for ever. I knew I could easily balance both. I had more time than ever managing the clinic and only worked four days a week.

I slumped back in my chair and thought. Why was everyone so against this?

Before I knew it, I had opened a new tab and searched for job opportunities within NHS Glasgow and Clyde, and there it was.

Coming soon: Lead surgical ANPs – A team of highly skilled nurses striving to take the profession to the next level.

As I became absorbed in the job description, there was a loud knock on the door and Tom's face appeared.

'Sorry, you got a minute?' he asked, stepping into the room.

I smiled, feeling slightly flustered at getting caught checking a job ad. 'Of course,' I said. 'Come in.'

'I'm aware that there are big things in the pipeline with Raj in Dubai, so I was thinking it would be nice if we all visited him?' His voice was warm and deep. I could smell his expensive musky cologne and he was still a few metres away.

'Awk, Tom, that would be amazing, but I don't think we could afford to cancel or compensate the clients. It would be such a nice gesture, but . . .' I shrugged my shoulders. 'We can't shut down the clinic for a holiday.'

Tom sighed a little and pulled the seat out to sit down opposite me.

'Yes. I understand. I just wanted to show our support somehow. He's been wonderful with me.'

'I know. He has with me too. Let me look at the diary. Maybe in a few weeks, or months, we could try to schedule a few days off together?'

'Yes, I suppose the entire team was rather optimistic.' Tom smirked and stood up, ready to leave.

'Tom,' I said suddenly.

He slowly swivelled back around on his heels. 'Zara.'

'Oh, it's OK, never mind. Nothing important actually, it's not a big deal.' I laughed, blushing.

Tom raised one eyebrow. 'Hmm,' was all he managed back, but the eye contact remained.

I sighed unintentionally and there was a brief silence.

'Is this about lunch with Jason? The ANP roles?' he asked.

A smile spread across my cheeks.

'So, Jason told me about the jobs coming up, and it got me thinking of how much I missed the hospital, the acute stuff. I was thinking of picking up a few shifts in the next couple of weeks again, and I don't know for definite, but maybe applying for one of the ANP jobs. I know I probably wouldn't get the job straight away, but if I let them know I'm keen, then maybe one day.'

Tom's face lit up. 'You would be an excellent surgical lead nurse.'

I blushed slightly at the compliment and felt grateful for a bit of support.

'But Andy . . .' I continued. 'Well, I mentioned it this morning, and he said it would be a step backwards and that financially, for both of us, it wasn't a good idea.'

Tom looked thoughtful, taking a moment before replying. 'It's difficult, Zara. I make a lot more money working here with you girls than I do in the hospital. The work is very easy money here too. But if I had to decide, and pick one job, it would be the hospital, every single time. I didn't go into medicine to do Botox, and I know you didn't either. I do it for the pace, the unexpected nature, the learning, the people. *Maybe* explain that to him. But, perhaps, people don't understand that element unless you've experienced the rush. The miracles. The team. If I may suggest . . .'

I smiled, urging him to go on.

'Well . . . if I were you, I'd absolutely do a few shifts and get your face noticed. Although, I doubt they've forgotten it.' Tom raised one brow cheekily.

I felt an unexpected wave of relief wash through me. 'Yeah, thanks, Tom,' I said gratefully, finally glad of a positive reaction. 'I think I'll text Anne and ask if her ward has any shifts going!' I pulled my phone from my back pocket and began typing.

He clapped loudly. 'That's the spirit!' He winked and exited the room.

Chapter Four

After lunch, I felt my mood lift from the morning's sulk. Maybe I was just being sensitive about the whole thing? Logically, Andy had a case, but ultimately what I did and where I worked was always going to be my decision.

Ashley, Tom and I were sitting on the white sofa, waiting patiently for the product meeting to begin. Finally, Andy walked through the door and grinned towards me.

'All right, darling.' He bent over and kissed my forehead. 'How's it going, Ash, Tom?'

'Aye, not bad,' Ashley replied, filing down her nails as she was booked in for an infil the next morning.

'Well, thank you,' Tom replied.

'OK, good, let's jump to it. I'll set up for Raj and we'll make a start, one second.' Andy pulled his laptop out of its case and loaded up the scheduled Zoom call. Since Raj had left, we tried to Zoom whenever possible, to ensure he was still up to date with the sales figures.

Suddenly Raj's smiling face appeared on the screen.

'Hi, everyone!' He waved to the camera, and we huddled around the screen happily, forgetting that we all spoke to him most days anyway.

'Hey!' we shouted together.

'Zara, I've tried to call you the past few days!' Raj tutted.

'I know, *I know.* I'm sorry, I've been busy running your business, boss!'

Raj smiled. 'I take it Andy told you about the Dubai Mall?'

'Yes, he did. And I am so buzzing for you, honestly!' I replied.

Ashley's head lifted. 'What about the mall? What mall?'

'I was going to see if you guys were free next week to come over to the sandpit?' Raj asked. As he waited patiently for a response, I felt slightly uncomfortable having just turned down the opportunity with Tom.

'*Argh* . . . Raj! Don't do this to me! To be honest, I'd love to, but we're jam-packed here.' I covered my face in guilt.

'I know. I knew you would be. I just didn't fancy doing this event on my own. It would have been nice to have a bit of male company this time as well. You two girls almost ruined my Dubai experience the last time,' Raj teased, rolling his eyes towards Ashley.

'Well, you two could go?' I looked between Tom and Andy. 'I would rearrange and try to do more late nights to cover your clients, Tom. Let you see Raj and support him during the mall display, and I'm sure your boss wouldn't mind, Andy? You've organised the full thing.'

Tom and Andy traded a puzzled look and the room fell silent for a few seconds.

'It's not a trap. Have fun, see Raj and make us jealous!'
I said, but the longer the silence went on, the more I
wondered if I was making the right decision or not.

'And Ashley?' Tom gestured politely.

'Fuck, I'm staying here. I can imagine Dave if I even
hinted about Dubai again. He'd be ramming the past
down my throat.'

I laughed loudly. 'Well, it was the throat ramming
that got you into trouble in the first place!'

Ashley gasped. 'Zara!'

We all chuckled as Raj squirmed at the reminder.

'I mean I'd love to,' Andy said, 'but I have the dog.
Jen is going away next week, and I'm supposed to have
the dog in between. I'd need you to help take care of
him, Zara. Would that be OK?'

I tried to look pleased. 'Erm . . . *yeah*, sure. You guys
will probably have to leave Monday to fit everything in.'

Andy agreed. 'Aye, Monday to maybe Thursday?
Tom?'

'I mean I'm there, of course I bloody am!' Tom
replied, looking ecstatic.

'I could get a dog walker during the day when you're
working, Zara,' Andy added.

I smiled back reluctantly at my handsome boyfriend.
That dog was going to kill me one of these days. 'Yeah,
course.' I went over to him. He raised his arm for me
to lean into his warm body, and I felt him kiss the top
of my head.

'Well, that settles it then. It looks like the boys are
going to Dubai,' Raj called out from the screen, and

both Andy and Tom looked like they had just won a free pass to Diamond Dolls.

Andy resumed the meeting, and we ran through sales figures, strategies, and incoming concepts. Next, we worked through training ideas, focusing mainly on the new starters by discussing their skills and ways to evolve the business. Finally, Ashley talked us through the social media ideas and videos for autumn trends and her opinions on how to get 'that Individualised glow' trending. When the meeting finished, Ashley and Tom went through to the staff room, eager to finish up for the day. I held off to chat to Andy.

'That went well,' I said, as he packed up his laptop.

His teeth glistened. 'Aye, for me, it did. A trip to Dubai! You sure you can spare us for a few nights?'

I lingered and gave it a thought. 'It's going to be hard, very hard.'

I pressed my body against him, and he slowly turned around to face me. I pushed in harder against him, and he smirked back. I could feel him surge with excitement.

'Think of the gift you'll get when I'm home, darlin'.' He raised his eyebrows suggestively and I giggled, wrapping my arms around his neck.

'*Mmm* . . . What kind of gift do you have in mind?'

Andy leaned into my ear and whispered, 'Come back to mine, and I'll show you.' He bit my earlobe playfully and I felt goosebumps travel down my body.

The staff room door opened, and we were suddenly interrupted.

'Fucking hell, get a room, Za,' Ashley yelled out, shielding her face. Tom stood calmly behind her, completely expressionless.

'Oh, stop it!' I said back, tugging down my dress and striding away from my Andy.

'You coming for drinks?' Ashley said.

I nodded then glanced at Andy. 'Are you sure you don't want to come with us?'

'I can't tonight but call me if you want a nightcap at mine.' He grinned back.

Tom tutted. 'Don't leave me with them, mate.'

Andy laughed and pointed at Tom as he headed for the door. 'You're going to have me all to yourself next week, Thomas. Don't you worry!'

'Indeed!' Tom replied, and Andy departed the clinic.

'So, where are we going?' Ashley asked, pulling out her phone.

'The Social?' I suggested, like we ever go anywhere else, and both of my friends agreed.

We headed out of the clinic and walked the short trip towards Royal Exchange Square. The streets were quiet. Even though it was a summer evening in the city, it felt wonderfully calm. Tom and I walked together while Ashley walked a few steps in front to call Dave.

'So, Dubai, eh?' I said to Tom while he adjusted the collar on his black shirt.

'Yes. Wonderful.' We walked a few more steps before Tom stopped in his tracks, seeming hesitant. 'Are you sure you're OK with me going and doubling up your clientele?'

I smiled. 'Of course, it's only for a few days.'

Tom's dark brown eyes met mine. 'Yes, but I know you wanted to do more hospital shifts for this potential job in the pipeline.'

I gently patted his shoulder. 'I can do more shifts when you're back. Plus, I'm not one hundred per cent even going for it. I'm still thinking about it all, and will need to win over Andy with the idea first.'

'If it's something you will regret not doing, I suggest doing it.' Tom held a meaningful stare with me for a moment. I began to giggle, as he didn't often offer up words of wisdom without a witty punchline to follow.

We continued walking while I rummaged through the overflowing bag from Andy's house in search of my phone. *Ah, got it.* One new message from Anne:

> *Nice to hear from you, Zara. I can put you down for a long day Tuesday and Wednesday in the ward next week? Let me know. Anne.*

Shit. Shit. Shit.

> *Sorry, Anne, slight change of plan. I'll have to leave the shifts for now, but I'll be in touch next week. I'm still really keen, though! Zara xx*

Read.

'Everything OK?' Tom asked.

I forced a smile onto my face. 'Yes, fine, now let's have a good night!'

★

The Social was alive and vibrant, changing the atmosphere from our chilled walk in an instant. A DJ in the back corner played house music while a group of young girls danced drunkenly around the room. Tom immediately made his way to the bar.

'Two Soleros and an espresso martini, please.' Tom turned to us as we scanned the room for seats. 'There's a small booth in the corner; I'll bring the drinks over if you girls grab it.'

I tugged Ashley's arm and scurried along to the booth. We sat down and smiled at one another.

'So, how do you feel about your boys going on holiday? It is a bit weird, is it not?' Ashley grimaced then laughed.

'Is it? It's a business trip for Raj. And besides, I trust Andy,' I replied, shrugging the conversation off.

'Does Andy know about yours and Tom's past though? Like any idea?' Ashley asked as I spotted Tom walking back from the bar, carefully holding the tray of drinks.

'Of course not. There's not exactly much to tell. And besides we're literally best mates now, not one flirty comment or look since Andy. *Shhh,* change the subject. Here he comes,' I muttered, not wanting to discuss my old psychotic feelings or past life where Tom was involved.

'Cheers, ladies!' He held his glass up. Ashley and I grabbed our fruity Soleros, and we all clinked, beginning our night.

The evening was flowing well and taking its ordinary course of slagging Ashley and calling Tom a pervert every time he opened his mouth or ogled the girls at the bar, while I laughed at the two bickering like Isa and Winston. A decent number of cocktails later, Ashley nipped to the loo, giving me and Tom an opportunity to discuss the upcoming trip.

'You know, Zara, I'm surprised you're letting Andy go to Dubai without you,' he said, sitting back in the booth and swirling his martini around like James fucking Bond.

'Why? He'll love it,' I replied, feeling confused.

Tom seemed to think carefully about what he was going to say next, and tried again. I suddenly noticed my heart was beating faster in my chest, wondering if Tom was about to bring up our past. 'I suppose I'm surprised you didn't want to go with Andy and leave me here to cover you.'

I paused. That thought had never crossed my mind, and a glimmer of guilt washed over me.

'You mentioned it just before the meeting, and I'd already kind of said no. It would be snide of me to jump in when you suggested it in the first place, that was all. But, of course, I'd love to go on holiday with him.' I laughed a little, trying to lighten the conversation.

'*Ahh*, I got you. Well, thank you, Zara, it was very, *erm*, sweet of you. Very sweet indeed,' he replied, slurping his drink.

I glanced at his smug face, not knowing why I felt Tom was being arsey. What was he trying to imply? That I didn't want to spend time with my boyfriend?

44

'I might head back to Andy's. He'll be waiting on me, and all this holiday talk has made me realise how much I'm going to miss him.' I felt my eyes scrunch tightly with how much I was exaggerating my grin towards Tom, who simply raised an eyebrow back. 'What? What? What's with the face, Tom? You keep staring like you want to say something but you're not?' I felt my voice getting louder in response to his calm but clearly patronising face. The warmth of anger rushed through me.

Tom slowly sat upright, put down his cocktail glass, gently patted his mouth with his paper napkin and replied, 'Are you happy, Zara? Are you happy with your decision?'

My decision. What did he mean? I had a sudden flashback to standing in my staff room a few months prior, sick with nerves with both Andy and Tom, and choosing Andy. Choosing a boyfriend and a future, not a fuckboy with posh suit. Was that what he was referring to? Or was it my decision to stay in Scotland while they travelled to Dubai? Of course, both were the right decisions. Tom had hurt me so much in the past. His condescending voice and smug face made me feel even more irritation as the alcohol backed me up.

'Well, right now, I'm no happy, Tom. I'm fuckin' ragin', to be honest. I'm ragin' you're suggesting I'm not happy when I've finally met someone who loves *me*, who wants to show *me* off and take *me* out. Who wants to give me a motherfuckin' *drawer*! So please don't question it. Just be happy for me.' My voice lowered

45

as I felt emotionally drained all of a sudden. 'And just, please, move the fuck on, or something.'

I grabbed my bag and stood up. Tom remained silent, slowly sipping his cocktail as I stepped out of the booth and exited the bar.

I walked to the end of the square and let out a large scream of frustration. *Why does he have to ruin a perfectly good fucking night?* I stood there on the pavement, feeling my racing heart slowly return to normal, then took a breath of the humid Glaswegian air.

I was happy, and I wouldn't let Tom fucking Adams play mind tricks on me. So, I hauled over a taxi and went straight to Andy's flat.

I bashed drunkenly on the door, and Andy welcomed me with a sexy smile and a glass of water. *Aww.* My heart wasn't the only thing that gushed immediately. He looked casual in his grey shorts, and I couldn't help but lustfully admire his tanned, muscley, tattooed arms against his crisp white top as he leaned against the door frame.

'Hey, baby,' he said.

I immediately knew this was where I was supposed to be. I'd missed him. I stumbled through the doorway, and as soon as the door shut we were kissing. His lips were soft and wet, and I could feel his tongue wrap around mine in a familiar rhythm. I stepped further into the hallway and we began undressing one other. With a slight fumble, Andy picked me up by the arse and carried me towards his bedroom. I giggled between the kissing until a very horny bastard lowered me to the ground and pushed me against the wall, moving my arms above my head. *How is it possible for this man to get even sexier?* I wondered. He knelt to the floor, slipped off my shoe and licked all the way up. *Jesus Christ,* my fanny was clawing its way out of my knickers like a scene from *The Shawshank Redemption.*

'Did you miss me?' Andy whispered, glaring up from my thighs.

I nodded, not wanting any conversation, just to be rode like the fucking Knight Rider. That's exactly what he did.

The following morning, I woke up hungover but pleased I'd gone back to Andy's flat and not mine. I bent over the side of the bed and lifted my bag to retrieve my phone.

Six missed calls from Ashley.

One new message from Tom.

Apologies for last night, kiddo. I think my martinis made you mad. Enjoy your day off. T

I lay back in bed and remembered what Tom said. *Are you happy?* I thought about my sexy night with Andy and immediately smiled. I was happy, and this was the most comfortable I'd ever felt with anyone. He was playing mind games with the wrong fucker.

I started to reply to his text:

No probs. I just woke up with a hefty hangover! I can't even remember why we argued. Ha! x

I let out a large sigh, dropping my phone back into my bag.

With the thud, I felt Andy stir. His breathing sounded lighter as he rustled around on his side of the bed, but he didn't wake up yet. He was lying back to back with me, so I gradually moved my bare arse closer to his to see if that would wake him. Nothing. I was having flashbacks of his shiny, ravenous face eating me out the night before like he was competing for the world's biggest pie-eating contest, and I felt a sudden waft of the hangover horn. Thinking I'd give my man a little surprise to wake up to, I reached my hand backwards under the duvet covers.

I began by gently rubbing his balls. He always enjoyed getting them tickled. I rolled them around my palm, gently caressing them with my thumb. He let out a sleepy puff of air. I carried on rubbing and stroking, but even after a couple of minutes, getting more heavy-handed, this cunt was still out for the count. I began moaning in a desperate plea to alert him to my horni-ness. I was still too tired to jump on but I wanted to make him horny enough to do all the work.

'*Mmmmm . . . Ahhhh* . . . Andy.'

Fuck sake, I was still half asleep myself and although my eyes were tight shut, I was expecting him to turn around and give me a nice tap on the back with his dick stick. But he didn't move a muscle. Wait. Had I done something wrong? I started to wonder. *What if I've drunkenly confessed about my past with Tom? Is* he mad at me? Shit, did I say something out of order

48

last night? I tried to think back as a million questions were flying through my confused, dehydrated head. The more I continued to rub, the more awake I became until I had a sudden realisation . . . His balls felt really, *really* small.

My heart skipped a beat and I froze, unable to move. I could hear my heartbeat in my ears. *Da dun, da dun, da dun.* Surely not? Please, God, no. I frantically pulled back the bed covers as the realisation hit me.

No.

No.

NOOOOO!

This can't be happening!

Lying open-legged and wide-eyed, staring directly into my eyes, was Tyson, Andy's little Staffie. I was fucking molesting his dog! I screamed loudly and Andy jumped up and turned to me in a blind panic.

'I've been rubbing Tyson's baws,' I wailed. I had chills all over my quivering body, retching and convulsing all over the place.

'What? What?' Andy was startled but was trying his best to calm me down.

'I'm so, *so* sorry. I thought they were yours,' I started to explain myself while desperately rubbing my hands up and down his Egyptian cotton sheets in absolute disgust.

'Jesus Christ, Zara.' Andy erupted into a ball of laughter while Tyson jumped around, wagging his tail happily from across the room at the commotion.

'You're not angry?' I whimpered, not yet able to find the funny side of my molestation.

Andy choked a little in his laughter. 'Angry? I'm fucking jealous! Come here, ya wee pervert!' He grabbed hold of me, and together we spent the entire day in bed.

Chapter Five

The following few days flew by far too quickly, and before I knew it I was waving Andy off from his flat door to spend his 'boys' vacay' with my ex. *What a fucking situation.* Andy seemed excited about the whole idea of voyaging to Dubai, even if I could sense the slightest hesitation about leaving me in charge of his most prized possession, Tyson. The thing was, I had never been a massive animal lover. I do think they're cute and automatically want to touch them, but my allergies to animals have prevented me from being overly affectionate throughout my life. One touch or kiss from a dog resulted in me resembling Sloth from *The Goonies* for twenty-four hours, which I found out the hard way at sleepovers during high school. But I was willing to suffer for Andy, even if I had downplayed the odd sniffle in front of him. I walked back into his notably quiet kitchen and smirked at the detailed list he'd left on the kitchen worktop labelled 'Tyson'.

'Well, it's just you and me, boy.' I sneezed instantly.

Tyson let out a yelp.

'Yip, that's exactly how I'm feeling, too,' I replied apprehensively wiping the snotters from my face.

★

The clinic was busy that Monday morning. A fresh wave of trendy girls visited for dermal piercings with Olivia, and Lisa had back-to-back clients. Ashley was in her element, meeting the new clients, keen to make a good impression with the younger crowd and get them to follow her as well as the clinic on social media. As it was approaching lunchtime, and my itching calmed down, we assembled in the staff room for a quick break and a chat. When Ashley and I headed in, the two new girls were chattering away about boy problems, which slowly drifted off as I joined the table with my squashed-up ham sandwich and packet of pickled onion crisps.

'What's up?' I asked the girls, who still seemed shy around us.

Lisa shrugged and Olivia giggled. 'We're moaning about our man dramas,' she said, smiling and looking a little embarrassed.

'Well, spill . . . We love boy drama, don't we, Ash?'

Ashley was approaching the table, having prepared her Mug Shot, and she gasped. 'Get it told! Yir Auntie Ash will tell you straight,' she said.

The two girls glanced at one another, then Lisa let out a small puff.

'OK, so my kid's dad. We're off and on a lot, but we've been getting on great again. He stayed over the other night and showed me a video of James he took earlier that day, but a screenshot of a girl's Tinder profile popped up on his phone that was saved to his photos.'

Ashley tutted under her breath and shook her head in disapproval already.

'Did you question him about it?' I asked.

Lisa nodded. 'Yeah, he said his mate sent a screenshot of the girl to him because he's chatting to her.'

I shrugged, thinking that was a reasonable explanation.

'But tell them what he said after that,' Olivia added.

Lisa's hands were on the table, and I watched her fidget nervously with her fingers while she spoke.

'I said, well, what friend? So I could ask them. I'm literally friends with all his friends.' She sighed. 'And . . . he said no way because it was none of my fucking business. Getting really defensive. So, now I don't know what to do. He basically stays over half the week. I keep thinking we're getting back together. But now I'm in limbo. I'm not moving on, and I'm scared he might be on Tinder.'

Ashley and I made brief eye contact, and I prayed she would be kind with whatever left her mouth next.

'I smell shite,' she stated.

'Ash!' I warned her.

'Don't you, Zara? If it were innocent, he would show you the chat and reassure you. But instead, he's turning it into a big deal. He's making you feel crazy to defend his actions. But clearly wanting a weekday girlfriend.'

Olivia agreed enthusiastically with Ashley as she gulped down a can of Diet Coke.

'But I'll never know one hundred per cent,' Lisa said. 'What if I'm being insecure? I love him so much, and James adores his dad.' She raised her hands to her head and sighed.

There was a brief pause. My heart was heavy for her.

'I have an idea!' I sat upright as it entered my head.

The three girls looked my way.

'Download Tinder and see if he's on it. Narrow your search down for his exact age and location, and you'll find him quickly . . . if he's on it.' I smirked at my clever detective work, having used this method several times to track down 'strangers' I fancied and wanted to date.

Olivia laughed. 'Genius! *Yes*, do that, Lisa!'

Lisa paused for a few seconds. She looked worried and shook her head. 'I can't. If he saw I was on Tinder, to spy or not, he would never speak to me again. Someone could spot me and send him it or anything. We share an iPad, and if the app uploads to that or something he'd kill me.'

'Use mine!' I offered. I reached into my back pocket and retrieved my phone. 'Here.' I passed my iPhone across the table, disabling the passkey.

'Eh, why do you still have Tinder, mate?' Ashley threw me a surprised look.

I laughed. 'I don't use it, obviously.'

Ashley stood up, glancing over to the home screen on my phone. 'You're literally still logged on.'

'I have the upgrade where you can see everyone who's liked you. It's paid till the end of the month, so I may as well have a snoop from time to time. It's just a wee ego boost,' I insisted, pulling my phone back towards me as I suddenly felt scrutinised by my colleagues.

Olivia laughed loudly, clapping her hands. 'Does Andy know?'

I was puzzled. There was seriously nothing to know. I wasn't interested in any other man. I occasionally popped on Tinder when men messaged or reacted to my photographs, but I hadn't once replied.

'There's nothing *to* know. I would be fine giving Andy my phone for him to look through. I haven't messaged one guy back since we started dating, and he would see the dates.'

'Aw, well, that's OK then . . .' Ashley sounded sarcastic.

I looked up at her rolling her eyes in my direction.

'Well, I think it is,' I snapped back.

'Well, I think it sounds like you're keeping your options open.' She giggled.

I felt annoyed at her. I would never hurt Andy, and I certainly didn't feel like I was keeping my options open. Maybe having Tinder was just my little safety blanket. I'd had it so long, and I enjoyed the attention, but deep down I knew I would never act on it.

'OK, Lisa, are you gonna check this out or not?' Olivia broke the tension.

Lisa's hand hovered. 'OK. Thanks, Zara. How do I change the settings then?' she asked, edging closer towards me.

For the remainder of our lunch break, I helped Lisa track down and ultimately spot her on/off boyfriend on the dating app. But observing her reaction made me realise she seemed more relieved than anything, that her gut was right. I wondered how Andy would feel if he knew I was on it. Surely, he would understand it wasn't a big deal? I mean, I wasn't entertaining anyone else, but I couldn't help but feel a tad guilty after the reaction from my friends. Lisa carried on her shift like an absolute trouper despite me offering to cancel her clients, and left that night looking more robust than ever, ready to confront her partner.

That night I headed back to Andy's flat and was greeted by a bulldozing Tyson. I opened a dog food can and popped it in the bowl down on the kitchen floor before refreshing my WhatsApp. I hadn't heard much from Andy since he'd been on the flight most of the day, but I was waiting patiently to see if he'd arrived safely in the desert. He should have arrived a couple of hours ago. I was in two minds whether to send a needy text or download the flight tracker app to ensure there were no delays. I was staring at my screen, considering my options, when I was knocked to the side by a friendly pooch in desperate need of attention. I couldn't help but smile as I glanced down at him. Perfect. I turned on my camera and snapped a photo, half me looking sad and half Tyson with the caption *'we're missing you already'*. Send.

I lay down in bed, awaiting the two ticks to appear under my message, indicating he'd read it. I tossed and turned, replaying the conversation from lunchtime. I mean it's not that big of a deal to keep an app open on my phone? After all, it had come in useful to poor Lisa today.

I lay back and sighed. My phone suddenly radiated through the dark room.

One new WhatsApp from Andy.

Aww. Miss you more, Darlin. FaceTime in five? xxx

My face lit up, and I felt a surge of happiness and warmth buzz through my veins. His plane had landed safely, he had signal, and he missed me, *phew*. I smiled towards my phone and instantly replied.

Of course! I can't wait xxxx

Bolting to the mirror, I brushed down my hair, pulled off my Christmas fleece pyjama top and exchanged it for a booby vest instead. *I'll make sure he knows what's waiting for him at home*, I thought. Sure enough, within five minutes, I was face to face with my handsome boyfriend. We'd parted just a few hours ago, but as soon as I saw his face, I missed him. He began by excitedly giving me a complete walkthrough of his luxurious apartment, from the walk-in shower to the balcony. It was like an episode of *Cribs* as he paraded the phone through the spacious, glamorous rooms. Everything was stunning. He was like a kid on Christmas Day and his energy was infectious.

'So, how is Tyson?' he asked, finally halting and relaxing down on his bed too.

'He's great! Don't worry, I haven't killed him just yet,' I said, rolling my eyes.

He laughed. 'He'll be loving having you there. I just know dogs aren't your thing . . .'

'If they're your thing . . . they're my thing now.' I blushed at my soppy reply, feeling a need to be overly cute as a slight glimmer of guilt passed through me about my Tinder profile.

'I miss you already. I wish you were here.'

I wished I was with him too. 'Only a few days. Where's Tom? The apartment seems quiet.'

Andy sat upright and chuckled. 'He's *erm* . . . meeting an old friend for a bite to eat and some drinks. They ran into each other in the bar downstairs.'

'And you didn't join them?' I asked.

Andy shuffled around a little, seeming to think carefully about his reply. '*Hmm* . . . Naw, man. It was more of a dinner for two. I know when I'm not wanted.' He laughed.

I felt my face screw up in disgust. 'Seriously! He's thinking about his dick already? He hasn't even unpacked yet. He needs to remember this week is about Raj, he can be so selfish.'

'Awk, the guy's single!' There was a brief silence, then Andy's bright smile spread across the screen. 'So, Zara Smith, how do you feel about phone sex? I've not stopped staring at your tits in that vest. I wonder why I only get the fleecy Grinch PJs when I'm with you!' Andy's eyes glimmered with excitement.

I giggled. 'I mean . . . I could get on board with phone sex. But I haven't got any toys at your place. I took my big dick home after you slagged it off.' I felt my cheeks blush as I remembered the awkward encounter.

'Aye well . . . It's time to go auld school, darlin'. Coz you have another few days of this to get through. Now, will I start, or will you?'

I laughed loudly and before I knew it, I was participating in my first phone sex session in a very long time. My cheeks hurt from smiling at Andy's face, his sweet, warm face. His sexy body.

I rested my head on Andy's side of the pillow that night, inhaling his scent and squeezing his duvet tight, missing him more than I had imagined, and repeating affirmations in my head until I finally fell asleep.

He is perfect, we are perfect, and everything about my life is going perfectly.

Chapter Six

That Wednesday afternoon was predominantly spent glaring at my phone. It was Raj's day to showcase his skills in front of the Dubai Mall, and Andy had promised to share the experience in photos, videos and anything else he could think of. I was in between clients and still hadn't heard a thing.

I paced the floor nervously, thinking about Raj and hoping to God it was all going well.

'I hope Raj is OK,' I said to Ashley, who was unboxing our latest delivery from Juju.

'Aye, so do I. If he messes up, it might affect business for us.'

'*Ash!*' I giggled, shocked at her lack of empathy.

'I'm joking. We all know Tom would stand up there and take over the full thing. He won't let shit go by him, that cunt.'

'Aye, if he even turns up! Andy said he's been out with an "old friend" basically every night.' We both laughed. 'Are you surprised?' I asked.

Ashley hummed a little, then continued to unbox. 'Surprised? Not really. He hasn't dated anyone in months, though. So good on him. His balls must be like watermelons.' She shrugged.

'How do you even know that?' I asked.

'Well, if he hasn't had sex, his balls will be massive?'

I giggled. 'No, not that. I mean how do you know he's not dated in months?'

Ashley shrugged. 'He's chatted about it to me. He said he needed time to heal himself. I don't mean after you chose Andy or anything, I mean after he lost his clinic. He said it was a bad time for him and he wanted to get his life back on track.'

I was mid eye-roll when my phone pinged, and I slipped it out of my back pocket.

One new message: Marion dog.

Hi Zara. Sorry, but I can't make Tyson today in my run. One of the pups I have just now has cut its paw and I need to take it to the vet. I will speak to Andy when he's back and give a full refund. Sorry. Marion.

I let out a large sigh and threw my arms down in a strop.

'Who's shat on your cornflakes, Princess?' Ashley asked. 'Oh my God, is it Raj?'

I stomped my feet. 'No, Marion, the dog walker. She can't take Tyson today, so I'll have to go back to Andy's and walk him.'

Ashley shrugged. 'You finish at five today, you have the full day and night.'

'I know. But I was looking forward to going to my place for a bit. Having a shower, washing my hair, getting ready for Andy coming home tomorrow in my own flat. It's not the same staying somewhere else.'

'Why don't I come with you? It's a night for a walk, plus Dave has football.'

'*Aww*, that would be so good. Yes!' I replied, walking over and squeezing Ashley's shoulders, grateful for her suggestion.

'OK, get finished, and we'll go a stoat about the shops!'

'On it!'

We finished our day and headed to Andy's flat to walk through the city with Tyson. I had only put on his harness and I was already scratching and sneezing like mad. I took his reins as Ashley was in heels, and he sniffed his way through every street, post and alley in the city. I still hadn't heard from Andy and as much as our walk was distracting me, I was still desperate to hear how they'd got on.

'So, are you going to get a drawer at Andy's then?' Ashley asked out of the blue.

I shrugged. 'It makes sense. I'll end up with bigger biceps than him if I keep lugging my bag every day.'

Ashley smiled. 'Oh, so exciting! Next, babies and marriage!' She leaned into me for a hug, but Tyson tugged my arm and pulled me forward.

I gasped. '*No* way, not next. Like way down the line. If ever.'

'If ever? Is that your decision or Andy's?'

'We haven't spoke about it, but I suppose I kind of like my busy life just now. I don't think I'd have time for a baby. It's stressing me having this big eejit for a few days never mind a baby.' I cast a gaze to Tyson, who was licking an old kebab off the ground.

'God, you've always wanted things like ASAP,' Ashley replied.

I nodded. 'I know, but I don't know why. It kind of scares me now. Suppose I was younger and a bit more desperate.'

My phone pinged, and I jumped with excitement. One new video from Andy. Ashley rested her head on my shoulder as we waited for it to load. I was reining Tyson back so he'd remain still while the video played.

Wow, there Raj was. Mic'd up to a massive crowd in the Dubai Mall. He was chatting about aesthetics. Andy videoed the vast group observing his skills. There were even girls hanging over the railing from the level above, keen to see Raj work his magic. The model sat elegantly on the chair, and every time he got close to her, the crowd would scream in appreciation.

'He's like a celebrity, Ash. Listen to that crowd!' I was impressed and trying hard to hear what he was saying behind the screaming crowd.

Ashley squinted from over my shoulder. 'OH. MY. GOD. He's not the celebrity, arsehole! It's . . . it's . . . it's QUINN FOXX!' Suddenly Ashley snatched the phone from my hand and started leaping around Sauchiehall Street excitedly. 'I can't believe this. I can't!' she bellowed. She clasped her hand over her mouth and jumped high. Tyson thought it was some kind of game and tried to imitate her while I was getting dragged along trying to control him.

'*Jesus,* Ashley, fucking calm it,' I hissed, conscious of people staring at us.

'Zara, do you know who she is? Do you know what this means?'

'Quinn Foxx?' I shrugged, having never heard of her until a few seconds before.

Ashley crouched down in a struggle to breathe from all the excitement. I looked around at an entire street of people, wondering what was happening.

'She is *sooo* famous. She is like Princess Diana for the millennials. She is this like amazing feminist woman who is on a mission to ban face filters and photo editing, and all of this stuff. So, the fact she's allowing Raj to inject her face will be massive. It will hit headlines that even *she's* getting work done.'

I was still lost in the commotion but tried to appear as if I knew what was happening.

'This . . .' Ashley aggressively pointed at my iPhone screen. 'This video could be on the six o'clock news tonight! Jackie Bird, Shereen Nanjiani, the lot will be fucking onto it. And do you know who her ex is?' Ashley kept going, throwing her arms wide with excitement.

I shook my head.

'Robbie fuckin' Cran, mate! Robbie Cran!'

I felt my face twisting. 'God love her.'

Robbie Cran was a *huge* American actor who had a string of celebrity girlfriends and was a party boy until he turned his life around and joined a weird religion. He now preaches at any chance about his cult.

'Are you joking! It's fucking big Rab! Together they started this worldwide campaign to stop journalists and newspapers from airbrushing pictures. She doesn't allow one picture of her to be cropped, filtered, airbrushed or anything!'

I glanced back down to the screen and watched the six-foot-something slender woman sitting on the stool. Her golden-blonde beachy hair hung effortlessly down to her waist as she smiled and waved charmingly to the yelling crowd. Even from a distance I could see Quinn had the brightest green eyes with stunningly symmetrical teeth. I tittered to myself, thinking of her whole take on filters. If I looked like that, I definitely wouldn't need to use one either, but, come on, hen, don't ban them, give the rest of us a fucking chance!

'Oh, *and*,' Ashley continued, 'she's into the full war on plastics. She basically championed the plastic straw to paper straw intervention! She's on the news more than that Greta woman.' Ashley took a large breath after exhausting her Wikipedia knowledge on Quinn.

'Well, she sounds like the girl next door! Perfect advertisement for us,' I replied, raising my hands.

'More than perfect. I don't know how the hell they've managed this one, Zara, but that man of yours is a genius if he's had anything to do with getting her on board! Why didn't we go to Dubai? *Why, oh why, oh why!*' Ashley moaned loudly, raising her hands to the gods like she was waiting on a sign.

I giggled, then noticed my phone vibrating in my hand. Anne was calling.

Shit! I hadn't gotten back to her about what days I could work in the ward. 'Ashley, I need to take this.

I'll be back in a second.' I passed the lead to Ash and sprinted inside Waterstones, needing a quiet setting to take the call.

'Hi, Anne. How are you?' I asked.

She cleared her voice, and I immediately remembered how stern she could be. 'Yes, well. I spoke to Jason today, and he mentioned you would be interested in the new advanced nurse practitioner post.'

I paused and felt my heart bang loudly in my chest.

'Yeah, I mean yes, I definitely would be. But I know I haven't been in the hospital for a while, so I know that might look bad,' I replied, seeking some sort of reassurance from her.

'Yes, it may indeed. I take it that's why you wanted extra shifts?' she asked, getting straight to the point.

I nodded, still feeling the intimidation I used to feel when I was a student and she entered the room.

'*Well*?' she asked.

'Yes! That's what I was thinking, keep my skills up before the interview.'

'Well, the job is going live tomorrow at three p.m. I am willing to vouch for Jason and yourself. *But* you will need to work more shifts in the hospital. A few per week before the interview takes place, to ensure you haven't lost all the good qualities I've taught you.'

'*Wow*, yes, absolutely, Anne.'

'It won't be a done deal. There are lots of people interested, Zara. People who have been qualified for a lot longer than you. I'll send you what shifts we require covered tonight. The interviews will be here

66

before you know it, and they will only take the best of the best.'

'I understand that. Thanks, Anne.'

I hung up the phone with a bubble in my belly.

Yes, Anne was willing to vouch for me! She was well respected in the hospital and such a hard cunt to crack, so I knew how much her word meant for me.

I walked back out of the bookstore and glanced around to find Ashley. The street seemed busier, with a sudden rush of people storming down toward Hope Street. Car horns were peeping loudly as the rush hour traffic increased. Again, I scanned the street for Ashley.

'Ash!' I called out.

I was half waiting for her to jump out from behind me like she usually did. As the lowering sunset glared overhead, I raised my hand to my eyes so I could see, when I noticed the red bumpy rash all over my hand. I began pulling up my top and noticed a bad case of the hives travelling up my arms. For fuck sake, Tyson!

'What was all that about?' Ash came up behind me and asked.

'Just work stuff. Look at my arms. Andy's back tomorrow and I am like a dot–to–dot!' I blurted.

Ashley's face fell in disgust.

'Ewwww. That better not be contagious, Zara.'

I raised my hands up at her lack of empathy.

'It's that cunt there. I swear to God, he's killing me by the day.' I was scratching my arms frantically, while Ashley looked conscious of the passers-by staring at my flaring reaction.

'Come on, let's get you home before your face starts swelling. I have a reputation around here and I'm not getting associated with the elephant woman!'

I pierced her with a death stare and she threw her arm around my neck cackling hysterically at my expense.

Chapter Seven

That night I cooled and applied enough Eurax cream to be mistaken for Mrs Doubtfire, keen for my irritated skin to be gone just in time for my man to return from his travels. I checked in with Lisa to see how she was after discovering her baby daddy on Tinder and felt so thankful to be away from the dating scene. The way I was shagging every Tom, Dick and Harry, literally, before I settled with Andy made me realise how much easier my life had become.

I dropped Tyson back at Andy's and returned to my place, enjoying the familiarities of my own surroundings for the night. After I cleaned the house and myself, I finally got settled on the sofa to catch up with the events from Dubai.

As I rewatched the video of Raj performing in the mall, I couldn't take the smile off my face. He looked wonderful, relaxed and completely professional. I hadn't heard much from Andy since the event, but they were probably all out celebrating the day's success. After scrutinising Raj's work creating the perfect lips on Quinn, I proceeded to go full-blown stalker mode on Quinn Foxx's Instagram, Twitter and fan club pages. *Wow*. She was just as captivating as Ashley had described. Quinn was the first model ever to get the front cover of *Vogue* sporting no make-up at all. She'd also dated Robbie Cran for over two years and even attended the Oscars with him. Most recently she had been campaigning for climate change in Dubai and was part of the annual summit earlier this week. I clicked for up-to-date articles and noticed *The Daily Showbiz* had just written a story – '*Quinn Foxx – queen of 'natural' beauty. Contradictory or courageous? As she gets filler treatment in Dubai.*' I flicked through the article and beamed with pride when I saw Raj's name getting a mention, *bingo!* And screenshotted it immediately to Ashley for the clinic's social media.

Next, I searched on Quinn's social media to see the public's reaction to her new look. Her Instagram was full of messages of admiration about her first ever cosmetic procedure being done so honestly, live on stage in front of an audience. She shared a live stream on her Instagram account and tagged Raj in all of the slides. There was no media or press at the event as you needed to apply for a special permit to take pictures in Dubai in a public venue. So, I could only see the pictures and videos Quinn herself posted.

I turned to Twitter next to scrutinise the opinions.

According to FlyKitty86 on Twitter, *Just seen @ QUINNFOXX with a bunch of random hot Scottish guys in Dubai partying! Day made!*

My arse suddenly dropped, and I sat up in shock.

Why is this flawless, activist dream woman sniffing around my man? This knowledge triggered a stab of insecurity. Why had Andy never mentioned he'd booked Quinn for the shoot? That should have been something he was excited to share. One of the most influential women in the beauty and economic industry had allowed Raj to perform aesthetics on her in front of the entire world – so why hadn't Andy shared it with me? I could feel my stomach twisting with anxiety and dread. I needed a nervous poo. Was something going on with Andy and Quinn? I glanced down at myself sitting in fleecy Primark PJs still stained from last month's period and suddenly doubted everything about myself.

I stood up and paced the floor. I was panting, close to hyperventilating. I needed to call him. I needed to know where he was and hear his voice. *But what if he thinks I'm crazy?* What if I started an argument and it brought him closer to Quinn? *OK, play it cool, Zara. Play it cool.* In fact, maybe I could ask what time he'd be home tomorrow, or tell him a random story about Tyson. *Hmm . . . What could I say?* My head was spiralling, full of excuses I could construct to call when I hit the green button.

Dialling.

My heart began throbbing, and I became aware of my foot tapping involuntarily on the wooden floorboards.

Call cancelled.

A surge of cold blood drained from my face instantly. He'd hung up the phone on me.

I was reliving every humiliating moment with Tom, all the stuff with Harriette, all the mind games. And then there was Cameron and the double life he'd been living. I'd believed it all.

I swiped my phone once more and called Ashley.

'Ash?' I asked when it connected.

'Hey, you OK?' she answered, crunching hard while she spoke.

'Are you eating?'

'Aye, why?'

'Aw, for God sake.'

'I'm in my bed eating a fucking apple, Zara. What's up?'

'I think Andy's having an affair with Quinn Foxx,' I spat.

There was a pause and then a roar of laughter came down the line.

'Ashley, I'm serious!' I yelled.

'He fuckin' wishes, mate,' she replied, still giggling but still crunching.

'This isn't a laughing matter, Ash. I swear!'

'Oh God. Right, tell me your evidence, Clouseau . . .'

'Firstly, he didn't mention that he booked her for the shoot. Why wouldn't he tell me that? Why wouldn't he tell you? You're the social media person. And secondly, I just called him, and he hung up, like totally didn't answer. And . . . and . . . lastly . . .' I rushed as I knew Ashley was about to jump in. 'FlyKitty86 said she seen Quinn partying with a bunch of hot SCOTTISH men in Dubai!'

'FlyKitty86? Seriously? FlyKitty's needing a volley up the kitty if she thinks any of the Scottish men we know that are out there are hot in the first place. Sorry, babe, but tell me there is something juicier, like a sex tape or something substantial, Zara. I'm halfway through the *Hollyoaks* omnibus, and you've interrupted a potential murder here.'

'Aye, well, there will be an actual murder tomorrow when I see him if this is true. I know something is going on over there, Ash. I can feel it!' I slumped down on the sofa, feeling wild, weary, and pitiful.

'Get to bed, babe. He's home tomorrow, and you can ask him all your crazy questions then, OK? Andy loves you and he's not a cheat. He's just not. He wants to give you a drawer, hen. Plus, you are amazing, pretty, smart . . . a *tiny* bit crazy, yes. But in a good way. So get off Twitter and get more of that cream on your face. You looked like you had the mumps earlier,' Ash replied.

'OK, night.' I huffed and hung up the call, feeling reassured but more self-conscious of my allergies.

Ping. One new message from Andy.

Hey babe, sorry we're out celebrating in the club, it's too loud to answer. See you tomorrow xx

I shook my head in disgust, grabbed the end of the blanket draped over the couch, and swaddled myself in it. I felt cool tears trickle down my cheeks. I knew I had no evidence. I knew I was being crazy. But something was happening in Dubai that just didn't feel right.

*

I woke the following day to a voice note from a croaky-throated Andy who was boarding the flight and promised that he was looking forward to seeing me. I was still resentful that he hadn't taken my call the previous night, so I wasn't entirely convinced. But I'd promised to walk the dog, so I reluctantly ordered an Uber back to Andy's and waited like a desperate housewife to confront him.

I rehearsed the dramatic scene over and over in my head. One where I'd unmask this great scandal and my not-so-perfect boyfriend would be outed once and for all. I would head to the *Daily Record* and slander Quinn's stellar reputation for wrecking my perfect romance. As the clock ticked closer to 3 p.m. my anger turned to dread and when Andy was due home, the butterflies in my belly turned to moths. It was my day off from clients and I'd promised to go through the mound of orders and invoices but I couldn't concentrate on anything.

Just on time, Andy entered his apartment with a sun-kissed glow and a giant grin on his face. Tyson immediately steered towards him while I stood back in the kitchen, rinsing a mug.

'Where's my boy? Did you miss me? Did you?' He had dropped his bag and was showering Tyson with love and attention.

I looked on, holding my poker face. His eyes met mine from the ground, and he smiled.

'Am I not getting a hug from my best girl too?'

I didn't move.

He stood and moved towards the kitchen. 'What's up with you, darlin'?'

'Why didn't you call me back last night?' I asked sternly, getting straight to the point.

Andy's thumb grazed his mouth in an attempt to hide his smirk. 'Seriously? Dubai is three hours in front. I left the club at one in the morning. I didn't want to phone you at four a.m.'

'Why? I would have been up!' I snapped back.

'What? Why are you acting like this?'

'*Me?*' I felt my face grow warm with anger. 'Why are you acting like this more like? So here I am in Glasgow walking your fucking dog like a right fanny – who, by the way, I'm highly allergic to – so you can swan around Dubai with fucking supermodels while I am stinking of cream and scratching like fuck. All so you can hang out with so-called goody-two-shoes models who you've completely failed to mention to me this entire trip!' My voice was raised, and I could feel my eyes glaze over with tears, still not knowing how this was about to pan out.

'So that's your issue? The girls?' Andy shook his head and let out a small tut of disappointment. 'Can we rewind to last week when you suggested I go to Dubai without you? You could have come, but instead you sent your fuckin' workmate. And the reason I didn't mention the girl – and I assume you're talking about Quinn Foxx – is because she's not my story to tell. So, I was leaving that to someone else. And hey, as for Tyson, I had no idea you were *highly* allergic, I thought he made you sneeze a little, yes. But, if that was the case, I'd have asked my mum to

75

help out while I was away. I just thought you liked hanging out here.'

Andy sat on the sofa. All positive energy from the trip seemed to have been stomped out of him by myself, Zara the elephant woman.

I burst into tears.

'Why are you fucking upset, Zara?' he asked, standing up immediately and coming towards me.

'I don't know. I thought last night you were . . . I don't know . . . with another girl or something,' I mumbled, bubbling into his shoulder.

He patted my back gently.

'Why would I be with another girl when I have you? You're more than enough of a headache for one man!' he said and chuckled softly, rubbing my back.

I rubbed my snot onto my sleeve and tried to smile back, feeling slightly ashamed at my vulnerable outburst.

'How was your flight?' I asked, staring up into Andy's bright blue eyes.

He shrugged. 'Better than Ryanair, that's for sure. Tom's flying home tonight. He missed his.'

I rolled my eyes, not surprised at Tom fucking up the plans one way or another. 'Are you serious? He better not miss his clients tomorrow.'

Andy giggled and kissed my head. 'He's catching it late tonight. He'll be there.'

'I did miss you, you know,' I said.

'I know, darlin', I know,' he said with a grin, reaching over and gently kissing my forehead.

I leaned into Andy's arms and felt comforted. *Why was I being so crazy?* There was nothing more this man could do to reassure me. I finally felt happy and content. He was home and I didn't want him out of my sight again.

Chapter Eight

After an entire night dedicated to sixty-niners and reverse cowgirl, I waltzed into work the following morning like John Wayne, feeling like a new upbeat woman. I felt refreshed and revitalised but my fanny felt like it had birthed ten hedgehogs overnight. Ashley was sitting at the desk as I entered the clinic and she immediately bopped her out from behind the computer screen.

'Morning,' she said.

I beamed back. 'Morning.'

'Oh, someone feels better?'

I nodded, feeling a little embarrassed. 'Much better!' I replied. 'I had a serious shagathon last night and it was just what I needed!'

Ashley laughed. 'You caught up on what you missed while he was away then?'

'We didny half.' I laughed. 'Where's Tom? Doesn't he have a morning appointment?'

Ashley pointed with her large acrylics to the door behind me just as Tom strode in.

'Ah, good morning, ladies. How are you both?' His masculine, musky scent immediately filled the air, and I couldn't help but inhale deeply.

'I'm good. How was the trip? I see your timekeeping in Dubai is just as bad as it is here, eh. Missing flights? I hope that's coming out your own pocket and not mine?' I said all in one breath.

'You mean Raj's?' Tom replied smugly.

'Same thing while I'm managing the accounts, basically. Well, c'mon, how was Dubai? And how amazing was Raj!' I beamed.

Tom seemed unusually nervous as his eyes shyly stuck to the floor darting up only occasionally. 'Yes, it was wonderful. The entire trip was just a dream, Zara.'

'Aye, well, did you leave your tan in Dubai, Tom?' Ashley interrupted cheekily.

'My tan and my heart, Ash.' He looked down once more and smirked. 'Are the girls here? I want to chat with you all.'

'Through the back.' Ashley gestured to the staff room, and Tom walked over, calling on Lisa and Olivia.

Soon we were all gathered on the shop floor. I shot Ash a questioning stare, and she shrugged toward me.

'Come, come, everyone, please,' Tom said, gesturing us to the sofa.

We all sat down. He cleared his throat, and I could hear a flicker of nerves in his voice that I had never heard before.

'I have news for you all,' Tom began. I couldn't help but giggle as Ashley and I made eye contact at his intensity level. 'When I was in Dubai, I rekindled my relationship with an old partner, Quinn Foxx.' I heard gasps from the other girls. It all started to make sense in my head. 'We had the most wonderful few days together, and, consequently, we have decided to tie the knot.'

The room erupted into cheers while I sat still in perfect shock. I felt like I had been punched in the gut by Tyson Fury. The girls swarmed around Tom, hugging and embracing him, but I couldn't move.

'No way! No way! No way!' Lisa screeched.

'Congratulations, like seriously, Tom. You deserve to be happy,' Olivia replied sincerely.

Ashley squeezed him, 'Mate. Mate. Quinn Foxx! I am stunned. How did you manage that one? Seriously though, congratulations.' Tom thanked and giggled back at the girls one by one.

Eventually, I felt his eyes on me, awaiting my reaction.

'Sorry, *erm* . . . sorry. I'm in shock here,' I said. '*Erm* . . . Yes, congratulations!' I walked over and clasped him. I could feel his body against mine and suddenly felt emotional. *How the fuck is Tom engaged?* I let him go and stepped back.

'Quinn Foxx! Tom, she is like my idol!' Olivia screeched in disbelief.

He nodded as the compliments about his new fiancée filled the space, but I remained frozen, trying to absorb the information.

'Can we meet her? Is she coming to Glasgow? And when the hell did you date Quinn Foxx?' Ashley asked.

Lisa gasped. 'Please say she's coming to Scotland!'

'Yes, yes, I'd love all of you to meet her! Of course, I would. We dated many moons ago, just after I graduated and she was slightly less known as she is now. We've always kept in touch with Christmas and birthdays but it sort of feels like fate when she's staying at the same bloody hotel as you in Dubai!' The girls let out a whimper hearing Tom's soppy fucking speech.

'So, Quinn is currently organising our engagement party. We are spending a few days in Milan with our families and friends, then travelling to Bellagio, a small island just outside the city on Lake Como for the big bash. It's in two weeks' time. You are, of course, all invited. But I know it's short notice with the clinic, Zara?'

The group turned to face me. I was still dazed, not taking anything in.

'What?' I replied.

'My engagement party is in two weeks' time in Bellagio, just outside of Milan,' he repeated.

'I know where Bellagio is, Tom.' I tutted through my lies, knowing geography was never my strong point. 'But, in two weeks. You want more time off?' I said, feeling stunned.

He looked just as shocked. 'Well, yes, it's my engagement party, Zara. And unfortunately, Quinn's work commitments are pretty intense.'

'And so are yours, Tom. We have a business to run here.'

The room suddenly felt very silent.

'Let me look at sorting the clients; it is his engagement party. I know we probably won't be able to make it with short notice but let's try to get the groom there, eh, Zara?' Ashley's eyes widened at me to say something.

'Yeah, see what you can do, please, Ash. I'll do extra late nights.' I cleared my throat. 'Again.'

Tom smiled slightly. 'Appreciated, ladies. Another thing, the tabloids want to break the story of our rekindled romance. It's all moving very quickly. I suspect I'll be in the press later today or tomorrow.' He rolled his eyes. 'I wanted to tell you all first. Quinn's publicity manager has put a hold on it being released for a few days to let me get home and tell family first.'

'Well, let's hope the clinic gets a mention, eh? There is always that.' I tittered, still trying to make sense of it all.

'Absolutely!' Tom agreed. 'I am emailing you all invites to the party right now.' He brought out his phone and typed for a few seconds. 'Even if you can't make it to the party, come meet me in Milan. The invite has the dates that I'll need off . . . Done.'

In sync all of our phones pinged and the girls yelped in excitement pulling them out.

'OK, well, girls, will we all get set up for today? I don't mean to cut your moment short, Tom, but I have lots of admin to catch up on because you were away winching.' I attempted a laugh. 'So I guess I'll make a start, eh?' I glanced at Ashley, who gave me a sympathetic smile, then I withdrew into my office.

I closed the door and felt my entire body shake.

Why do I feel sick? I shut my eyes. I felt dizzy with confusion. I could still hear the chatter from outside my door as I rubbed my head, hoping it would all stop.

There was a knock at my door that made me jump because I was still resting against it. I hitched on a smile and opened it. It was Ashley.

'Hey, you OK?' she asked.

'*Shhh.*'

She came into the office and shut the door softly behind her.

'I'm fine. Why wouldn't I be?' I asked, pacing the floor.

'You just look . . .' She paused, searching for the right word.

'Shocked. Yep, I am. Shocked that Tom wanted time off work to woo a girl none of us had ever met. It is a bit of a coincidence if you ask me – he was the one that suggested that trip in the first place? *And* he expects us to attend this party? With two weeks' notice? No fucking chance. To travel to Milan for some tree hugger's engagement party? And I thought she was meant to care about the environment? All of these unnecessary flights back and forth to Dubai and Italy are giving Tom a carbon footprint the size of fuckin' Bigfoot's. But no one seems to be batting an eyelid.'

Ashley appeared taken aback. 'Aye, well, you clearly are. I never knew you cared *so* much.'

'How can Tom, *Tom*, want to settle down? It's *Tom*, Ashley.' I whimpered.

'Maybe it's his time, Zara,' she said, giving me a gentle hug.

I tried to embrace her, but my entire body felt stiff.

I couldn't understand my feelings. I loved Andy more than I could say, but I was so annoyed at Tom. Maybe

I didn't expect him to ever settle down. Maybe I didn't want him to be happy after everything he'd done to me in the past. Maybe part of me didn't want anything to change between us all. I had no idea why I felt so irritated by him. I knew I'd made my decision to pick Andy, and I would still make the same choice now, but knowing Tom could be so happy with someone else made me feel completely out of sorts.

That afternoon I gazed at the empty application form on my computer screen for the advanced nurse practitioner job, questioning all of my decisions. Was there any point? If Tom was getting married, would he up and leave, so I wouldn't have anyone to work at Individualise? Could I even do the job? Andy was right, it was such a highly skilled position I wasn't sure I'd have a clue what to do. I remained fixated on my computer screen with a sore head niggling and an almighty desire to be left alone.

The door knocked in a familiar beat; I knew who it was before it opened. I forced a smile, pretending to look busy shuffling some papers on the desk as Tom entered the room.

'Hey, come in, Tom. Everything all right?' I asked, barely taking my eyes off my screen.

He sat down opposite me. 'Apologies for springing that on you today, Zara.'

I continued to scroll down the blank screen, making myself look occupied. 'Springing what?'

'My engagement?' He sounded confused.

'Oh *yes*. Don't be silly. I'm genuinely happy for you.'

Tom relaxed back in his chair, stretching out his long body. 'You seemed shocked.'

I glanced at him. His white shirt was open at the neck, exposing a sliver of his hairy, tanned chest.

'Hmm . . . I suppose I was. You went on a business trip for a couple of days, and you come back—'

'With a spouse. I know,' he interrupted.

'Well, not yet, is she?' I grinned. 'I suppose from a business side of things, I was surprised, but I'm happy for you as a friend.'

Tom's head swayed gently.

'But, then again, I'm surprised you've never mentioned dating Quinn Foxx before.' I shrugged my shoulders, curious about his reasoning.

'I suppose . . . I didn't feel the need. I don't often speak of exes. Firstly, I suppose most women would feel intimidated by her and all the positive work she's accomplished.'

I laughed. 'Really?'

Tom cleared his throat and looked at me. 'Like her abolishing plastic straws?'

'Did she? *Hmm* . . . Well, I wouldn't lead with that one around here. The people of Glasgow won't be too happy knowing she's the fucker to blame for turning our straws soggy on a cocktail night, ha!'

'Zara, you shared the campaign on Facebook, I remember. All that information on the poor baby sea turtles? You were a fan.'

Damn, has this cunt got the memory of a fuckin' elephant or something?

85

'Really? Hmm, don't think it was me.' I paused. 'Oh, wait! Wasn't that the video with Robbie Cran talking about them too? That's clearly why I shared it, *ooft*!' I pretended to waft my face with a piece of paper from my desk feeling somewhat nervous and fidgety all of a sudden.

'Hmm . . . Perhaps. Robbie and Quinn dated a while back. So, possibly.' He seemed unfazed even bringing up one of Hollywood's biggest movie stars.

I gasped, pretending I had no idea of their association. '*No way*. Robbie Cran and Quinn! No. No. You're joking? Jesus Christ, Tom. You have big shoes to fill there!'

Tom scoffed. 'Hardly. I think you're taller than him, Zara. And that's certainly saying something!' As he chuckled casually, I felt my face twist in resentment.

I pretended to laugh until the chuckling slowly died between us. There was a brief silence. 'So, anything else?' I asked.

Tom smiled. 'No, just making sure you're OK.'

I nodded extra enthusiastically. 'Perfecto!' I said and gave an awkward thumbs-up to show some form of acceptance.

The door closed, and my body flopped down with exhaustion.

Why does he get his happily ever after?

Chapter Nine

I walked home that night, keen to return to my own flat. The streets were dark and silent, but my head was messy and full of questions. As soon as I opened my front door, I dropped my bag to the floor and pulled off my T-shirt and trousers as I walked through to the bedroom to locate the comfiest pair of pyjamas I could find. I forced my hair into a top knot at the front of my head and settled down to zone out in front of the television.

Around nine, my buzzer rang, and I dragged myself over to the intercom.

'Awrite darlin', it's me,' Andy's husky voice came out of the speaker. I pressed for him to come up.

Shit, my house was a riot. I quickly volleyed the earlier discarded pile of unwashed clothes into a bundle and shoved it into the cupboard just as the door handle turned and Andy came in.

'I wasn't expecting you!' I said, feeling slightly flustered at the mess.

Andy grinned. He was wearing a pale blue polo shirt that made his eyes seem even more intense.

'Aye, well, I missed you. Nice bun,' he joked, reminding me how much I looked like the Peru

Two. *Fuck*. I grabbed hold of my hair, but Andy reached for my wrist. 'Keep it. It looks cute!' He leaned forward and kissed my forehead.

I laughed, thinking this cunt seriously needed to update his prescription from Specsavers. I returned to my spot on the sofa, and Andy followed.

'How was work?' he asked.

'Yeah, it was fine.' I sighed. 'Sorry, I don't feel myself. I've had a migraine all day,' I said, feeling too tired to converse much.

Andy hummed gently under his breath. '*And* . . . any news from Tom about the holiday?' he asked, raising his brows.

'You knew?' I replied sharply.

Andy tilted his head to the side, looking confused. 'Of course I knew.' He raised his hands defensively, taken aback by my tone of voice.

'I was with you all last night, and you didn't think to mention one of my staff had just got engaged to a fuckin' celebrity?' I could feel myself warm with irritation.

Andy tutted. 'Your staff member is also your mate, Zara. I wasn't going to tell you *his* good news. That was for him to say.'

'Good news?' I said sarcastically.

Andy's face screwed up, and he got to his feet. 'Why is it not good news?'

I suddenly felt stuck. I didn't know what to say, or why I was even reacting like this. 'Eh, well . . . he'll be jet-setting around the world instead of working for a start?' I snapped, stuttering slightly at the confrontation.

'Have you asked him that?' Andy asked.

I shook my head, trying to conceal the emotion coming over me. I couldn't let Andy see me upset over Tom. I wasn't even sure why I was upset. We had become good friends *finally* and I didn't want the dynamics of the clinic to change already.

'I've worked so hard to get the clinic where it is. We both have. If Tom goes, I'm not sure I'd manage on my own.'

Andy stepped towards me with his arms wide. 'Tom's replaceable, Zara. You would just pick up his clients for a few months, work longer days temporarily and put in the graft until you train someone else. That's how this industry works. Plus, you don't know if he's going anywhere.'

A few months. My heart was dampened at my dream ANP job getting further out of reach as my responsibilities firmly remained with Individualise. But I knew Andy wouldn't understand my wish to return to the wards, and realised there was no point in confiding in him.

'Look, Zara, people meet, find love and move on. You can't get ragin' at one of your best pals for finally meeting a girl he actually loves?'

There was a silence in the room and I felt like I had been punched in the gut.

Was Andy was right? I've moved on so why shouldn't Tom?

'I'm here and I can help sort the clinic with you, babe,' he continued.

I turned to him and bopped my head, finally attempting a smile.

'I know. I'm sorry. I just don't want you to hold anything back from me, Andy. Especially when it's to do with the clinic. I could have been better prepared today if I knew all this drama beforehand and it wasn't a complete fuckin' surprise.'

'OK, darlin'. Noted. Now come here, I've missed you.' He reached over with his muscley arms and held me tightly, close to his warm chest.

After our second argument, we embraced and eventually got cosy on my couch. Andy briefed me all about Raj's successful debut in Dubai. He explained how his wife and son held banners during the show supporting him and how the television channels and press gathered in the car park outside the mall desperate to report on what Quinn Foxx had got done to her natural face. My cheeks hurt from smiling as Andy filled me in on Raj's success, and it made me realise how much I had missed Raj.

'That's where he proposed, you know?' Andy said.

I felt another blow as he mentioned it. 'What's that?' I asked.

'Tom. He proposed at the mall. So, after the show, he took the mic and did a full grand choir instrumental thing from the crowd. Then, random people in the crowd started singing. It was class.' Andy smiled, reliving the moment.

'*Oh*, like a flash mob?'

'Aye, that's it. They sang that song . . . erm . . .' Andy cleared his throat and attempted to sing. 'I had died every day . . . that one.' He giggled at his rendition.

'Sounds like a funeral rather than a fucking proposal if you ask me.'

'Ha, naw! It's like a love song.' He giggled.

I smiled at Andy trying his best to recite Christina Perri's 'A Thousand Years'.

'I know the one, it sounds perfect,' I said.

'The full thing made me think of us, and where we were going.'

I felt my heart quicken, not sure if I was ready for a deep conversation after today.

'I mean, I can't wait to marry you one day, Zara. Have kids and everything. I know it's soon just now, but we're settled, you know? I feel like it's just around the corner for us.'

I paused, not knowing how to react. I wasn't even sure if I wanted to get married. I was still figuring out how to keep a boyfriend for more than five minutes never mind a husband. Not to mention a child.

I smiled back at Andy, and nodded.

'One day, maybe. The thought of having kids just now scares the shit out of me. But I'm happy at where we are.'

I leaned over for a kiss, hoping a distraction would temporarily pause the conversation. His lips felt juicy and soft, and he let it go deeper, pushing himself onto me.

'*Mmmm . . .*' I murmured as the change in atmosphere ignited the room. His tongue felt soft against mine, and my body pressed into his, desiring more. I pulled down on his muscular shoulders and felt his firm chest against mine.

'What do you want me to do?' Andy asked, panting between kisses.

'Fuck me,' I ordered.

With one tug at my waist, Andy had yanked my bottoms to my ankles and then pulled down the zip in his jeans. No foreplay, no touching. He took hold of his hard dick and thrust it inside me. I moaned as I felt it push inside.

'Fuck me,' I called back once more, and he grabbed hold of my leg, bent one of my knees up to his shoulder and leaned his face into mine.

'Do you want it deep like this?' Andy asked, pushing his dick further inside me.

'Yes,' I called loudly, desperate to feel something else other than today's confusion.

'Good girl.'

Andy started fucking hard in and out. Over and over. I watched him pound me. His enormous shoulders and large arms draped in tattoos looked so masculine on top of me. I loved watching his handsome face tower above. I loved watching his big dick slipping in and out, feeling every stroke inside me. I loved being here with him.

'I'm gonna cum,' he growled. The way he took control was unbelievably sexy.

'Me too,' I replied. Even though I wasn't quite ready, I sort of felt obliged as he had done all the graft.

Andy began moaning and grabbing the sofa tightly. 'Aw, yes, yes, ya fuckin' beauty!' He roared as I did my best fake orgasm, yelping simultaneously.

'*Ohh, yes, yes, mmmm . . .*'

With a sweet, satisfied smile, he bent down towards me; I felt his damp face kiss me lovingly. He seemed completely unaware of my Oscar-winning performance and rather proud of his.

'Oh, that was good. Do you want a glass of juice? You're roasting,' I asked, pulling my trousers back up with a slight sigh, ready to do the cum run to the bathroom while still feeling my itch hadn't been thoroughly scratched.

'Aye, just water is fine for me, babe,' he replied, still catching his breath.

I returned from the bathroom and ran the cold tap while watching Andy pull off his top in a bid to cool down. His upper body was sculptured neatly, and he sported the tiniest little potbelly, which I adored. There was something so manly about it, and it made me feel less self-conscious about my muffin top. I loved waking up in the morning and resting my head on it as we chatted carelessly about work and life.

'So, what do you think about Tom and Quinn then?' Andy asked, approaching the kitchen.

I shrugged. 'I don't have an opinion. I don't know the lassie. What did you think of her?'

He smirked. 'She's sound, total perfection, similar to Tom, I suppose, so, yeah, good match all round.'

I hummed as I passed the glass of water to him.

'But to get engaged after a few days is just mental. Like they haven't even lived together or spent enough time with one another. I just think he's gone in head first,' I replied.

93

'Yeah, but there were fireworks, Zara. They had something, you know. Everyone could see it. But I know what you mean. Unless you live with someone, how do you know you'll like each other's quirks?'

'Like, when someone grinds their teeth in their sleep, for instance.' I laughed and looked playfully at Andy, a serial grinder.

'Or when someone farts out the balcony,' he returned smugly.

I gasped as I felt my face turn beetroot. 'What?!'

'Yep, sweetheart, Mike next door told me. He said you nearly blew him to Greenock with that arse.'

Both of us erupted into laughter as my cover was blown.

'I honestly don't know what you're talking about.' I was holding my side from laughing, still wanting to deny my farts.

'Babe, it's fine. I was impressed you had your cover well thought out. I usually run the shower and turn up the GBX so I can fart like a machine gun all at once!' Andy and I were laughing so loud my cheeks were hurting.

'So, here, seriously right. Like I was saying, I was thinking about us,' Andy said. His expression was suddenly serious, more so than usual. 'I can't ask you with a brass band or anything cheesy like that, but, if you want, would you like to move in with me? Like, permanently.'

I paused. My heart thumped in my chest.

I had never lived with a man before. I could feel my face stick with sheer surprise.

Say something, Zara. Say something?

'Wow!' I responded. 'I know I'm there all the time but do you think it's OK this soon?'

Andy looked unnerved and shrugged his shoulders a little.

'Well, I've been thinking about it for like a month. *Awk,* I just think it makes sense. We want to spend the future together so let's stop wasting time and start now, darlin'?' Andy puffed slightly, trying to explain himself. 'When I watched Tom and Quinn together it made me realise you can't put a time limit on these things. You're my future, Zara, and I think you need to start thinking about doing grown-up things now. I know it's scary, and you've never lived with a guy before. But we're not getting any younger, darlin'. We need to start planning for the next stage of our lives.'

Shit. He was right. I was in my early thirties with not much to show for it. But the thought of not having my own quiet place to stay terrified me. Making plans for my future terrified me. Living with a dog who would have me scratching and sneezing the rest of my fucking life terrified me. But then, I thought of Tom. How could he make a decision like that in just a couple of days and I was swaying over moving in with my boyfriend who I practically lived with anyway? I took a deep breath.

'OK.' I nodded, still taking in Andy's proposal. 'OK. Let's do it.' I leapt over to my beautiful boyfriend, splashing his glass of water all over us and we squeezed one another.

And just like that, with a cheer and a fanny half-full of jizz, I, Zara Smith, made plans to leave my single life city apartment behind and officially move in with my boyfriend.

Chapter Ten

The following morning, breakfast at Eusebi's with Ashley and my sister Emily was more of an exciting prospect than our usual catch-up breakfasts were. Before Andy, I was usually the hungover singleton spilling my guts on my list of Tinder dates that I'd rattled that week but now the breakfast dynamics had changed; I felt like a responsible adult catching up with friends and conversing about everyday life, finally having a *normal* monogamous relationship. I had been wholeheartedly lifted from my Dubai slump, and I swaggered into the Italian deli with a huge grin and a whole lot of chat to tell the girls.

'Morning!' I called out as I approached them, where they were sitting glued to Ashley's screen. 'Hello?' I said, not getting my usual hug greeting from my sister.

They fluttered their hands at me, ushering me to take a seat beside them and coorie in.

'What are we watching?' I asked.

'Tom's engagement video in the mall! It's been leaked on the showbiz websites. You need to see this, Zara, it's the most amazing thing,' my sister gushed.

I reluctantly glanced down and grinned. 'Looks like a poor man's *Love Actually* with the band and shit.'

'There is nothing poor about that man, Zara. Fuck, you should know that!' Ashley laughed back.

Emily gasped loudly. 'Oh my God, Giuliana is doing a profile on Tom! We could phone into *E!* and give them the details!'

Just then, a young waitress approached the table and we momentarily forgot about Tom in favour of the menus.

'Morning ladies, are you ready to order?' she asked.

'Can I have . . . erm . . . the roll and steak sausage, please, and a Diet Coke.' I handed my menu back.

'And can I have the eggs sugo and a black coffee,' Emily said, immediately returning to the phone.

'*Mmm* . . . I'll have the same, please,' Ashley said.

My sister leaned forward and squeezed my hands as the waitress walked off. 'So, how are you feeling about it all?' she asked.

I shrugged my shoulders. 'I dumped him, remember? I think it's a farce, but hey.' I smiled back.

Ashley giggled. 'Savage, Za!' She was engrossed in her phone again. 'God, they want to know every inch of him, don't they?'

I chuckled. 'Been there – and trust me, it ain't impressive. Two, maybe three if he's lucky!' I whispered, and we all giggled round the table.

'You've changed your tune,' Emily said, blushing slightly. 'I remember you wouldn't shut up about his dick. What did she call it again, Ash?'

I felt myself turn red.

'Oh shit, what was it?' She was bopping up and down on her seat, desperately trying to tease me.

'The devil dick!' they shouted together, then exploded into laughter as I urged them to be silent.

'Or wait,' Ashley imitated my voice, 'Tom with the magical dong!'

'Shhh!' I hissed. 'I've changed my tune because it was like dealing with fucking Voldemort at the end. Nothing but dark magic.'

The waitress came over then with our drinks. I received mine and took a slurp.

'So, I have something to tell you both. Put down the phones!'

Emily sat back in her chair, looking uneasy.

'Go on,' she said.

'Andy asked me to move in with him last night, and I said yes!' I raised my hands in the air, and they both gasped in excitement.

'Aw, Zara. Wow!' Ashley said.

'*Oh my God!* Yes! When are you thinking of moving?' Emily asked. 'Me and the kids could come up and help you get packed up.'

'It's amazing and like wow! But it's only been a few months, Zara? Have you even told him you love him yet?' Ashley questioned.

I paused.

'You know I feel awkward saying things like that out loud. I'm not a lovey dovey girl. But of course I do. He's my boyfriend! We're together all the time and have so much fun. It makes sense.'

Ashley looked a little worried, 'Me and Dave were with each other for like two years before I moved in and even then, I found it hard!'

'I think it's great, Zara! Like you are finally growing up and settling!' Emily was clutching her hands with excitement.

'No, I think it's great too. But I'm like *wow*, super-fast, babe!' Ashley replied, looking more cautious.

'I know it's quick, but I stay there all the time anyway. And I'm older now, Ash, I have to settle down at some point. I'll need help though packing up, it's ridiculous the amount of shit I have in that flat.' We laughed at the table.

'I'll rope Dave into it as long as the football's off; we can help. Obviously, I won't be packing much because of these nails, but I'll keep you lot in check.' Ashley smiled over to me.

I giggled warmly at them. 'Thanks, both of you. I was just going to start moving things gradually over the next few days, then hopefully move in next week or so. What's the point in prolonging it? God, Mum will be so happy I'm finally moving out, won't she, Em?'

Emily nodded over her coffee.

'She'll be happy to get the flat back,' Emily added, as my mum regularly made remarks about moving back to her city home as soon as I moved out.

'You will need to make sure it's clean, Zara. You know what she's like.'

I was slightly insulted. 'I've actually been keeping it clean lately. Andy just pops by unannounced, so I don't want to be sitting in a shit tip.'

Emily laughed. 'Like proper clean though, like a company should come in or something. Years and years of God knows what will be in that flat.' My sister shuddered at the thought.

'Aye, if someone walks in with a UV light, the place will shine like the Blackpool illuminations, full-blown cum scene . . . sorry, crime scene!' Ashley said, and we all erupted into laughter.

'Oh, what about a moving-in party? We could invite Mum round to see Andy's flat and get crisps, dips and wine? Really impress her!' Emily suggested.

'Oh yeah, I'm totally down for that!' I replied, then paused. 'I'll need to get the arsehole dog out the way, though, or he'll hump Mum's leg all night.' I laughed and added in a snooty voice, 'She might not approve of that!'

Ashley made a face and flicked her hair back. 'I think your mum's a dark horse. Bet she's no shy of a hump or two!' She laughed as Emily and I hit her arm, hoping she'd stop.

Our breakfasts arrived and we all began to tuck in. Eusebi's was in the heart of the West End, overlooking Kelvingrove Park. It was family run and always had the most delicious food.

'So, when do you want this house-warming?' Ashley asked, while delving into her breakfast.

'Hmm, next Saturday maybe? I'll have to confirm with Andy, but I'm sure that'll be fine. I'll keep the Sunday clear for the football for the boys,' I replied, rolling my eyes between mouthfuls of sausage.

'Tom leaves on the Thursday,' Ashley said.

The table fell quiet for a few seconds.

'Ideal, then I won't have to invite him!' I eventually shot back, having already thought of the dates in my head.

Ashley's long blonde hair was hanging down past the table, and she tugged it slightly in thought. 'You know we'll need to get them a gift,' she said.

Emily chuckled. 'What the hell do you buy Quinn Foxx?'

'Something keepsake like. Tom cherishes all the sentimental things in life. He's big on cards. But I've no idea what she'd like,' I said, remembering the mounds of thank-you cards from patients he'd keep.

Ashley's large green eyes rolled. 'OK, that helps. *Not*. Fuck it. After this, I'll nip down the Forge Market and get him something cheesy.'

We all laughed, thinking of his disgust.

After breakfast, Ashley headed to the clinic while Emily and I wandered through Kelvingrove Park. It was a mild, fresh morning and the joggers and dog walkers were out in full force.

'How're things with you?' I asked, linking into my sister's arm.

'Good, thanks. Boring compared to your life.'

I laughed. 'Boring is good. Trust me.'

'I'm excited for you and Andy, Zara.' She smiled at me, and I nodded, appreciating the compliment. 'He's a good guy. It's obvious he cares for you a lot.'

'Yeah, he is. I really do for him too. He pushes me, in a good way, he keeps me calm,' I replied, breaking into a smile when I thought of Andy's cute face.

'That's exactly what you need!' she said, squeezing me eagerly.

We continued our walk onto a bustling Byres Road. Emily's husband was picking her up so they could spend a day at the safari park with the kids. I waved them off and blew kisses to my niece and nephew. I loved seeing their little snotty faces and it always cheered me up. As I walked back towards the park, I thought more about Emily and her little loving family and felt nervous as I realised moving in with Andy would be a step closer to settling down. *Was I ready for that?* As worries and doubt set in, I felt a twinge of nerves contract my arse. I mean, I loved spending time with Andy. Of course I did. But was this it? What happened next? What did he expect from me? I knew these were all normal worries people go through, but our relationship seemed to be moving so fast it never dawned on me what Andy wanted or expected to happen next. Fuck, I didn't even know what I wanted yet.

Groups of doting mums pushed past, conducting a theatrical teddy bears' picnic in the park, and I guiltily thought I'd rather drink the pond water fermenting behind them with an ice cream cone stuck up my arse than participate in that kind of activity. All the high-pitched singing and clapping, not to mention the sheer responsibility of keeping another human being alive – it was too much, especially when that very morning I had congratulated myself for remembering to brush my teeth. It just wasn't for me.

I continued walking to the skate park that swirled around the centre of Kelvingrove, and sat on a bench observing the skaters. This was one of my favourite spots in the whole of Glasgow. From the left, I could see the peak of the university's turret through the blowing trees and from the right, the grand fountain sat so elegantly, water catching the sunlight. I took a moment, shut my eyes and breathed. I was panicking, and I knew I had to stop. *You are making the right decision, Zara. You are making the next appropriate step. This is what adults do.* I brought out my phone to text Andy.

> *Don't want to scare you off, but I'm thinking of a moving-in party with my family (and Ash, obvs) in yours next Saturday. What do you think? X*

Sent.

It's your place too! Sounds great to me, babe xxx

I couldn't help but smile at his message. He was always there for reassurance, always so loving and welcoming – something I'd never experienced with anyone before. I sat for a few more peaceful minutes, taking in the beautiful morning in Glasgow, before hopping on the subway and heading back to pack up my home.

Chapter Eleven

A week passed, and I was working hard shifting my entire life into boxes as the big move to Andy's loomed closer. That was in between my *Judge Judy* and *Homes Under the Hammer*, work at the clinic and catch-ups of course. But no matter how much I packed up the flat, it still looked like a work in progress with lots more shit to organise. I loaded all my sentimental things and dismissed and bagged the ridiculous hoarding of size six dresses that I finally accepted I would never fit into again. Twelve bulging bin bags of rubbish were lined up in my living room for the dump. I was gobsmacked by some of the items I'd kept hold of after all these years: old Westlife concert tickets, the lid of my first Buckfast bottle (neatly chewed around the rim), the packaging of the condom I used to lose my virginity, not to mention piles of odd socks and enough batteries to sell to fucking Putin to blow up half of Europe. It felt quite refreshing to know I was moving on, to know my life was about to be condensed and only the necessary parts of my past would be joining me on my next chapter with Andy.

It felt somehow significant that I finished with my clearing out and packing up the day Tom was leaving for Dubai. Although I hadn't seen much of him since his announcement, I planned to pop into the clinic and wish him luck as Ashley had organised a small do for his trip. I knew I was dodging him as much as I could. It wasn't because I felt sad or jealous, it was just awkward and weird chatting to him so openly about other women. Well, another woman. I suddenly understood how he must have felt with Andy and me groping one another all the time.

As I arrived at work just after five as the last customer was leaving, I immediately gasped. Ashley had decorated the entire clinic with balloons and banners, all Italian themed. She stood us all in line at Reception and made Olivia and I rehearse party poppers going off while Lisa was to video it as Tom walked in. She wanted to 'capture the moment', but we all knew she was hoping for a retweet from Quinn Foxx. There was always a business-related ulterior motive with Ash, but I relished it if it benefitted the clinic.

As Tom walked through the door as planned, the group cheered and clapped just as Ashley had conducted us. Tom's face shone as he was taken by surprise.

'Congratulations!' we called out and he laughed at the effort.

He was wearing black denim jeans, a plain black T-shirt and a pair of Ray-Ban sunglasses.

'I like your fit, Tom. I'm getting Alex Turner vibes,' Olivia said as the cheering simmered.

'Who?' Tom asked, raising an eyebrow.

'Say Elvis Presley, he's more familiar with that era, eh, Tom?!' Ashley giggled, and we all joined in.

Tom curled his top lip and gave his best Elvis 'Uh-huh, uh-huh' impression then turned to me and gave a playful grin. I laughed and handed him a glass of limoncello.

'So, are you looking forward to Milan?' I asked in between eating the mallow top hats I'd just spotted.

'Absolutely. Lots of alcohol, good people, and my new bride, of course.' His voice sounded so confident, not a hint of nerves about publicly celebrating his life-long commitment to one of the world's biggest stars. It took me a little aback, knowing how un-committed he had once been with me. I hadn't thought he had this in him.

'This is so unlike you, Tom.' I puffed my cheeks out, still unable to take in the past few weeks. 'You must really like this one.'

Tom paused and turned to me with his arms folded coolly across his chest. 'I've wanted to settle down for a couple of years now. It's time.'

I passed him a fleeting smile while memories of how we'd finished went through my mind. It had been so abrupt and so messy.

'I'm glad you found her. You deserve to be happy. And I know we all wind you up, but, yeah, you really do,' I said, feeling more humane now that I'd said something positive and heartfelt.

Tom lowered his sunglasses, and his eyes looked into mine.

'Thank you, Zara. Out of everyone here, I nee—'

'Didn't want to miss the excitement, my man!'

I turned around as Andy bulldozed through the door and made a beeline for Tom. The two men hugged one another, and I glanced at Ashley, who was smirking in my direction.

'We're gutted we can't make it, mate!' Andy said, pulling back from the embrace with Tom.

Tom grinned. 'I understand. I hope to do a similar party here or down in London for my family. Hopefully, one day we can all celebrate together.'

'Aye, definitely, ma man. It's a shame you're missing our celebration on Saturday too. Not exactly on the same scale, but . . .' Andy shifted to me and smiled lovingly. I felt a stab in my chest. *Shit,* I hadn't mentioned to Tom I was moving in. Not for any particular reason other than I was trying to avoid him for the entire week.

'Oh, I don't think I'm aware of another shindig, Zara Smith?' Tom's loud, deep voice sent shockwaves down my body.

'*Hmmm . . .?*' I pretended not to hear, trying to buy myself more time to think up a reply.

'You didn't let on you were celebrating Saturday night?' Tom seemed a little edgy.

I smiled as if I had just remembered. 'Oh yes, that. I didn't want you to think I was stomping all over your good news. But Andy and I are moving in together.' I fist-pumped the air awkwardly. 'Way hay!'

'Oh, tremendous. Congratulations to you both,' Tom said, nodding in our direction as Andy came closer and squeezed me.

'Aye, we're buzzing, aren't we, darlin'?'

I smiled at Andy, feeling my nose scrunch up, and took a sip of my Italian cocktail.

'For a minute there, I thought you were about to say you were expecting,' Tom proclaimed with a slight chuckle.

I nearly spat out the drink. 'Fuck no!' I exclaimed, answering at an unbelievably fast pace.

'Ching-ching!' Tom joked, nudging my arm while Andy remained silent.

I turned to look at him and noticed his face twist as he bit his lip agitatedly. Tom caught the tension and swivelled on his heels, walking over to the desk where the alcohol was posing.

Andy's chin pierced into my shoulder. 'Fuck no?' he whispered in my ear. 'That was awfy dismissive. Especially after our conversation the other night.'

'Was it?' I replied, conscious of anyone overhearing a potential argument.

'Aye, well, put it this way: it hurt my feelings, Zara,' Andy said.

I paused, wondering why he was so tetchy.

'I'm sorry,' I said, keeping my voice low. 'It was a joke. I didn't mean "fuck no" to kids with you; it was "fuck no" to kids in general.'

'What do you mean by that?'

Fucking hell, I thought. My cheeks were suddenly warm with the interrogation.

'What I mean is, I'm still young,' I said, trying to be diplomatic. 'I still want to accomplish things before even considering having a conversation about that. God.'

'You're in your thirties, Zara,' he said.

'That's right,' I snapped. 'Still young.'

I took a breath, conscious of where we were, and gazed around the room, making sure no one was witnessing the intense conversation. The girls were too busy taking selfies with Tom while Ashley rearranged the tray of bruschetta for any potential photographs.

'What else do you need to accomplish? Climb fucking Kilimanjaro or something? Because, let's face it, both of us are at the top of our careers right now. I don't mean to be dicky, hen, or pressure you, but you need to start growing up a little here, Zara. What is going on with you, man? All this talk about taking shitty jobs and not moving forward.' Andy puffed out a large, loud sigh, and I noticed a few glimpses from the others thrown our way. 'Look, I'm sorry but that was a snidey comment from you, and you know it.'

I started to tear up, stunned by Andy's reaction.

Don't cry in front of everyone, Zara. Don't cry.

'I'm sorry if I hurt your feelings . . . I just . . . it just came out. I didn't think. I honestly haven't thought about kids seriously before. It's not something that I even know I want, Andy. We've only been together a few months, maybe I just need more time to get used to that idea.' I didn't want any drama, especially here, and bringing up that I wanted to accomplish more in my nursing career would have gone down like a fat kid on a seesaw. I retreated.

'I know. Right, OK, I'm sorry, darling.' He kissed my head from the back and he draped his arm around my shoulder. 'I just didn't expect that to be your reaction. I think I'm just so buzzing that this is happening and thinking of what it means for us. For the future. You know I want to marry you one day, Zara, and I'd do it tomorrow if I could.'

'I know. I'm sorry, Andy. I didn't think. I'm just not used to proper relationships like this. I like going at a bit of a slower pace, that's all,' I replied, feeling ever so slightly better about our misunderstanding. Andy had one serious relationship his entire life before me and I knew he wanted the *dream life*: married, good careers, nice house et cetera whereas I'd struggled to live off one dick for a week before him, never mind the rest of my life. I wanted Andy but I knew I wanted to go along with my own timeline.

'OK. Yeah. Yeah. I get you.' He smiled, pulling me closer to him again.

I stood on my tippy toes and leaned forward for a make-up kiss.

'Let me get you home, baby,' he said, his voice lowering cheekily.

At the sound of me laughing the others briefly turned to us before resuming their conversations.

'I hate when we argue,' Andy said. 'Well, disagree.'

'I do too. I hate confrontation full stop.' I sighed.

'Awk, I'm sorry, darling. I know you do. I feel bad I got so touchy. Here, mon home and I'll go down on you for a good hour, I promise!' He smirked, grabbing my waist.

'Stop, stop! That's blackmail!'

He shrugged his shoulders playfully. 'That's facts!'

I stuck out a petted lip, knowing I couldn't factor in a shagathon on top of all the packing I had to do. Besides, I knew all too well that a man may promise an hour lick-out sesh, but he would take at least forty minutes to find the clitoris and by then, his tongue would be as limp as a silk handkerchief.

'I honestly can't. I have so much to clean and a few things to pack before tomorrow. I need to go back to mine. You could come up and help me?' I hinted at some much-needed assistance.

'Can't, babe. I have Tyson getting dropped off at six, I'll have to head in five.'

'Well, it looks like you'll need to wait till move-in night then, sunshine. I'm totally tied up with boxes.' I winked at my boyfriend and attempted to walk away. But instead, he grabbed my arm and pulled me back.

'I'll tie you up, more like!'

'Stop. I have to mingle!' I giggled.

And Andy kissed me once more. 'I'll go and call you later then, babe.' I nodded and watched him approach Tom, shaking his hand and leaving the clinic. I went over to the others and when Tom joined us I laughed as they quizzed him on the celebrities he thought would be attending his engagement party.

'OK, what about Sebastian Stan? They done that Hugo Boss advert together, didn't they?'

Tom just smirked at the quickfire questions.

'Did they?'

He didn't flinch.

'What about Donald Trump?' Olivia asked.

Tom sat down on the chair behind the desk and crossed his legs casually, giving a brief dramatic pause. 'No, Olivia, Donald Trump will not be attending my engagement party.' We all laughed. 'However, Quinn has invited bishops and diplomats from Rome and around the world,' he explained.

'No way. Are they going?' Lisa seemed shocked.

'I believe so. Next week, Quinn is delivering a speech about global warming at the Vatican.' Tom seemed wholly impressed as he boasted about his new bride's accomplishments, and I couldn't help but feel slightly uncomfortable at his newfound, utterly intimidating fiancée's celeb status.

The party continued, and an hour later, we packed up the mess and said our farewells to our friend.

'So you'll FaceTime me from the party? Take pictures, and if you see anyone famous, you'll get them to send me a personalised video saying hello? Like the ones Wagner does?' Ashley demanded as she hugged Tom.

'I . . . *erm* . . . promise.' He embraced her in return and over her shoulder mouthed to the group *Not a fucking chance.* We all giggled; Ashley was blissfully unaware.

I watched as Tom made his way around the group one by one, receiving advice on what to do, what to wear, how to be a good husband, and, eventually, we were face to face once more.

'So, when you come back, you will be one step closer to being officially off the market, Thomas Adams,' I joked. 'The women of Glasgow will be in mourning!'

He nodded. 'Indeed.'

We looked at one another without saying a word for a sweet, fleeting moment.

Eventually, I cleared my throat. 'Well, come here.'

Tom's long muscular arms reached out, embracing me. It was a warm, heartfelt and wholesome hug. I closed my eyes tightly to be in the moment. It felt meaningful, yet it felt like something else too. It felt like we were saying goodbye. I knew he would only be away a week, but as I watched him leave the clinic, I also knew it was the end of an era for us.

Chapter Twelve

The following day I only had morning clients booked in, so I cut from the clinic early to get hammered into my packing. I had left Ashley in charge of the clinic with Lisa and Olivia's appointments full. It felt strange observing my flat declutter. As the rooms emptied one by one, I couldn't help but feel a little empty myself, but I knew this was a necessary step into adulthood. I was finally moving out of my mum's flat and going to be living with a man and creating a life together – *Jesus,* how scary? For a few years there, I'd worried about the future. I honestly thought once I got to a certain age, my life would consist of lying about in week-old BO-smelling, fake-tanned, mahogany-brown bed covers with only my Rampant Rabbit and a few jars of Nutella to keep me company. Not that that doesn't seem appealing from time to time by any means. But I supposed I had something more with Andy. Something genuine and real. And *yes*, I was shitting my pants a little to move in, but it was the right time for us. Plus, he was saving me a fortune in batteries.

That night I gaped at the bareness of the flat. The kitchen drawers were cleaned. I was leaving the pile of mismatched plates I'd randomly acquired over the years as Andy had some decent Royal Doulton ceramics that all matched. I'd cleared the bathroom – all the shampoos and conditioners were bagged and only a shrunken toilet roll perched on the bath panel remained. The living room was tidied and wiped down. I decided to leave the sofa but packed the TV to put up in the bedroom. As I walked around, I could hear my footsteps echo throughout the flat, and it made me smile – *end of the shag pad, Zara.*

Andy buzzed on the intercom, and I let him up.

'Wow, this place looks like a ghost town, babe. Good work!' He smiled, kissing my forehead. 'Will we start loading the van?'

I nodded.

'I sort of feel guilty leaving it behind. All those memories!'

I felt Andy's large, heavy arm hang around my shoulders as he squeezed into me. 'C'mon, babe.'

Together we lifted the boxes and the overloaded Ikea bags and carried them down to his borrowed van. I strategically picked the lighter loads, pretending to be struggling as he stumbled down the concrete stairs behind me. Soon, the move was complete.

Andy and I walked back up for one last scoot around. I sat quietly on the edge of the sofa while he bopped his head in and out of the rooms.

'Babe, you have hunners of clothes hanging still?' I heard Andy's voice call out from the bedroom.

I let out a puff of defeat. *Nooooo!* I couldn't face more packing.

'Shit! That was my rack of undecided – keep or not. I forgot about them,' I moaned.

Andy laughed. 'Do you want me to pack them for you? We have to do it quickly, though. I've left Tyson in for a while now.'

I beamed at his kind face. 'Nah, don't be silly. You go. I'll sort it. I'll have my last night here, and we'll have the party tomorrow.' I squeezed my fists excitedly at the very thought of my first grown-up party. I had done a complete M&S party food order for the occasion too, which would probably leave me skint for the rest of the month, but it was worth it to impress my mother.

'Are you sure?' he replied, rustling his fingers through my hair.

I nodded, feeling nostalgic. 'Yeah, I'll sort this out and get to bed.' I rose to my tippy toes and leaned into his juicy lips. 'See you tomorrow!'

Andy leaned forward for another few kisses. 'Can't wait, roomie,' he said, then smacked my arse so loud it resounded around the now empty flat.

I waved him out just after ten, then glanced in the direction of my bedroom and huffed. *OK, the last mound of clothes and then bed.*

I reluctantly returned to my bedroom, pulled the last clothes pile onto the floor, and knelt down to tackle it. I lifted each item individually, analysing it and placing it in the keep or bin stack. I had sequined dresses, flared trousers, and snake-print leggings. Every item held a special place in my heart, and I giggled at the memories as I considered each piece of clothing. I squeezed my arms into the red Berghaus I'd acquired during my ned days at high school and thought back to the time I wore it getting winched against Mohammad's shop shutters; when wee Tam the Bam slipped the hand, and my vagina was touched for the very first time by a boy. I remembered boasting about it for weeks to my friends – not that he did anything remotely satisfying beyond stroking a few of my wiry pubes down. Still, I remembered that exhilarating feeling of being a dirty badass bitch that night.

Definitely keep the Berghaus.

I was combing through the items until I came to a black blazer that made me pause. Instantly I smiled as I recalled wearing it not too long ago. It was the night Tom and I went out to Cut for his leaving dinner. We had just come up with the Individualise prospect having turned the clinic around from months of struggling, and thought Raj was returning the following day. Tom was only working there temporarily at the time and we all thought it was his leaving night, so I'd taken him for a thank-you meal. That was also the night I bounced into an Uber and got the driver to race like Dick Dastardly to Tom's place for one last shag after the meal. Sitting on the floor, I went through each moment that night. Even replaying it in my mind sent a rush of blood down below. I experienced an immediate pang of guilt for just reminding myself how good it felt to be in something so risky, so passionate, so fucking hot. I threw the blazer into the bin pile, hoping to rid myself of the memory along with the jacket. But, as it hit the floor, I noticed a small piece of folded paper falling from the pocket.

Curious, I picked it up from the ground and stood up. The paper felt stiff from being pressed in the same position for a while, but, as it unfolded, I felt my heart quicken as I recognised Tom's handwriting.

What the hell was this?

My eyes skimmed over the neat, privately schooled handwriting, and I began reading.

Miss Smith consultation.

Your nose has a small dorsal hump – a three-point technique could disguise this.

You have laughter lines when you smile – Botox would straighten these out.

Your top lip is much smaller than your bottom lip – 1ml of filler would amplify this.

Bear with me, PTO . . .

Please turn over . . . *Fuck sake, Tom*. I wondered how much more of my face the cunt wanted to scrutinise. But somehow it made me laugh, knowing how much of a perfectionist he was. As I turned the note over, I replayed this very night out in my head, mapping one another's faces in the restaurant. I remembered how we tried out the Individualised concept on one another. How I had read out all my suggestions of what Tom needed, and when he was about to read his suggestions, this very note, out loud, I stopped him. I was far too insecure to let my ex list the physical changes I required to be perfect to him, so he popped it in my pocket until I was ready. I couldn't help but smile as I continued to read his suggestions.

Your nose is unique and unsymmetrical. Yet somehow I am plagued with butterflies each time you scrunch it up.

Your laugh is one of the greatest sounds I've heard on this earth – and I love your laughter lines, as even when you're not laughing, they remind me of when you do.

Your top lip is small but one of the purest things I've touched on this planet.

I know you asked me for a list of things to fix, but it's wholly impossible when your imperfections are utter perfection to me.

They are the reason I'm here, the reason I smile and the reason I won't ever go away.

Always yours,

Mr Tom Adams

My head was spinning. I was numb, paralysed completely.

It can't be. Was this a joke? Was he taking the piss? My fuzzy head was flashing back to that night and I replayed every second, every thought. My legs shook and with a thud I was slumped onto the floor. I reread the note over and over.

Why did I have to find this tonight? The night before I was due to move in with my boyfriend? *Surely this doesn't mean anything now? Time has passed since this. Tom's engaged. I've settled down. Jesus, why now?* I felt the coldness of watery tears pour down my face without making a sound. Why had he never said any of this to me before? Would it have changed how things ended, or was it just a way of getting me into bed that night? Would it have changed what I thought of him? Would it have changed who I chose that night at the clinic?

What do I do now?

Chapter Thirteen

That night I lay awake on my empty bedroom floor, rereading the note surrounded by a jumble sale of clothes. My entire body was achy and tired, and my face felt as if it had been stuck in a fucking beehive for ten hours. The inside of my head was full of anxiety and what ifs until the sound of my phone cut through the silence.

One new message from Ashley.

Hey, do you want me to bring some Whispering Angel tonight? A client left some at the desk for you xxx

I scrolled down my phone to see an earlier message from Andy.

Morning darling, I'll pick up the buffet. On my way to get a haircut. What time will you be HOME!! Xx

I automatically broke into a guilty sob. *I'm such an arsehole. He's getting organised for my moving-in party while I'm questioning choosing him entirely. What kind of a person does that?* I moved up onto my knees, my body stiff from lying on the hard floor, and brushed myself down. *It's only a wobble, Zara. You love Andy.* I knew deep down I was an overthinker. Surely, it's natural to have this type of reaction when you're taking a big step in life? I lifted the rest of the items and decided to put them all in the bag for the charity shop, peeling off the Berghaus that was now stuck to me from hours of sweating. *Out with the old and in with the new.* Andy was my future, and I had to seriously stop living in the past with made-up fantasies of *what ifs.* I knew I was no longer the wee lassie getting poked off behind Mohammad's shop and I knew I wasn't the insecure mess of a girl who once got messed around by Tom Adams.

I walked through to the bathroom, soaked my face with cold water, and took a breath. *Get it together, Zara.*

As I walked back to the living room, I took out my phone and replied to Andy.

Morning, Fab! I need to drop things off at the charity shop and get ready. I'll meet you at the flat for everyone arriving. Xxx

He instantly replied with a single red love heart. I had to stop overthinking. Life with Andy was simple, uncomplicated and moving like a real relationship should. *This is what I want, he is who I chose.*

That afternoon, I walked down a dry, sunny Argyle Street and handed in some bags to the local charity shop, hoping they'd make use of my old clothes. As I passed the overflowing Ikea bag to the smiling lady behind the counter, I felt a massive weight lift from my shoulders. I was letting go of the past and I felt upbeat. *This is what adults do.* On the way back to my flat, I wandered through Primark and scoured the home section looking for accessories to add a bit of femininity to my new gaff. I grabbed a few beige vases, a fleecy throw for the sofa and some candles. I also couldn't leave without purchasing a new silky pyjama set.

At the till I felt a pair of giant hands grab me from the back.

'Eh, hello!'

I turned to see Jason, and I immediately grinned and hugged him as I lifted the bag off the counter. We took a few steps away from the checkout and stopped.

'So, do you not return any texts now, Zara?' Jason asked, putting a hand to his heart dramatically.

I laughed, suddenly remembering the umpteen voice messages he'd sent about this new job opportunity.

'I'm so sorry. I've had the craziest few weeks, honestly.'

He nodded his head, briefly pouting, waiting for a better excuse.

'Tom went to Dubai. I'm sure you've heard what happened there. I've been running the clinic by myself, *and* Andy's asked me to move in with him, so I've been spending all my free time getting packed up. I move in tonight!' I felt a smile explode over my face.

Jason gasped and squeezed my arms excitedly. 'Aww, chick! So happy for you! That's amazing.' He paused then and looked more serious. 'Tell me you've had a chance to put your application in between all of your madness?'

I felt a weight in my chest, having completely neglected the new job at the Royal.

'I haven't,' I admitted.

'Zara!' He groaned.

'I know, I know. It's probably not the best time for me to be doing something like that, to be honest. But I can't wait to see you smash it.'

Jason's face screwed up. 'When will you have another chance, though? I've waited ten years for a job like this to come up. There's still time. The application closing date isn't for a few weeks.'

I nodded, having googled the job description at least one hundred times that week. 'I know. I know. It would be amazing.' Being around Jason again made me realise how much I loved the old acute nursing side of my life. 'But . . .'

'What's stopping you? The clinic?'

I swayed, slightly uncomfortable at his direct questions. 'Yes, and my inexperience. And Andy, to be honest.'

Jason looked confused. 'Andy? Your boyfriend?'

I nodded. 'When I mentioned it to him, he sort of . . . well, he sort of thought it was a bad idea. He thinks my life running the clinic is much more . . .' I thought carefully about my next words when Jason interrupted.

'Boring?' he replied sharply. 'I'm sorry, Zara. But what do *you* want to do? It's not Andy that will be doing the job.'

I paused, feeling guilty for talking about Andy when he wasn't here to defend himself. 'No, I get it, though.

I'd be working much longer hours, and financially it wouldn't benefit me as much as the clinic does.'

'That's fine, babe, if that's *your* decision. Just be true to yourself, though. I'd hate to think you're passing on an opportunity you want because of a man, you know?' He looked at me kindly, and I felt a sudden burst of emotion that I was trying to hide.

'No, I get you – one hundred per cent. I think it would be the ultimate job, but even applying would rock the boat with Andy just now.' I shrugged as I moved a few steps out of the way of some impatient shoppers.

Jason hummed a little. He went to speak but then stopped himself.

'I know. I know what you're saying,' I replied without him having to say a word.

'Have you spoken to Tom about it?'

Hearing his name again made my face red.

'Tom?' I repeated.

'Well, you value his opinion. And I'm sure he gets it more than Andy,' Jason said.

I nodded. 'Yeah, he said go for it.'

'Ahhh, we agree on something, Thomas!' Jason giggled.

I laughed, and we began to walk towards the shop entrance together.

'Think, Zara. But don't write it off because your latest boyfriend disagrees. Promise me you'll do what feels right for you. OK?'

I smiled, realising how much I'd needed the advice. Even though I didn't see him often, he always looked out for me. 'Thanks, Jason,' I said. 'You know we're having a little house-warming tonight if you're free, just my mum, sister and the girls from the clinic are coming over. You could meet Andy properly. I promise he's lovely.' I laughed.

'Ohh . . . I have hot yoga, but that beats it. Send me the details. I'm dying to meet your mother!' He laughed, knowing the stories of her harshness.

'Oh, I've been the favourite daughter since I met Andy. No more problem child Zara! She's very proud!'

'And why wouldn't she be? You're fabulous, darling.' Jason winked, and I hugged him.

'OK, I'll text you the address. See you about seven?'

Jason gave me a thumbs up, and I waved him off down the street.

As I walked back up a hilly Glasgow to my flat for what might be the very last time, I thought about what Jason had said. I knew deep down I wanted the job. However, I wasn't sure if I would get it. What if I caused arguments with Andy even applying for a position just to be told no? It would all be for nothing. Still, something in me wanted to be back in the hospital. I knew I would have to talk to him about it, but it wouldn't be today. Tonight was about us: me and Andy. So, I walked back to my flat and started to get ready with Lizzo blaring from my iPhone.

Chapter Fourteen

Three hours later, after a nap and an entire bottle of Barefoot consumed, I was running fashionably late to my own party. It was half seven and I was dressed in a white skater dress with my leather jacket draped over my shoulders. I still had a few bags of necessities to bring to Andy's, like my make-up, charger, my folder of documents and invoices. I glanced around the bare, simple-looking flat and sighed nervously, feeling a weird sort of guilt that I was leaving it behind. Through it all – my dramas, my highs and lows – it had been *my* place of refuge.

As I did one last wander, I noticed Tom's note still lying on the floor exactly where I'd left it. I reached down without giving it a second thought and scrunched it up into my pocket.

OK, time to go.

I went on my phone and ordered an Uber, locked up the flat and then walked down to meet the cab with a couple of bags for life at either end of my arms.

'You set?' the driver asked.

'I guess,' I replied, smiling, but watching as we drove away from my empty flat for the last time.

My stomach was achy with nerves. I glanced at my phone to see a screed of text messages.

Andy: *Where r you? Everyone here?*
Zara!?
Call me? You're out of order.

Ashley: *Hurry up, Zara! Your mum is asking where you are xx.*

Mum: *Timekeeping Zara.*

I grunted and replied quickly to Ashley: *Sorry on the way. Had more stuff to pack up. Tell Andy for me xxx*

The taxi pulled up on the opposite side of the road from Andy's flat, right at the riverfront.

'Is this OK for you here, hen?' the driver asked.

'Yeah, of course, thank you.' I automatically went to tip him, but as I delved into my pocket, the note from Tom fell out again. I seized it, disguising it from the unaware driver, handed him a few pounds, and jumped out of the car.

The road to cross was busy, and I glanced up toward Andy's apartment. I could see figures illuminated inside as the balcony doors were slightly ajar. I was still clutching at the note. A feeling of dread overcame me. *Was I doing the right thing?* There was no way I could bring it into the apartment, this was the start of my next chapter and I didn't want the curse of Tom holding me back, so I turned and made a few steps to the water. I leaned over the painted railing with my bags resting at my feet. *Let go, Zara. Let go.* I wanted to rip it apart and forget I had ever seen it. To throw it into the Clyde and watch it sink to the bottom along with the Tesco trolleys and cans of Stella. But something was stopping me. Why could I not let go? My eyes darted back to Andy's apartment; Ashley was staring out the window at me. She held her hands up, confused about what I was doing, and I placed my finger on my lips for her to stay quiet. I needed a couple of more minutes alone to think. To breathe.

What was I doing?

I pulled up straight, my heart beating so loudly I could feel it in my ears. Yet I stayed fixated on the dark river below. *I can't do this. I can't.* I had to make sure I was doing the right thing. I had to make sure I'd made the right choice that night I chose Andy in the clinic. I was clutching the note so tightly I could feel my hand begin to shake. I had to see Tom.

I brought out my phone and texted Andy.

I'm so sorry but I can't do this right now. There's somewhere I have to go.

I picked up my bags and ran back to the taxi I had just gotten out of, which was still waiting at the side of the road.

'Can you take me to the airport instead?' I asked.

Chapter Fifteen

Four hours later, I was navigating myself onto a seat on an easyJet flight to Milan with a three-hundred-quid dent on my credit card for the flight and two overpriced bottles of Prosecco in the airport. After sending Andy the text I switched my phone to flight mode; no one, not even Ashley, knew where I was going. Half of me didn't want to admit my destination or my intent to anyone out loud because I knew they'd tell me I was crazy, they'd try to make me see sense, and, the truth was, I didn't want to. I wanted to take a risk. I want to be wild. It was better than possibly regretting not knowing how Tom really felt. I wanted to confront Tom about the letter and look into his dark eyes and hear him tell me whether every word in that letter was true or not true. Either way, I'd have my answer.

The other half of me didn't want to deal with the shit show of a mess I'd left back home in Glasgow. It didn't want to deal with Andy. I didn't want to be reminded of how much of a horrible person I was to do this to someone. Or hear from my mother about how this was just another disappointing stunt from Zara to be spoken about at every Christmas and family get-together from now until one of us died.

So, I switched off from it all, helped nicely by the Prosecco bubbles and an evening flight with a budget airline to Milan's biggest airport.

The plane landed with a thump and I woke from a broken, slightly drunken sleep. The reality of waking up in a foreign country with only two bags for life for luggage neatly stowed in the overhead compartment packed with paperwork, basic make-up and a charger was sinking in, and I started to feel my body turn into a pool of sweat. What the fuck was I doing? I hadn't booked a hotel or anything, yet here I was in the middle of Italy with not even a clean pair of knickers.

Everyone began disembarking from the aircraft, and I followed behind, still numb from the night before. *Maybe I should call Raj?* I knew he was attending the pre-party events and he'd certainly pick me up from the airport, but he'd also tell me how mental my plan was. Maybe force me on a flight back to Glasgow and I wasn't ready for a lecture or to deal with any consequences.

I stood in line for passport checks and scrolled down my emails until I found one from Tom sent a few weeks prior.

Miss Quinn Foxx and Mr Thomas Adams invite you to celebrate their engagement party.
August the 19th at the Grand Hotel Villa Serbelloni Bellagio, Lake Como.

7 p.m. till late
RSVP for the dress code.

The party wasn't for two days, and I knew I had to see Tom before then. He was in Milan, but I had no idea where. I felt shivers creep down my spine with nerves then suddenly I felt a shove from behind.

'You want to go, hen? We're all waiting,' an impatient man said, gesturing, and I realised it was my turn.

Once through the passport checks I continued ploughing my way through the lavish airport towards the trainline terminal.

'*Erm* . . . Milan Central station, I suppose,' I said to the man behind the desk at the ticket office, and with a nod of his head and a train ticket in hand, I was suddenly on an express train to finally get some answers.

As the train stopped at Milan Central, I grabbed hold of my bags and walked along the platform. The rush of the busy tourists thundering their way past me made me feel dizzy, and I began to wonder if I had done the right thing. *Am I crazy?* But then I'd always think back to the note Tom left me. *I need to know. I need to know I'm heading in the right direction with Andy. I can't spend my life with him always wondering what if?*

I wandered out of the terminal building, and Milan was in darkness. I took a small breath of humid air and smiled at the night-time bustle. The buildings were architecturally cultured, just like I'd seen in photographs. Old fairy-tale-like buildings with huge windows and the odd small balcony that overlooked the street. Taxis and bikes lined the road waiting to escort passengers to their destinations. But I had no idea where to go. My body felt exhausted from a day of travelling, but my mind was alive with a new determination to find Tom.

I walked along the city, admiring the small bakeries that were still serving customers late into the night. I took a breath, inhaling the rich smells of Italy, knowing that at this time in Glasgow the only smell I'd be able to inhale was the 240 bus exhaust and some weed from passing teens. I passed by the bars, which echoed loudly with laughter from inside. I peered into each one wondering if Tom would be inside, but deep down I knew finding him wouldn't be so easy. Finally, I stood at the lights, allowing a tram to pass by, and crossed over the road heading to the first hotel I could see.

'Hey, can I have a room, please?' I asked the small Italian man serving.

'Do you have a reservation?' he asked, not breaking eye contact with his screen.

'No,' I replied nervously, praying I wouldn't be homeless and sold to the Italian mafia on a whim to confront my ex.

'Hmm . . . How many nights?' he asked.

Shit, I hadn't even thought about that. If I found Tom tomorrow before he left for his party on Bellagio, I could return to Glasgow that night.

'Erm . . . one.' I hesitated, doing the maths in my head.

'Fill in your details here. And that will be three hundred euro, miss.'

134

My stomach cramped as I felt another considerable dent on my credit card.

Great. I'll be paying this back till my next breakdown, I thought.

'Here you go,' I replied, handing back the pen and tapping the screen with my credit card.

'Third floor. Room 313.'

I smiled at the man as he handed me my key.

'Welcome to Milano!' He grinned, finally glancing up at me.

I felt butterflies engulf my stomach at his words. I was in fucking Milan! I was on an adventure. I felt exhilarated but terrified all at once. I struggled to go to the toilet alone on a night out, never mind travel to a foreign country.

'Thank you!'

I pressed the elevator call button and headed up to my room. As I opened the door, a smile sprinkled across my face as the city lights met my gaze. Wow. I threw my bags onto the bed and looked out at the skyline. He was near. I just wasn't sure where. I could feel him around me. I paused, feeling my hands shake with apprehension. Tomorrow I'd have my answers, and I'd know exactly where my life was going.

Chapter Sixteen

I woke up late the following morning with the ultimate fear. Here I was in Milan by myself with not even a clean pair of knickers to my name, trying to approach a hot-shot surgeon engaged to a famous celebrity. What the fuck was I thinking?

The Prosecco buzz had well and truly worn off and my mind swarmed with doubts. But I still found myself rereading the note over and over. *He loves my nose, my lines, me!* I am not imagining this. I had to get some answers.

I sat up in bed and examined the beautiful view. The city was alive with shoppers and tourists scouring the small winding streets, snapping up every unique sight. The sun was warm and beamed over the multi-coloured buildings, almost hurting my eyes as I admired it. Everything in my room seemed peaceful and quiet, yet I could feel apprehension grow in the clammy air. I could feel my nerves echo throughout the room. I wanted to talk to someone – Ashley, Raj, Emily or Jason, but I knew none of them would understand. They'd talk sense into me, and I'd be admitted to the Priory as soon as my flight landed back in Glasgow.

I had to see this out and be true to my feelings, and I was committed. It was too late to go back now. I'd already left Andy and my house-warming and I didn't have much else to lose. So, I took a deep breath fuelled with worry and began to get ready, back into last night's outfit.

I had to meet Tom today, before he left for Bellagio. I had to explain to him why I was here. Maybe he'd realise he was making the wrong decision when he saw me, that he was marrying the wrong woman. Maybe he would tell me that I was in the past and Quinn was his future, and I'd then know I had made the right decision that night in the clinic all those months ago. If I hung around the town centre, even googled Quinn's whereabouts, I'd hopefully bump into him. But my phone was turned off and there was no way I was switching it back on, not after boosting to Italy on a whim. I hoped my friends hadn't called out a search party from my disappearing act. I thought about them all back home and my stomach twisted with anxiety. I flopped back onto the bed. *What would they think? What would Andy think?* I squeezed my head in my hands and shook it off. *You're here now, Zara.* This was something I had to do. Putting them all to the back of my mind I stood up, grabbed hold of my bags for check-out, and headed to the hotel reception. I needed to buy new clothes, have a coffee and plan exactly what I would say to Tom.

I headed back to the reception and returned my room key. I had one day to sort my life out, and this was it.

As I wandered through the warm city at just 11 a.m., I quickly realised that I seemed to be getting nowhere. After an hour of winding roads I realised I had absolutely no sense of where to go in the city. The tall buildings limited my views of where I was headed, and behind every corner was a different sight, from parks to small delis to large built-up city buildings.

I examined every person that passed me, hoping I'd find him, or a clue that would lead me to him. The fashion capital was full of large groups of diverse people. Men were wearing high heels, and women were in power suits. I was utterly captivated by them all, knowing they'd, unfortunately, last about three minutes in Glasgow without getting egged or taunted for their uniqueness.

As my legs became weak and my arms heavy from gripping my bags, I found a small restaurant and sat outside, feeling slightly deflated. It was like finding a needle in a haystack. With no phone, no friends, and no idea where he was. As the waiter approached me with the breakfast menu, I glanced over it, craving my typical roll and sausage with fried onion fix. He stood beside me, waiting on my order.

'Erm . . . the panettone, please and a strong coffee.' I smiled back at him as I returned the menu. I flopped my head onto the table as he returned to the counter. It was only midday, yet the humidity was building up, and I could begin to feel the effects on my underarms, having not washed or had a spray of deodorant. I couldn't see Tom like this. What was I thinking?

'Some coffee, *la ragazza*?' a deep voice said behind me, and I lifted my head quickly.

'Thank you, yes!' I replied, feeling slightly flustered at the dramatic way I was sitting.

A tall server set down my coffee, and I couldn't help but admire his colourful eye make-up and acrylic nails.

'I love your make-up,' I said.

'Grazie!' he replied and attempted to walk away, then turned. 'Hey, why are you so blah? It's still so early! You can't be so blah already!' He giggled, reaching up to the bright sky in delight.

I puffed slightly. Where the fuck did I start without sounding like a complete psychopath.

'Awk, I know. But, look at me! Look how I'm dressed,' I shrugged. 'I'm in Milan alone, I have no idea where anything is, and I'm chasing someone I have no idea where to find!' I laughed a little, shaking my head at my shitty situation, beginning to break off a piece of bread.

'Well, I can help you with the shops. Head straight up this road for ten minutes and find The Galleria Vittorio Emanuele. It's to die for!' He winked.

'Thank you,' I replied gratefully with my teeth filled with bread.

'But just a warning, I passed Quinn Foxx heading in there about twenty minutes ago so that place might be overrun with the press!' He tutted a little sassily.

I felt my face fall and almost choked with shock.

'Quinn Foxx, the American actress?'

'The American queen! Yes!' He shimmied his shoulders happily.

'Ha!' I screeched. 'You have no idea how much that helps,' I replied quickly, wolfing down my sweet bit of bread and taking a large slurp of coffee.

He broke into laughter, and I pulled out my card to pay the bill. 'Can I pay? Like, just now?' I asked, still pressing the bread into my mouth.

'Si, I'll get the machine!' He giggled, heading back through to the cashier's desk. When he returned, my coffee was downed, and I was wiping off the crumbs, eager to move on.

'Twelve euros,' he said with the broadest grin. I tapped my card against the reader and smiled warmly at him.

'Hey, one last thing. Don't come to Milano to chase a man. Come to chase your dreams!' He winked again. This time his shimmery glittered eye caught a glint of the sun, and I smiled at his sparkle, then nodded back confidently.

'That's exactly what I intend to do!' I replied happily, feeling empowered, and began power-walking, budging through the crowded city with a coffee buzz and a tiny glimmer of hope that I was finally heading in the right direction.

As my walk continued, I pushed through my stitch and, ten minutes later, I stopped. There stood the most magnificent cathedral I had ever seen. It was over one hundred metres tall, smack bang in the shopping district, and my jaw dropped. This place was insane. Its white gothic pillars, statues of saints, and crosses fixed onto the building make it look like it had been wholly transported here from another era. I stood in awe, wishing I had someone to share the moment with. It almost lit up the square. I read the sign outside the church, Duomo di Milano. I held my face in disbelief at its beauty. I strolled around the building, trying to take it all in, watching couples pose for selfies outside it. I couldn't help but think of Andy. He would love this: the culture, the food, the romance. I started to feel a pang of guilt. Then I noticed another grand building across from the cathedral, Galleria Vittorio Emanuelle II. I gasped. This was it, this was where Tom must be.

As I headed through the arched entrance and onto the shiny marbled floors, I looked at the enormity of the centre. It stood four storeys high and was more like a five-star hotel than my usual jaunt to Silverburn. The ceiling was bright, with large glass domes pushing the sun through and brightening the space. Where was he? I wondered. I began walking through the shops and quickly realised that shopping in Milan wasn't the same as in Glasgow's town centre. Ferrari, Louis Vuitton, Gucci, Prada and other high-end shops I wouldn't even dare to pronounce. I trundled past countless women in classy branded outfits with small dogs in their bags, casually smoking through the mall while chatting to their friends elegantly in Italian accents.

'Quinn, Quinn, over here!' I heard someone call out from above me and immediately felt sick.

My eyes darted around the chic space until they fell on an escalator, and I began scurrying towards it. *What would I say to him?* I wondered. I hadn't planned my speech. Even if I could see his reaction to me being there, maybe I'd know. Perhaps he'd know. The escalator seemed to move slower than George W. Bush, as I barged through the crowd till I finally reached the top. Groups of people and paparazzi swarmed, calling out Quinn's name. I could feel the adrenaline ripple inside me as I pushed through the crowds to catch a glimpse of her and finally see Tom. White flashes and screaming fans echoed in the background, but I felt like I couldn't hear a thing as I edged in fuelled with adrenaline, wanting to say my piece finally.

'Quinn, Quinn, over here, Quinn!' The crowd began yelling.

I found a tiny hole between the paparazzi's shoulder, raising my head through the crowd, and noted the screams becoming louder as she turned my way. Then, finally, I spotted a tiny woman with a huge sun hat, cream maxi dress and humungous sunglasses waving towards the crowd. Oh my God. *Was he here?* I peered around the entourage of staff she had, desperately searching for Tom, but my eyes fell on Quinn instead. *Wow.* She was beautiful. She was fascinatingly perfect. I leaned forward, taking in her beauty between the gaps of screaming fans, and watched her long blonde hair blow effortlessly like silk. My jaw dropped as her perfect smile took centre stage in one of the most beautiful buildings in Italy.

'We love you, Quinn!' the crowds called out, following her steps.

'When is the party?' one person shouted.

'Tomorrow night! I'm heading there soon!' Her American accent sounded like she belonged in Hollywood. 'It will be a private affair, so please respect that for mine and my fiancé's friends and family!'

Fiancé. Fuck, even the word made me feel nauseous. I felt a cold trickle of sweat run down my back.

With a flick of her hair, Quinn was quickly escorted out of the building, and I pushed and prodded out of the way by the adoring fans keen to snap her for a picture.

I stood like a statue, remaining remarkably still, taking everything in. Then with one hard thump, I sat on a bench in the shop foyer. I hadn't anticipated her beauty, her class. *What the hell was I doing here?* I looked down at the floor and noticed my shoes were black with footprints from the stampede of fans. Great. Quinn looked almost shiny with her fresh skin and designer clothes, and here I was, looking like I was on a three-day bender. But still, I couldn't get the note out of my head. Tom wasn't the type to express his feelings, all the time I'd known him. It had to mean something. Even if I wasn't sure what it meant to me, I needed a conversation. I thought back to all the moments he'd tried to speak to me, at work, even that night at the bar – *are you happy, Zara?* And I'd dismissed him. I'd gotten angry at him. Tom deserved some closure from me after writing all of those things. I couldn't give up. But I also couldn't let him see me like this. So, I stood up, brushed down my once-white dress, and headed towards the first shop that caught my eye.

Chapter Seventeen

I entered the shop and was immediately eyeballed by beautiful assistants wearing immaculate outfits. 'Ciao,' one greeted me at the door.

'Hi.' I smiled back. I walked over to the ladies' section, conscious of the time I had to pick an outfit, get changed, and find Tom before he left the city for his party. I pushed and examined the rail, hoping to find a pretty dress or perhaps the old jeans and a nice top combo. I knew the weather wasn't ideal for jeans, but the reality of not shaving my legs for a few days was beginning to show as my once-smooth pins felt as rough as a badger's arse.

'Can I help you?' One of the workers approached me.

'Do you have this in size twelve?' I held up a plain white jumpsuit with halter-neck detail.

The woman gave an unconscious eye roll. 'We only stock up to a UK size ten. Perhaps some of the other shops will be best suited, size-wise.' She attempted to take the item from me, but I held it tightly.

'Miss, we don't have your size.'

I paused. Aye, nae bother hen. *What sort of shop doesn't cater for the average dress size?* I wondered. But I didn't have time to go on a fucking shopping spree.

Despite the insult, I breathed deeply, then said, 'I will try the ten then, *please*.'

'Well . . . OK. Follow me, *please*.' She walked towards the fitting rooms, and I stood in the doorway while she went to a room through the back. She returned with the jumpsuit and passed it to me.

'Grazie.' I gave an over-exaggerated grin to the worker and pulled across the thick velvet curtain to get ready.

As I yanked off my skater dress, which felt sticky against my skin from all the walking, I began hauling up the jumpsuit. I felt my fingers admire the touch of the thick silky fabric. *This might be the one, Zara.* I felt a ripple of excitement, imagining myself approaching Tom in my new classy outfit. But as I pulled it over my stomach with a tug, I began to feel how restricted it was. Fucking hell. *Why don't they have a size up?* I continued hoping it would all come together and when I had finally fixed the halter tie, I glanced at the mirror. My camel toe was feasting on half the material. Jesus! With an almighty clawed attempt to pull it out of my vagina, not wanting to cause permanent damage to my love button, I suddenly felt a pop. Relief at last. But then, as I turned, I noticed the large split up the arse exposing my bum hole to the mirror. *Oh, no!* I paused and held my hands to my face.

'Is everything all right? Would you like me to adjust anything, miss?' the shop assistant asked.

I began to sweat profusely.

'Would you like me to come in?' I noticed the curtain twitch from the side.

I'd like you to fuck off, hen. That's what I'd like.

'Erm . . . no. No, thanks. It's a stunning jumpsuit, but I'm not . . . I'm not too fond of the material, to be honest,' I mumbled, trying to pull it back over my stomach.

'The material? It's the finest Italian silk.' She sounded offended.

Italian silk? *Shit.* I began unfastening the neck and pushing it down my body, kicking it off at the legs, and lifted the tag, €2,100. I gasped. No wonder it had its very own Kevin Costner at the curtain.

'You know, I think . . . I think I'll leave it,' I replied.

With my dress thrown back on, I pulled on the curtain to see her standing with her hand on her hips.

'Grazie!' I returned the jumpsuit and legged it back through the shop onto the mall floor.

My heart was racing. I hurried back down the escalator towards the entrance and onto the street, hoping a security guard wouldn't come after me and demand me to pay for the damages.

I turned to the vast cathedral facing me once more. *Please, please help me, God.* I was on the verge of a breakdown and felt my bottom lip quiver, feeling completely defeated. As I lifted my head from the ground, I spotted a young girl clutching an H&M bag. I felt my face lift immediately, and continued further down the street until I spotted the huge flagship store. Ha! *Yes! Yes! Thank you, God!* I ran inside and immediately felt at home. Rails of discounted dresses, T-shirts and shorts. Hallelujah! With a quick supermarket sweep bustle, in under ten minutes, I was standing at the till paying for three dresses, a pair of sandals, two tops, jeans and shorts – all for €109. I felt exhilarated, clean, and like I was finally a step closer to accomplishing my mission.

I returned to the square and sat on a bench overlooking the grand cathedral. *OK, so where would Tom go?* I wondered. I felt myself reach for my phone instinctively but remembered it was switched off and dropped it back into my bag. I people-watched, hoping he'd pass by me at some point. Whenever I heard a posh English accent, my head turned, almost causing me whiplash. But he wasn't anywhere. Groups of school kids, couples, and best friends gathered around the church, capturing memories as I sat like a grumpy gargoyle trying to lure him in.

I knew he'd be leaving soon to head to the Lake and begin the party preparation, but there was something about this church that gave me hope and I didn't want to leave it.

About forty minutes later, I eventually stood up as two pensioners looked like they needed a rest more than I did, so I wandered to the top of the high steps. It overlooked the entire square, and I watched the bustle as the restaurants and cafés surrounding me attended to their guests. I raised my hand to my forehead, blocking the sun glare, wishing I had spent the extra €4 on cheap sunglasses, but then I spotted a familiar smile. I closed my dry eyes and opened them again. It couldn't be. Across the square, leaving a fancy restaurant was Raj. And following directly behind him was Tom. Suddenly, everything stopped. My heart quickened.

I waved my hands in the air frantically hoping they'd spot me, but I saw Raj pointing in the opposite direction towards the tram line. My legs felt like jelly. *Please turn around, Raj, please.* They began walking away, and I tried to move but felt stuck with nerves.

This was it. Move, Zara, fucking go.

I started hurling down the giant stone steps, two at a time. *Please don't fall. Please don't fall*, I prayed and barged through the crowds approaching me.

'Tom, Tom,' I screamed. But he was too far away. 'Tom! Raj!' I started to feel out of breath and I couldn't see them anymore. Crowds of tourists lined the street admiring the landmark, and they had completely disappeared amongst the group.

Finally, I stood at the edge of the pavement, scanning up and down the street and road.

'TOM!' I screamed out at the top of my lungs, but nothing came back, bar a few strange looks.

I heard a squeal of a passing tram, which made me step backwards, but as it continued, I noticed Tom and Raj on board. Their faces were laughing at one another, seeming carefree from their day exploring the beautiful city. 'No! Tom, Tom!' I began racing to the edge of the tram, as my new purchases fell from my bags. I briefly halted to pick them up, but then continued chasing down the tram hoping he'd hear me or turn around.

'TOM, RAJ!' I ran and ran as fast as I could, hoping they'd spot me. Hoping Tom would hear my voice and tell the driver to stop, but he never noticed. The tram continued down the tracks much quicker than I possibly could and when it eventually disappeared out of sight, I stopped, laden with half-empty bags. I felt tears run down my exhausted face.

He's gone.

I heard an almighty yelp escape from my lungs as my body gasped desperately for air.

I felt myself leaning into an old stone building.

I only had two choices left now: going home or going to Bellagio, and I needed to decide fast. I wasn't sure which was the easier option, to deal with Andy and try apologising for running away and live with never knowing how Tom really felt. Or to put on my big girl pants and head to the party, risking ruining the whole thing – my friend's engagement – for a silly note from months before.

I paused and closed my eyes.

'Taxi!' I called out.

A black car stopped and rolled down its window.

'Can you take me to Bellagio, please, driver?'

Chapter Eighteen

A dark cloud of anxiety loomed over me. The journey out of the city at rush hour was much longer than I'd anticipated and the humidity was catching my breath along with the taxi driver's Columbian cigar. I felt dizzy with nerves and adrenaline, replaying the possible situations over in my head, with only my mind for distraction. *What if I saw Tom and Quinn in the lobby?* Would I just come clean? Explain that I had to see him and ensure his feelings were gone? Or would I wish him luck and hope he came to me? I had no idea. I slumped into the leather hotbox replaying possible scenarios in my head. I imagined Tom seeing me and realising instantly that I was the one and I wouldn't have to admit any of my crazy journey and what brought me here in the first place. I imagined him completely rejecting me and humiliating me in some form of evil toast in front of all his guests. At one point I even wondered if the taxi driver was secretly some kind of axe murderer who captured young-*ish* women travelling alone by taking them to his secret cottage in the hillside, and then quickly realised that would still be a better option than living with Tom's toast humiliation. Eventually, almost two hours later the taxi came to a stop.

'We are here, miss,' his deep voice called from the front seat, and I sat up.

All I could see was dark water in front of us, as the sun was setting around us. 'Where is this Grand Hotel?' I asked. The taxi driver sniggered as panic began to set in as I could only see the stillness of water. 'Driver, is this Bellagio?'

'No. This Varenna. You need to get on boat to Bellagio,' he answered.

'The boat?' I repeated.

He laughed and pointed to the bright lights approaching us from the water.

'This boat?' I asked, watching a large ferry come towards the dock.

'Yes. Yes.' He held his card reader up to me to hurry me along. I tapped my credit card on top to pay, then looked nervously at the dark choppy waters surrounded by mountains and gulped.

'OK, well, thank you.' I hopped out of the car and closed the door. Then looked around the small deserted village. I spotted a small queue of people waiting to board at the side of the dock and joined them anxiously. Truthfully, I hadn't been on a boat since my younger Ibiza days where I was spewing over the edge after two many slut-drops and Jägers. *Where the hell was I going?* I struggled to navigate myself through Braehead on a busy afternoon never mind travelling alone in a foreign land. Why couldn't Tom have a normal engagement party in the Normandy or down the Alona like everyone else? I wondered.

'BELLAGIO, BELLAGIO!' A man dressed in a captain's uniform stood at the top of the boat deck and ushered the passengers on board.

Well, this was it. I began walking forward, tightly gripping the railings as well as my bags as my feet slid against the metal below me. I could feel the water wobble us, yet still continued on board, following the crowd towards the ticket office.

'One adult to Bellagio, please,' I asked a small elderly man behind the desk puffing on a cigarette.

He printed out a small ticket without any eye contact whatsoever and shouted, 'Next.'

A few minutes later with a loud sound of a horn we were leaving the quiet town of Varenna behind and speeding across Lake Como. There were no seats available on the ferry and I stood on the bottom deck getting sprayed by the water. If the taxi driver wasn't going to do me in, perhaps this was. I had no idea where I was going with only the dark night sky and shadows casting over us from the mountains.

Only ten minutes later, I began to see twinkling lights from a small island.

I had seen pictures of Bellagio on television, but they didn't capture the majestic element like the real thing. The entire town was built on mountainsides. The old cobbled streets and greenery seemed like I'd been transported to another era. I couldn't believe this place existed just outside the bustling built-up city of Milan. Everything was still and peaceful. As the boat came closer to shore, I spotted the small boutique designer shops lining the bay, and the fancy restaurants crowding the streets. I could hear very faint laughter combined with classical music as we pulled into the dock. It was peaceful, quiet, romantic. Nothing in comparison to the squeals of trams and groups of tourists like Milan had. The Grand Hotel Villa Serbelloni immediately caught my eye being the proudest and most majestic on the small island. It was situated right beside the waterfront and it was the most elegant place I'd ever seen. I felt my breath catch as I took in the night-time lights twinkling off the water. I carefully stepped off the boat and walked towards it. I smiled as I passed by the laid-back couples sipping on expensive wine.

As I got closer to the hotel steps, the door opened and I was met by one of the staff.

'Good evening, miss. Can I take your luggage?'

I smiled at the enthusiastic worker and passed him my two woven Tesco bags, and large H&M haul. 'That's it.' I shrugged, and he briefly bowed before leading me inside the building.

The lobby was like stepping into a movie set. Massive chandeliers hung from the ceiling with the cleanest white walls and gold fittings. The floor shone so brightly it took my eyes a second to adjust. It reminded me of a palace. I had never seen anything like it before in my life. *Wow.*

People were escorting huge flower arrangements through the lobby, and I knew almost certainly it was for Tom's party.

'Excuse me, can I take your name, please?' a voice from the reception desk called out, and I approached.

'Hi, yes. I don't have a reservation, but I would like to stay for a couple of nights, please.'

The man behind the desk laughed. 'No reservation? We are full,' he said, dismissing me in his Italian accent.

I felt my eyes water from all the stress. 'Could you check again, please?'

He shrugged and gestured for the next couple to approach the desk.

I felt a rush of panic.

'Listen, mister, I am attending a party, and I am a personal guest of Quinn Foxx. She assured me I'd have a room here. I don't think she'll be happy when I tell her about this,' I said, lowering my voice to a whisper in case any of her entourage could hear.

He immediately sat up on his seat, his smug face simmering into a helpful grin.

'Ahhh, you should have said. I have reserved the ground floor with an open terrace for VIP guests of the happy couple. Can I take your name?'

I felt a wave of relief wash through me. 'I thought so, it's Zara – Zara Smith.'

He began typing into his computer. 'I don't see your name,' he replied.

'I'm a news reporter from Britain. The *erm* . . .

BBC.' My heart was pounding as the lies spilled out of my mouth.

His eyes brightened. 'How many nights are you staying, Miss Smith?'

'Erm . . . maybe one, maybe two actually.' I thought about it and realised I hadn't booked my flight home or anything.

'How many nights?'

'Two.' If the party was the following night, I would need time to talk to Tom.

'Credit or debit card?'

I smiled back. 'Credit.'

'That will be eight hundred euro.' He reached over for my card.

'Can you convert that to pounds, please?'

He rolled his eyes, brought out his calculator and typed loudly. 'Seven hundred and sixty pounds, ma'am. We will charge you at the end of your stay if it's easier. Can I see your passport and card, and I will lead you to your room?'

I felt my jaw hit the polished marble floor. Eight hunner quid. Surely there was a Travelodge or something nearby.

'And does that include the event discount?'

He gazed at me, not amused, with his palm out, and just like that, I handed over my documents, life savings and the last bit of self-respect I had left.

'So . . . *erm* . . . I was hoping to catch the groom before the party. We have some things to go over. Do you know a room number perhaps?'

The man shook his head at me while typing on the computer.

'Please, sir.' I lowered my gaze to meet his. 'I really need to speak to Tom Adams.'

'It is simply not possible. The couple are staying at one of our sister hotels across the lake, at one of the other islands tonight. They are arriving tomorrow for the party. Your room number, keycard, and Wi-Fi code. Enjoy your stay.'

I exhaled.

'Ah, right, OK. Well, thank you,' I turned on my feet and made my way through the lobby.

I walked into the restaurant area and noticed a few scattered tables of couples eating the most wonderful-smelling pastas and risottos. But my stomach felt achey with nerves. I wandered through to the garden area overlooking the lake.

The sun had now disappeared completely, and the sky had turned a navy colour. I watched the commotion of staff setting up the party for the following night with anticipation lurking in my stomach. Everything was coming together with the flower arrangements and sculptures, and the team swept the early falling autumn leaves off the ground while chattering to one another in their captivating language. But as I watched on, the evening grew lonelier, and with no chance of speaking to Tom, I headed back through the hotel to my room.

I walked around the humungous bed towards the double doors that opened onto a private garden. I took a long humid breath, then closed the doors. My bags lay neatly on top of the bed for my arrival, and I rested my head on the pillow. *What if Quinn is the one for Tom?* I wondered. *What if I'm ruining his only chance of happiness by dredging up the past? God, what about poor Andy?* I thought about what he'd be doing right now. If he was mad, or angry, or just sad. I felt my body ache with guilt. I turned around in bed in anguish, doubting the entire trip until I caught sight of Tom's note that was tipping out of one of my bags.

> *I know you asked me for a list of things to fix, but it's wholly impossible when your imperfections are utter perfection to me.*
>
> *They are the reason I'm here, the reason I smile and the reason I won't ever go away.*
>
> *Always yours,*
>
> *Mr Tom Adams*

I shut my eyes and held the note to my face and inhaled a long deep breath in. I was doing the right thing. I had to see this through.

Chapter Nineteen

I woke up at midday starving and with a ton of pressure resting on my chest. I lay wide awake, wanting to scroll through my phone but terrified of the messages that would fill my screen, causing my anxiety to soar even more. I rustled around the duvet and sat up in bed.

I had to try to see Tom before the party. I had to say my piece and get off this island.

I got dressed quickly, and headed out of the hotel.

Walking down the steep hills of Bellagio my eyes were on red alert. I felt desperate to find him, but at the same time, I didn't want to risk seeing Raj just to be talked down from this ridiculous plan. I continued walking like some sort of spy, keeping close to the walls and bopping in and out of the tiny designer jewellery shops. At one point I almost gave a lady a heart attack as I hid behind one of the shop signs, convinced I could hear Raj's voice from afar.

The streets of Bellagio were alive with tourists, party-goers and press. I walked along all the tourist attractions wondering when Tom would arrive.

After an hour of camouflaging myself in bushes and almost giving myself whiplash convincing myself that any tall man could be Tom, I finally took a seat at one of the restaurants overlooking the dock. When he arrived on the island, I'd clock him from here.

'Can I take your order, Miss?' a waiter asked.

I immediately jumped as my hiding in plain sight was getting a bit too literal.

'Oh, sorry, yes.' I picked up the menu and skimmed over it quickly, humming and hawing.

'Oh, yes, sure. Erm . . . Can I have bruschetta to start, and some mushroom risotto, please?' I smiled back to him, mouth watering at the thought of finally having a decent meal.

'Certainly, and to drink?'

'A glass of dry white wine, please.' I paused. 'In fact, make it a bottle.'

I grinned at him and he smiled back, then took hold of the menu in my hand.

'No, wait. Can I keep this, please?' I asked, tugging the other end.

'Si, erm . . . OK.' He looked intrigued but turned back to the kitchen.

I opened the menu up and propped it in front of my face in some form of disguise, only the tops of my eyes peeking out as I scrutinised the holidaymakers. *Where are you, Thomas?! Where are you?*

My food arrived shortly after and I was munching away as a second load of passengers descended from the boat. I sat bolt upright, dropping my cutlery to the side, waiting. But still, no Tom. I felt myself getting more and more frustrated and slammed my hands down on the table.

'Is everything OK with the food?' the waiter asked, noticing my reaction.

'Yes! Oh my God! The food's delicious.' I paused, realising how crazy I must have looked. 'I'm waiting for my friend and I assume this port is the only way you can get onto the island?' I pointed out to the dock as holidaymakers gasped in awe stepping onto the island for the first time.

'Si, that's right.' He laughed. 'Unless of course . . .' My ears pricked up, and I turned to him. I could feel my mouth was still dripping with sauce.

'Go on!' I encouraged him, while grazing my hand over my creamy chin.

'Well, unless they are very wealthy, then they take the sky!' He looked up to the heavens and smiled.

'The sky? What do you mean?'

'Helicopter! Lots of rich don't like the busy boats, so they fly from island to island.'

It all made sense. Of course Quinn would summon a helicopter to transport her. While preaching about the environment. Such a bloody hypocrite!

'Is your friend rich?' he asked.

'Very!' I snapped back, closing the menu as my cover now seemed pointless. 'Can I just have the bill, please?'

'Si, right away.'

With yet another failed attempt to find Tom I trekked back up the cobbled hill to my hotel room.

It had just passed 8 p.m., and I was two bottles of wine down. I paced the floor of my room wearing one of the new dresses that survived the tram dash; it was pale blue with an off-the-shoulder detail. I could hear music and laughter in the distance, coming up from the gardens, and knew Tom's party had well and truly begun.

You can do this, Zara! Think of the note. I repeated over and over in my fuzzy head.

I could feel the vibration of the music rattle through the floor and smack off my chest as I approached the private entrance of Tom and Quinn's engagement party. My ears were ringing with nerves. *Just stick to the script, Zara. You've got this.*

As I got closer to the entrance, I admired the vast gated arch alive with pink and blue tropical flowers. Small diffusers sprayed the air with a gorgeous strawberry scent every few seconds. *Uhhh, damn.* This place was stunning. But I couldn't see any part of Tom's classy elegance peer through. It was bright and pretty. Not captivating and mysterious like him.

'Can I . . . *ahh* . . . help you?' a deep and sexy Italian voice said.

I turned and gasped at the sight of a vast green monster standing guarding the entrance. 'Holy fuck!' I screamed.

The green man smirked back.

'Oh, fuck, I'm sorry, you gave me a fright!' I laughed. I held my chest, trying to get my breath back, but the guy was standing there like a brick shithouse, as tall as he was wide, painted head to toe in green body paint.

'You're kind of camouflaged against the trees there,' I persisted, awkwardly laughing at my little joke.

'I'm Hulk.' He grunted and shrugged his shoulders.

I nodded back as the penny dropped. '*Ahh*, I see. Well, great costume. Yep, yep, I see it now.'

I tried to walk on, but his huge Hulk biceps blocked the gate.

'Oh, erm, excuse me.' I tried to smile, pushing to get past.

'You know the host?' His broken English and gangster-sounding accent was a bit more Al Pacino than the Hulk.

I smiled politely at him, trying to suppress a small, frustrated tut. 'Yes, I'm friends with the groom. I'm his . . . *well* . . . it's complicated . . . his boss, and his friend, I'm his ex too actually . . . but right now—'

'You have a ticket? I am security,' he interrupted, casually pulling out two cigarettes, one popped into his mouth and the other rested at the top of his ear.

'Eh . . . well, I have an email? You know Quinn doesn't like paper, does she?!' I glared up at the topless man, hopeful this was enough.

He nodded as I switched my phone on, ensuring flight mode was enabled and scrolled through old emails to the generic invite. 'All invites on the phone. Quinn's request,' he grumbled.

Of course, it is, Miss Goody Fuckin' Two Shoes.

'I've travelled from all the way from Scotland. So, I better head in.'

Hulk laughed. 'Yes. But, not without a costume, lady.'

I was hitting my limit now. I sucked in a large breath, then immediately coughed on the smoke from the doorman's roll-up cigarette.

'Costume?' I repeated, waving my hands in front of my face from all the smoke.

Hulk raised his shoulders, disinterested.

'What does that mean?' I imitated his shrug. 'I'm on the brink of a breakdown here.'

'No costume, no get in. Rules. No plastics, natural face paints and re-useable costume.' He looked off into the night sky, puffing on his cigarette.

I glanced through the gates and spotted the glamorous costumes the crowd wore inside.

Shit! The invite did say RSVP for the dress code. Why didn't I RSVP?

'Well, is there a gift shop or anything in the hotel then?' It would probably cost me a grand for a costume there, I thought. I was tapping my shoe on the marble tiles, impatiently waiting for a reply, which never came.

With a surge of anger, I reached up towards the tall security guard and screamed, 'Listen, I need you to get me into this fucking party. I don't care how, but my life, the lives of my future children, all depend on this fucking moment. Please!'

The jolly green giant looked down on me and smirked. 'You act more like Hulk, little woman.' Then he laughed again, puffing small smoke rings into the air. 'Try the lost-and-found box here from the pool. You can wear something from that.'

I immediately reached for his hand, and mine looked like a baby's in comparison.

'*Really?* Yes. Yes! OK. Thank you, thank you so, so much.'

163

He nodded and pointed towards a large wicker box in the distance alongside the pathway.

'Please, God, help me find something sexy.' I rummaged through the basket of misplaced towels, damp pool shorts, and snorkelling flippers. The only thing I could dress up as at this rate was Tom Daly or Sir David fucking Attenborough. Great! I placed my head at the side of the basket and felt my eyes fill with tears. After all the air miles, all the money, I wasn't getting in. I couldn't say my piece. All the hurt and pain I'd caused everyone. It was all for nothing.

I lifted my fuzzy head to the sky to let out a distressed drunken wail but, as I did, I suddenly noticed a garden terrace overlooking the event. Hanging there was a long, black, buttoned gown. I squinted staring at the costume just waiting on me. It was a sign. *Yes! Thank you, God!* I raised my hands to the heavens as a desperate, relieved, tipsy smile swept over my face. Then, before I second-guessed it, I hopped over the small wall and swiped the garment, making sure no one saw. Maybe it was someone's backup choice for the party? It could definitely become some sort of Grim Reaper idea, or be teamed up with a *Scream* mask. I yanked it over my dress and pulled it down. Wow. The material was thick and silk lined, not like my usual cheap Halloween costumes from doon the Barra's you could spit peas through. Some cunt had really paid a fortune for this badboy, and it did meet Quinn's reusable criteria. This was perfect. As I took a few small steps admiring the robe I realised it was obviously made for a man as it trailed a little on the floor. I buttoned it only to the top of my thigh to create a slight split, attempting to make it as sexy as possible, given the circumstances. *Tonight, Matthew, I will be Professor Snape!* I thought, tucking my dark hair into the tight collar, giving the illusion of a short bob.

When I returned to the path I crouched beside a tree, checking the ground for anything I could add to my costume. *Yes, yes, yes!* I found a branch which would play the perfect part as a wand for tonight. Fucking belter!

As I walked back to the gates, Hulk looked past me.

'You have an invitation?' he asked once again in his thick Italian accent.

'*Wa-ha*! It's me!' I pointed my wand at him, happy I'd managed to fool the bouncer, and he laughed deeply letting out a smoker's rattle from his chest. 'You didn't recognise me, did you?'

He shook his head, still smirking at my get-up. 'I thought you would wear a bikini from that box, not all of these clothes! So many clothes.'

I smiled warmly at the Hulk and nudged past him.

'That is a funny costume, little one. Go now and sort your future.'

I smiled back at the huge, green, shirtless man and nodded; it was exactly the encouragement I needed.

Walking through the gates, while switching my phone back I immediately saw crowds of people dancing and chattering around the pool area. Almost every woman was bandaged in some form of sexy cartoon remake with their tiny body showing costumes and diamond-encrusted underwear. While the majority of the men were going for Thomas Shelby, or gangster vibes. Strong American accents surrounded me as music blasted from a raised podium with fluorescent lights. I scanned the gardens of Great Gatsbys and superheroes, desperate to find a familiar face. *Where is he?* I thought. I nudged past the 'Quinn and Tom' light-up lettering with a bubbling pot of envy, resisting the urge to *accidentally* knock it over, and continued searching the grounds. People were dancing and singing loudly as glamorous waitresses passed out champagne willy-nilly to the guests. I turned to see a huge billboard-sized photograph of the couple mounted over the stage by the pool, it looked more like a Colgate advert than a declaration of love. But still, it made my stomach twist. Everything here seemed so fake. So corny. So unlike Tom. I continued pushing through the painted faces hoping I'd recognise his eyes beneath a mask. Hoping I still had time to say my piece.

Then suddenly, I spotted him. Tom was lying on a large beach bed on the terrace stage, just observing the party, alone. *Finally!*

At the sight of him, my heart began pounding. A surge of sweat streamed under my thick robe. This was it.

I walked towards him, not breaking eye contact, praying he would be pleased to see me. I watched him laugh, witnessing some of the dance moves from his partygoers while nodding coolly to the music as I pushed and edged through the crowds. I was getting closer, and as I watched his glistening smile I felt my heart warm. I paused briefly as the realisation came over me. Tom is the one. He is the one I want. Why hadn't I realised this sooner? I gasped, feeling nervous but excited. I had to tell him I felt the same way as he did on the note. I had to apologise for dismissing him at every chance. I began thundering through the crowd. I had to tell him that I wanted this. I wanted us. I was finally ready. I had been scared to think about Tom that way for a long time; I had faced many barriers to getting close to him again because of the past. But tonight, they were down, and I didn't care about the past. I only wanted to think about our future.

I was metres away when Tom's head suddenly swivelled and his attention cut from the crowd. Quinn. My feet halted immediately. She looked stunning and he couldn't take his eyes off her. His sunkissed arms draped around her tiny waist as she joined him on the bed, and they giggled together, completely carefree. My heart stopped. I felt everything I had suddenly fall out below me. I didn't think I would see a connection between them, but it was there.

I stood still, watching them. Quinn was dressed in a gold-and-turquoise belly top and matching cutaway shorts made from a shimmery material, which made her tanned skin seem to glow. Her hair was amplified into two bobbles and had changed to jet black overnight, which seemed to make her features even more captivating. Mounds of gold jewellery jingled up her arm as she playfully touched Tom. She was

Jasmine, he was Aladdin and I was dressed *and* acting like fucking Jafar.

What the fuck am I doing here? I couldn't do this. Not now. *Abort mission, Zara. Abort mission.*

I turned on my heels, feeling my face burn with embarrassment. I felt like I'd been kicked in the stomach by Jackie Chan. *What was I thinking?* I needed a drink pronto!

I approached the bar and noticed the triangular warning-shaped beer mats with Quinn's face printed on them and the message '*Don't edit our pictures tonight! We are beautiful, and so are you!*' I sneered at it. Not all of us were born with your bone structure and money, hen. Calm down, I told myself. I wanted to hate her. I wanted her to be the villain, but, deep down, I knew it was all on me.

A waiter approached me. 'Yes, sir, can I help?'

I felt my mouth drop a little. Surely, I wasn't that unrecognisable.

'A porn star martini, please,' I replied, with no fight left to correct him.

He turned and began mixing.

I looked out to the packed crowd, wondering where I would find Raj. He would most definitely be here somewhere, but I wasn't sure what he'd say. There was no way I'd be able to tell him my ridiculous plan and how I shat out of it when the time came, but there was no way I could lie to him either. I could really do with a friend or someone to talk to.

The waiter handed me my drink and walked away before I could retrieve my purse from the layers of costume.

Oh, I hadn't anticipated the free bar! This could be dangerous. The last place I went somewhere with a free bar was at Ibrox for the Harry Styles gig, and I was doing the worm in the hospitality lounge before nine. I gulped down my martini and then another three far too quickly, drowning my sorrows. But the more I drank, the more I wallowed in self-pity. I gawked on enviously at the bride-to-be, the idyllic setting, the entertainment. Her face was everywhere. People chattered around me while I sat alone, contemplating why I ever thought I'd have a chance. Mermaids swam in the pool, flipping their fins in time with the music, and aerial acrobats were catapulting from hanging silk fabric while the crowds clapped in awe. It was undoubtedly an experience for the hundreds of press and journalists there but I couldn't help but think how over the top it all was. What part of tonight represented Tom?

The evening was going on, and I hadn't moved from the bar. My eyes felt misty and I was deeply intoxicated. Who did I think I was? I didn't have the bottle to approach Tom, never mind tell him how I felt. I slid off the bar stool after watching a fireworks extravaganza commence, but I knew deep down I was the only banger that night. Stumbling towards the bathroom, tripping over my long robe, I was feeling woozy when a deep voice behind me called out.

'Excuse me, mate. The gents' is this way.'

I recognised the voice in an instant and stopped dead. It was Tom.

Slowly, I turned around, fixing my face with an awkward smile.

'Zara? Zara, is that you?' he exclaimed happily, thundering towards me and wrapping his arms around me.

Relief flooded my body as he held me. I laughed and squeezed him tightly. His arms, his hold, his smell all felt incredible.

'What are you doing here? When did you arrive?' he asked, leaning back to look at me.

'A couple of nights ago! I couldn't miss this. I wanted to see you!' I spat out of my drunken mouth.

Tom raised a suspicious eyebrow. 'Why are you dressed like a Jedi?'

'It's not a Jedi! I'm Snape!' I brandished my wand. 'Expelliarmus!' I tried to jump into some form of wizard battle pose while stumbling a little on the path.

Tom laughed. 'Oh! I've never seen it. Wait, you have to meet Quinn! Come, come.' He jumped excitedly and grasped my arm, tugging me along. He was completely caught up in his whole new world, and he wanted to show me it all.

'Tom, wait. Wait. I can't,' I said, pulling back on his grasp.

This is my moment, I thought.

'I kind of . . . kind of want to chat for a second.' I looked down, unable to hold eye contact.

'Sure. *Yes*. Are you OK? Is Andy OK?' he asked, placing one hand on my shoulder, seeming concerned. 'I can't believe you're here! Where's Ash?' He was bursting with excitement, laughing loudly.

'Andy's fine. I'm fine. It's just . . . *Oh God*, I don't know. I suppose I want to make sure you're OK? This is all so quick, Tom.'

He let out a small, confused laugh. 'Oh, Zara, I know it was a shock. But come meet Quinn and I'm certain you'll understand. She is wonderful,' he said, grasping my shoulder.

'No, I don't doubt that for a second. She seems beautiful and full of confidence, empowerment, and everything you want in a wife. It's just . . .' I sighed, searching for the words I desperately wanted to say. *Say the speech, Zara. Say it.*

Tom's hand lowered off my shoulder and he tucked his arms into his chest.

'I suppose . . . Well, this whole thing, like your engagement. It has made me wonder about you and me. And well . . . if I made the right decision . . . like choosing Andy?' I waited on a reply while facing the ground. I felt my face twist with nerves in the silence, then eventually glanced up at the horrified expression on his face.

'Sorry, what?' Tom's face dropped, and he took a step backwards. One of the guests walked past us and Tom lowered his voice. 'And you're telling me this at my fucking engagement party? Are you crazy, Zara?' he hissed. His warm smile had disappeared entirely, and coldness suddenly cut the space between us.

'I know. I'm sorry. I'm so sorry. I had to say something. I was questioning my decision. My whole life with Andy and . . .' I felt my bottom lip quiver, wishing desperately I hadn't said a word and I could make this all go away.

Tom paced the floor, shaking his head. 'Why would you fly across the ocean and say this to me?' His body seemed rigid and tense as he glared down at me. 'It always has to be about you, doesn't it?'

My mouth gaped open. 'What? No, I'm sorry, Tom. I'm sorry—' A cool clamminess descended on my perspiring body. I was nauseous.

'No, I'm sorry we even got embroiled in that, Zara. This is my fucking engagement party. What is this? Is this payback for Harriette?' He waited on a response, but I couldn't lift my eyes from the ground. 'I gave you every opportunity to change your mind over the past few months. I sat back. I gave you space. YOU told *me* to move on. You said that. And I have. Don't dare question your decision now, Zara.' He took a few more steps back. 'Trust me. It was the right one.'

He turned to walk away, then changed his mind. He came close to me. Silent.

I couldn't speak.

'Go home, Zara. Please. You've taken up enough of my time tonight.'

He looked at me and shook his head and walked off back to the party.

'TOM!' I called out.

But he had gone.

I stood entirely still, not wanting to move. It wasn't supposed to happen like this.

What the fuck had I done? Music and chatter rang in

my ears until my brain felt like it would explode. I had to get out of here. I could feel the embarrassment and rejection building up inside me, and I was so alone. I had no one. Tom's words played over and over in my head. *Go home, Zara*. But I knew I couldn't. I had ruined everything back home too. I had wasted everything: my friends, my relationship, my career, my life. I was a laughing stock to think Tom Adams would ever choose me.

Chapter Twenty

I bolted through the crowd, bumping and forcing my way through the rich people in their elegant costumes towards the exit. I felt claustrophobic, and as my chest crushed tightly I struggled to breathe. I needed out. 'Excuse me, please. Excuse me,' I whimpered, budging past everyone.

Eventually, I was back at the entrance and immediately fell onto my hands and knees as I left the party. I cried and cried as the odd person passed by me, but I didn't care. Neither did they. They shrugged and smiled at one other and went on into the party. *Another Scottish burd on a bender,* they probably thought, and they weren't far wrong.

The reality of abandoning my boyfriend on the day I was supposed to move in to make this ridiculous idea happen was sinking in. *Poor Andy.* I'd almost certainly just thrown away our entire relationship. There was no way out. There was no way I could fix this. *What the fuck was I thinking?*

'Have you finished with drama now?' a familiar deep voice said.

I looked up to see a large green figure towering above me.

'I'm finished more like.' I whimpered, watching my tears soak into the dry tiled path below me.

'Ha, you not finished. You have not even started yet. What age are you? Twenty-five or something? Just *bambino*.' he replied.

I attempted a smile between the tears. 'Thirty-one . . . and a half.' I sniffled.

He shrugged, still blowing small smoke rings out of his mouth. 'See, a baby,' he replied.

I got to my knees, stood up, and stepped over to the low wall overlooking the dark lake. He followed me.

'I thought the groom liked me. I thought he'd want me more than his bride.' I felt ridiculous saying the words out loud before feeling my eyes water once more.

'And he say no?' Hulk asked in his broken English.

I nodded, feeling my restrictive costume tug at my throat.

He leaned his hand on my neck and kindly unbuttoned the tight costume at the back of the neck. Finally, I could breathe.

'Well, I think he's *pazzo*. A crazy British man,' he said loudly, gesturing with his hands.

I looked up towards his humungous, painted Hulk face. Yet, behind the tough-guy persona, his eyes glimmered, a kind, compassionate stare, and I felt my body lean back into his for comfort.

'*Pazzo*,' I repeated, not knowing what insult I was even giving Tom.

Hulk flicked his cigarette onto the ground and pushed his spade-sized hand onto my lower back as he sat down on the wall beside me.

'Better, *bambino*?' he asked.

I shrugged my shoulders, feeling defeated.

'Oh, come on!' He pinched my chin and smirked.

'I left my boyfriend to come here. I was supposed to be moving in with him and I left everything for Tom.'

'Tom, is groom?' he asked, and I nodded my head back in response feeling tears stream down my face.

'Maybe boyfriend will ask you back now?' he replied optimistically, shrugging his shoulders.

I shook my head. 'He doesn't deserve this,' I muttered. 'I just feel so lonely over here, I thought I'd come and get answers but I have been invisible since I got here.'

'You are not invisible! There is no way. Look at that costume, little lady,' Hulk replied softly.

I looked beyond his green-painted brows into his dark eyes and felt an odd sense of comfort. 'Will you stay with me for a bit. Just hold me or something?'

Then, with one push, Hulk moved me onto his lap. 'You better now like this, baby? I give good advice, *si*?'

I laughed, enjoying the unexpected affection.

'*Si*, thank you for listening to me, Hulk.'

'Matteo,' he replied, grinning.

I smirked back. '*Hmm* . . . I prefer Hulk.'

We both chuckled. His gaze was intense on my face and I dared to look back, feeling somehow flustered by him.

'You know this is one of the most beautiful places in the world, *signora*.'

I used my hand to dry my tears and snot, sniffing self-consciously at my large excretion of body fluids.

'And yet you cry sad tears. They should be happy tears.' He swivelled my head to the view. 'You are in Lake Como, *bambino*.' His voice echoed loudly across the lake, and I giggled at his enthusiasm.

'I know, I'm sorry. It is very beautiful,' I replied, looking onto the still black lake below us. The water was surrounded by lush greenery and dramatic cliffs, and all along the coast lights from cafés, hotels and houses glistened from afar.

'It's so, so beautiful,' I said.

'You are also *bellissima, si*,' he added softly while rubbing my shoulders. I turned to face the giant green man again.

We looked into one another's eyes. I felt comforted and grateful to have one person in this country who didn't hate me.

I leaned towards Hulk and suddenly felt his lips on mine.

It was a bittersweet contrast to how I was feeling with Tom, but I welcomed the distraction. He was rough as he kissed me, heavy-handed, not sweet and soft like Andy. He was solid and unpolished.

I pulled away almost immediately. 'I'm sorry. I shouldn't have done that.' I attempted to stand but Hulk grunted and pulled me back down onto his lap. He stared darkly into my eyes, once more and I leaned forward, straight onto his lips, only this time we kissed passionately. His large tongue wrapped around mine while his hand rummaged through my hair, tugging it out of my costume. Then I spun my body around, wrapping my legs around him so that I could face into his gigantic body. I felt like I was doing the splits just straddling the big cunt. I felt my thighs burn from the angle I was sitting at. So, I manoeuvred my legs upwards around his waist, to be as close as I could get to him. All of a sudden, I became aware of him pressing into me. It felt thick, large and completely solid. One second later I could feel my fanny's jungle drums begin to beat like I had just begun a round of Jumanji.

Holy shit, this felt . . . good. And incredibly risky. We were only a few metres from the entrance of the party.

With his big, broad hands, Hulk pulled up my robe and dress, abruptly tugging my underwear to the side. He pushed his thumb deeply up and down my clit, stroking it ever so slightly while smiling.

'Wait, wait!' I winced, feeling a drunken rush of realisation. 'We can't, surely? Not here.' But he was still stroking with the biggest grin, knowing I didn't want him to stop.

'I make you feel better now, *bambino*?' His dark eyes were mischievous and full of desire.

I panted. Of course, I fucking did. It wasn't every day I had my clit massaged by an Avenger.

'*Yes* . . . But—' I was trying to think up a reason to stop. I hadn't had a public sexual experience since my teenage days.

'Hulk hungry!' he grunted.

I paused.

Jesus Christ, I hope that means the same in both languages.

Was the Hulk insinuating he ate pussy? He licked his lips exaggeratedly, the way only an Italian man could get away with. Fuck me. *He* certainly seemed more incredible by the second.

'*Mmmmmm . . .*' He winked at me, wiggling his tongue up and down and giving me a preview of how he'd caress my fandango. With one push he inserted a finger inside me. My back straightened up as tingles crept up my spine. Then he brought his hand out of my robe, held his finger to his mouth and began sucking it.

'Mmmmmm . . .' He hummed, teasing me with his mouth.

'Where will we go?' I asked, as all other problems drifted from my mind.

With my legs still wrapped around his waist, he stood and walked a few steps into the party. No one seemed to notice us entering as they danced around us completely carefree. But Hulk knew exactly where he was going, as he thundered through the crowd, turning left at the bar and transporting me into a little towel hut. It was within the party area but had been cordoned off and was in darkness with only a small glimmer of light spreading through the gaps of the thatched roof above us. I could hear the chattering of partygoers passing by and the music thundered through me as he lowered me to the ground and we stood in the darkness staring at one another.

Hulk was sexily biting his lip at me. I skimmed my hands upwards to reach his shoulders. His frame felt twice as broad as mine. He was the most macho-looking

scary man I'd ever seen, yet there was something undeniably sexy and warm about him.

'Get them off,' he grumbled, trying to dig through my
layers of costume to pull the elastic of my underwear.

I laughed loudly at the commotion, almost losing my
balance as I shoved my way through the robe, up my
dress and lowered my underwear to my ankles.

His breathing was getting heavy. As his chest crackled
with exertion and desire, I could tell he was a heavy
smoker. If he were my patient, I'd probably fetch him
some Amoxicillin and a nebuliser, but, right now, he
was my big Hulk, and I found his Darth Vader breathing
weirdly hot. There was a growing anticipation of heat
between us, just staring at one another in the little hut
as my underwear was now tossed on the floor. Then
with one grab, he lifted me by the arse, firstly to his
chest, then with another lift, my vagina was directly
in his face. I wobbled clumsily, not expecting to be so
high in the air, not knowing where to put my hands
as my head pressed against the roof. But, then I felt
an almighty paw grip holding me steady and I knew I
would be safe. I gripped the thatched roof hard with
my fingers for balance as I glanced down at his face
just as he looked up at me and smiled.

'I told you . . . Hulk hungry.'

With that, he buried his head deep into the robe,
deep between my legs and finally entrenched into my
vulva. *Jesus, Mary and Joseph.*

I could feel the warmth of his tongue caress my
clit, licking me up and down over and over again. I

threw my head back in sheer wonder as he touched me so passionately. It felt satisfying after the emotions I had been through just to have this one little bit of pleasure. A little bit of passion. A little bit of company. I was panting for dear life as he muff-dived me amid Tom's party. No one outside had a clue of what was going down. He was grumbling and smacking his lips loudly almost as if he was devouring some of his nonna's favourite spaghetti. Occasionally, the lights flashed towards us, and I was momentarily blinded, but there was something so exhilarating about hiding there in plain sight with only my big green body-guard beneath me. I was already in pleasure town, and nothing or no one was making me think of anything other than the hulky Hulk between my thighs. I felt his strong arms push my arse further into his mouth, and I wondered if it was his tongue or tonsils doing the work. Not that I cared, as he was utterly devouring me like it was his last meal before getting condemned to the electric chair. I felt my body twitch as my hands gripped the roof, my head was thrown back in some form of demon pose and shook frantically as I came over and over in his mouth.

'YES, YES, YES!' I screamed loudly, finally able to release all of my emotions.

He kept going.

Hulk was fucking starving, never mind hungry!

At least twenty minutes passed this way when I was disturbed by cheering along the poolside. My intoxicated eyes squinted through the cave-shaped window of the towel hut and I noticed people gather around us and cheer towards the party. Then, I suddenly heard Tom's voice echo from a microphone.

'I want to sincerely thank everyone who came along tonight . . .'

Shit, shit! I couldn't listen to his voice whilst getting oral, it felt so seedy. I was trying to distract myself from him.

I tapped frantically on my big boy's shoulders.

'We need to go! Hulk? Hulk?' I giggled. 'Matteo, we need to go.' I kept tapping.

'No!' He slabbered briefly, gnawing at my fanny lips.

A shiver of sheer horniness ran up my spine and I threw my head again back, enjoying it too much. 'Ohh, yes!' I whispered. 'There's lots of people just outside!' I whispered between drunken laughs, trying to get back in control.

'Your room, *bambino*?' he asked, looking up with his half-smudged shiny green face. He looked angry I had interrupted his last supper.

'What about your job? The security?' I asked.

Matteo shrugged casually. 'Your room?' he repeated.

'Yeah. Yes, come on.' I clambered off his shoulders, reassembled my robe and grasped Hulk's hand as we casually slipped out of the towel hut.

'Hulk make you feel better?' he asked, slowly running his thumb over his lips, catching any leftover pussy juice, and then sucking it.

I nodded, feeling a rush of adrenaline. I hadn't done anything this wild for a long time, and it was

182

exhilarating. I was enjoying the unexpected attention, excitement, and undeniable attraction.

As we exited the towel hut, I turned the corner to see Raj standing directly in front of us listening intently to Tom's speech while sipping on an orange juice. I froze. *Shit!* Hulk tugged on my arm to continue, and I shook my head.

'This way!' I redirected him around the back of Raj, tiptoeing and trying hard to bring as little attention as I could towards us. I kept my eyes glued to the ground the entire time and eventually headed back the long way around, through the streets towards the hotel.

We finally entered the hotel lobby, dressed as Snape and the Incredible Hulk, giggling and holding hands like mischievous teenagers. People glared, but when Hulk met their gaze, they immediately averted their eyes. Jesus, he was so intimidating, but every part of my vagina and shaky thighs were lusting over it. As we walked past the lift, I was grateful to be situated on the ground level as I was unsure if the Hulk would have breached the maximum six hundred kilogram capacity limit.

'How far now?' Hulk moaned, tugging on my arm. I giggled back as I tried hard to walk in a straight line from all the cocktails.

'It's just around the corner, be patient!' I pointed my finger towards him and with one large sweep I felt my body get lifted from the ground.

I screamed playfully as Hulk trudged down the corridor holding me and biting my ear. Suddenly he lowered me down to the ground and paused.

I looked up to my door and standing there was Tom.

'Tom?' I said, stunned, still panting for breath. 'What are you doing here? How did you know I was here?'

'The man at Reception gave me your room number.' My heart pounded. 'I thought we should talk, but apologies I feel I may have interrupted something,' he replied with a blank expression on his face.

'No, no. Please stay. I want to talk. I really want to talk.' I walked closer towards him and attempted to hold his arm, but he stepped away.

'I'll go. Good night little one,' Matteo said. I turned towards him gratefully.

How could I be so stupid?

'Zara,' Tom eventually said, when Hulk had left.

There was a brief silence in the hallway. I wasn't sure what was going to happen next.

'Tom?' I replied after a few seconds, reaching over to him.

He squirmed away, taking a few steps backwards.

'No, *no*. Don't. Don't touch me, Zara.'

'What? Why?'

'I came here to fucking apologise. I came here to tell you,' he stopped, and shook his head, 'and you're with him.' I could see the anger build behind his eyes. 'You unexpectedly show up at my fucking engagement party, and then half an hour later you're running back to your bedroom with the first man you see!'

'No, no. The guy, it's not . . . it's not what you think.' I felt tears pour down my face as Tom continued to look at me with his eyes heavy with disappointment.

184

'Tom! Please.' He slowly turned and began to walk down the corridor, 'Please don't walk away. TOM! It's not what you fucking think!' I called out, feeling a surge of anger at him.

'It's precisely what I think, Zara. What the fuck has happened to you?' He turned and shook his head disapprovingly.

I rushed down the corridor after him.

'What's happened to me? Ha! Are you serious? YOU! YOU are what's happened to me! *I was happy!* I was moving in with Andy! I was starting a normal life with someone, and YOU got in my fucking head again!' I screamed, unable to hold back the tears, feeling every emotion – anger, sadness, fear.

'And I fucking let you, Zara. It was fucking hard. But I let you be happy!' he yelled back at me.

'But I found the note,' I whimpered.

Tom stopped dead.

'I found the note when I was packing. The one from the night in the restaurant. The one when you were supposed to be listing my imperfections.'

His head bowed, and I could see his eyes glisten with tears.

'I had to know. I had to know if that's how you felt. How you *still* feel now.'

Tom turned to the side, putting a palm to his eye while rubbing it. Then he turned back to me and shrugged. 'It's not,' he said. 'You're not the person I met years ago at the clinic, Zara. Look what you've done to Andy tonight. The lying, the cheating, coming here and causing a scene. You are no different than me now. I should never have treated you the way I did with Harriette. It will always be the biggest regret of my life, and I'm sorry it's changed you. But, honestly,' he paused, 'I don't even recognise you anymore.'

'What? I haven't changed, Tom! Tom?' I repeated as he stood lifeless. 'I was scared. I chose Andy because he was the safe option. I know that now. I was protecting myself! You had hurt me so much, but I want this. I want to try.' His eyes remained fixed on the ground for a few more intense seconds, but then he began walking back down the corridor, 'Tom, for fuck sake. Please, please just stop and talk to me.'

My wailing cries rang down the hallway, but I didn't care.

'It's too late,' he said quietly, facing the floor. 'Enjoy the rest of your night, Zara. If you hurry up you may still catch your man.' He reached the end of the corridor and faced me one last time. 'But stay away from me and Quinn.'

I watched him walk away, his steps echoing off the marble floor.

'Tom. Tom! *Tom!*' I cried after him, but nothing – no second glance. No consolation. Nothing.

I leaned against the wall.

I had lost him forever.

Chapter Twenty-One

Around nine the following morning I heard my bedroom door open.

'Housekeeping!' a small elderly woman said as she let herself in, then immediately gasped. 'Oh, *mamma mia!*' she clamoured.

I sat up in bed and looked around the room. The crispy white bed sheets were stained with paint. I looked at my hands, which were bright green from touching and caressing Hulk's head while he was going down on me. I glanced down at my thighs, and they matched my paws. *Oh no, last night really happened!* I had been hoping it was some sort of fucking nightmare. To top it off, my head was pounding from the hangover and crying all night.

'I'm sorry,' I whispered. 'I'm sorry about the mess!'

The cleaning woman tutted dismissively and shooed me out of my bed, shaking her head.

I stumbled into the bathroom, too ashamed to show my face, and scrutinised myself in the mirror. My face was puffy, and my eyes were bloodshot and red. I had green, sticky, matted hair, and the Hulk's paint had stuck to the tiny hairs on my face, giving me the greenest moustache from all the snogging. *Great!* I felt like Luigi from Super Mario. I ran the shower and got straight in, washing my hair and cleaning all of what happened last night off me. I couldn't help but constantly replay it all, Tom appearing at my door over and over in my head. *What would have happened if I had been alone? Did he want to say something? Or did he just want to restore what little friendship I had well and truly shat all over?* I had no idea, but my mind was racing. I stepped out of the shower, dried myself off, and headed back to the bedroom, now sparkling clean once more with the minibar topped up.

I couldn't eat or drink yet, I was too nauseous from alcohol and emotions, so I lay back on my bed and began sobbing. I wanted to go home, but I couldn't face anyone. I had nowhere I could go.

There was a loud knock at the door, and I flinched immediately, feeling my hands shake.

What if it was Tom? Or what if the manager had come to tell me to leave after last night's commotion?

I walked cautiously to the door and opened it ever so slightly.

'Zara!'

I felt a small, slim pair of arms wrap around my damp hair, and I cried instantly. It was Ashley. I had never been so relieved to see anyone before in my life.

'What the fuck are you doing here?' I cried into her shoulder.

Ashley pushed past me and entered my room.

'What the fuck am I doing here? Mate, what the fuck are *you* doing here? I thought you were fucking dead! I've tried calling you twenty million times!' She stood with her hands on her hips lecturing me, but still wearing the brightest smile of relief.

I was wiping away tears, still utterly gobsmacked she'd tracked me down. 'I . . . eh . . . I . . . know. I'm sorry. I switched it off. How did you find me?' I asked.

Ashley flicked back her long blonde hair. 'Eh, I checked your emails, obviously. I saw your flight booking and booked the next one out here!'

I let out a large puff of air, relieved I had her with me.

'So, what the fuck? Are you going to explain yourself? You look like shit, Zara,' she stated, sitting down on my fresh sheets.

I didn't know where to start. There was a silence between us as I stood opposite her.

'Zara?!' she screeched impatiently. 'Your face is about to be printed on milk cartons back home. Get spilling!'

'OK, so . . . the other night when I was packing, I found a note that Tom left me, a few months back, like just before Andy and I got togeth— *Awk,* wait, I have it here.' I reached over to the bedside table and retrieved the slightly crumpled note, and handed it to Ashley.

I watched in anticipation as her eyes skimmed over his words, and then she turned it over. Her mouth widened as she took it all in.

'Shut the fuck up!' she bellowed.

'I know. I know.' I bit my nails nervously.

'So?'

'So, I wanted to ask him about it. If he meant everything he said . . . before things moved on with Andy. I didn't want any regrets,' I explained.

'So, you wanted to ask Tom about *this* note?'

I nodded back.

'Months later?'

I nodded again.

'At his fucking engagement party?'

I threw my hands through my wet hair, realising how crazy and reckless my plan sounded out loud.

'Oh God, I know it sounds mental!' I groaned.

'A fucking phone call wouldn't have been sufficient, Zara? Like, OK, if you *really* had to ask him?'

'I know. I know!' I cringed for myself.

Ashley stood up, pacing the floor. 'Well, have you spoke to him then?'

I nodded.

'And what did he say?'

Immediately my mind flashed back to the night before, and I buried my face in my hands.

'Zara? What happened?'

Slowly, I peeked up at my best friend and felt overcome with emotion again. 'He told me to leave. He didn't mean the note and he's happy with Quinn.' I felt my bottom lip tremble, completely mortified.

'Aww, babe. Come here!' Ashley wrapped her arms around me, and I wept into her shoulder. 'Why wouldn't you phone me?' she asked.

I shrugged. 'I was too scared to turn my phone on after bailing on Andy.'

Ash pulled back and looked at me, clutching my shoulders. 'You know I have your back always, Zara. I'm here, and I'm not going to tell you what to do. But fuck, I think Andy deserves a phone call, a text, or something. The poor guy's going Tonto back home. I didn't know what to say to him.'

'What does he think happened?' I asked nervously.

'Well, he's no daft. He knows you bailed, Zara.'

Thinking of Andy and what I had done to him made me cry even louder. I'd been pushing it all to the back of my mind, maybe thinking it would somehow be worth it if Tom had said yes. But I couldn't ignore it anymore.

'Not right now,' Ashley said, rubbing my arms, 'but soon. When you're ready.'

Still sniffling away into her shoulder, I nodded.

'Have you seen Raj?' she asked. 'He's here. I texted him this morning and told him I'd landed.'

I gasped, too mortified to explain my actions to someone else.

'I avoided him at the party. Oh no, please, please tell me you haven't told him I'm here, Ashley!'

She rolled her eyes, her long eyelashes fluttering. 'Zara, he's worried sick! I've had to arrange cover at the clinic. He had to know.'

I disentangled myself from Ashley and got up, pacing the floor. 'I can't tell Raj the truth, Ash. He won't get it. He'll think I'm crazy!'

'Well, if the shoe fits and all that!' she teased, attempting a smile at me. 'He needs to know, babe.

For the business too. We have two new starters currently running one of the busiest clinics in Glasgow! Have you eaten?'

I shook my head. 'No. Of course, I haven't . . . But the minibar's been stocked up?' I tried for a smile.

Ashley looked revolted. 'No way. I'm off it! Could we go to the hotel restaurant to get some food? I'm starving! We could meet Raj. This place is unbelievable, you know.'

'I'm not leaving the room. You get food. I'll wait here.'

She rolled her eyes once more in my direction. 'I'm not leaving you, Zara, I just got you back! I'll text Raj the room number, and he can bring our grub to us. How's that?' Ashley slipped her hand into the small Chanel bag hanging off her shoulder, retrieved her phone and began texting frantically. 'Done! Now get dressed if he's coming down. You know what he's like. All awkward and shit.'

I laughed a little, thinking of Raj and how uncomfortable he'd get around us when we got ready for a night out, or in Dubai last year.

'I have hardly any clothes. I ran into the H&M in Milan, but I hardly have a thing.'

Ashley looked more traumatised by that than me gatecrashing our friend's engagement party. 'Jesus, Zara. What would you do without me?' She bent over, pulled her bright pink case towards us, and opened it onto the floor. 'Try this.' She handed me a one-shouldered black maxi dress.

'Thanks,' I replied.

I pulled on the maxi dress and shrugged.

'Better?' she asked.

'A gold fucking Versace suit wouldn't make me feel better right now.'

Ashley laughed, and we sat on the bed together while she wrapped her arms around me.

Around ten minutes later, Raj came to the door with a slight puff of exertion.

'Zara, what the fuck? You've had us all worried going AWOL like that!' he said, wrapping his arms around me tightly.

'Ashley text last night saying she thought you were coming to the party but I searched and searched and couldn't see you.'

'I'm sorry. I only went for a bit then left, I'm so sorry for worrying you.' I whimpered, feeling slightly overcome at finally seeing my friend after months in the desert.

'Did you bring food?' Ashley asked.

He tossed her a paper bag of fresh pastries.

'Jackpot!' she said cheerfully.

'Let's sit on the terrace?' Raj suggested. 'Your room is beautiful, Zara. This is one of the executive suites, I think.'

I nodded, still feeling dead inside, and opened the double doors.

Bright sunlight shone through the room, and the stunning views of the lake took my two friends by surprise. While they drank it up, I sat on a chair on the balcony with Ashley's sunglasses on, still too fragile to enjoy the scenes.

'This is literally like a movie set!' Ashley screamed.

Raj skimmed around and eventually sat beside me at the table while Ash took out her phone and began snapping the picturesque lakeside views.

'How did you end up here, Zara? Why didn't you call me?' He sounded concerned, and I also didn't want to let him down.

'Honestly?' I huffed. 'I don't think you want to know.'

Raj shook his head, disagreeing. 'What? Of course, I do.'

'I came for Tom,' I blurted. 'I ditched my own house-warming party and got on a flight to Italy without as much as an explanation to Andy.'

His face dropped slightly, but I could see he was trying to disguise the shock.

I began explaining the note I found in my apartment and my set-to with Tom last night while Raj listened intently. When I was finished, he rubbed his chin, seeming lost for words.

'I know. I know. I'm an idiot. I'm a fanny. I shouldn't have come out here, blah blah blah.' I leaned back in my chair while dreading his reply.

Instead, he smiled.

'If you didn't come out here, would you have regretted not knowing?' he asked.

I looked at my friend and felt my eyes glaze with tears.

'I suppose,' I whispered.

Raj reached over the table to gently rub my hand. 'Well, it's not a regret, Zara. It's something you had to do. Something you had to know. And now . . . something you can move on from. Andy is an understanding person. Maybe you will patch things up, maybe you won't. But you don't have to think about that right now. OK?'

My bottom lip trembled as his words rang true on so many levels.

I had to know. And yes, it wasn't the outcome I had hoped for, but that note would have haunted me for years to come if I hadn't dealt with it.

'OH MY GOD!' Ashley screeched loudly, interrupting the first positive thoughts I'd had that day.

'What? What is it?' Raj chuckled at her energy.

Ashley held her phone up, and Quinn's face was on her Instagram, addressing her followers.

'There's been a pure drama at the party last night!' Ashley gave an evil laugh.

'That would explain the commotion at Reception,' Raj said. 'Camera crews everywhere!'

'Some priest was getting oral in the background of ALL Quinn and Tom's photographs! The newspapers have printed stories about it! Totally stealing the limelight!' Ashley erupted into a ball of laughter while my arse fell through the chair and landed smack-bang on the tiled floor below me.

'Wh— What?' I stuttered.

My friends laughed hard at one another, but time stood still for me.

'Yeah, look at TMZ. They're going live just now.' Ashley turned her phone around, and sure enough, there I was, on her screen, legs pinned around the shoulders of the Jolly Green Giant, head leaning backwards in mid-gasm getting well and truly muffed in a robe for the entire world to see.

No, no, no, no!

How could this trip get any fucking worse?

Ashley set her phone up for the live news broadcast in the middle of the table, then she and Raj crowded around to watch.

'BREAKING NEWS: Love wasn't the only thing in the air at Quinn Foxx's engagement party last night. Celebrity, actress and environmental activist Quinn, famous for NEVER editing her photographs, has been outed after she shared a clear picture of her and her soon-to-be husband on Instagram, not realising she was, in fact, PHOTOBOMBED by a gigantic green Martian and what looks like some sort of priest involved in oral sex at the very private lavish do, right here in Lake Como. The captivating beauty claims she was oblivious to what was happening at her own bash as it looks like a couple of partygoers got a little peckish during the celebrations last night. So, we are here live at Lake Como, uncovering what kind of party the prim and proper Miss Foxx was actually throwing. And we're all curious to know if the beauty will break her own cardinal sin and edit that picture! This is Fiona Rashbar reporting live for TMZ.'

Ashley and Raj exploded into fits of hilarity, but I couldn't take my eyes off the screen.

Please, God, tell me this is a joke.

'See, Zara, Tom will have much more to deal with this morning than your silly dispute. There is a muffing Martian on the loose! Damn, I can't believe I missed that last night!' Raj exclaimed, clapping his hands like a fucking seal. 'Zoom into the picture again, Ash,' he said. 'Let me see if I recognise them.'

'No, no, don't!' I pleaded.

'Aw, Zara, I know you're depressed, but this is funny! Let's go to Quinn's Insta!'

With a flash and a flicker of her long nails, Ashley held the phone around to us again, clicking on a video of Quinn looking visibly upset. Her American accent was strong, and she appeared with no make-up or filter present.

'Firstly, I want to start by apologising for the image I shared earlier today. I had no idea about the disgusting and vulgar content contained in the background. My page is never about negativity, and I don't respond to hateful comments or words, but this needs to be addressed. Last night my great friend and role model, Bishop Zamen, had his sacred robe stolen from his balcony. Robes that had been gifted to him by the late Pope. The intruder then accessed my engagement party with a man believed to be dressed as Frankenstein, who performed oral sex on the individual. Neither I, nor my fiancé had any idea this was happening, and I am so, so sorry to the friends, family, foreign diplomats, fans and followers that this has offended. I am known for never editing photographs, for embracing every situation as it happens, but now my images are tarnished with filth. I have one thing to say to these culprits. I and the Vatican have hired a team of

investigators who are working tirelessly around the clock to find you. You will be prosecuted for stealing sacred robes and performing sex acts in public. I will not stop until I get justice! You have ruined everything! If anyone knows anything about this, please contact me directly, or the police.'

The video had barely ended before Raj and Ashley were gutting themselves laughing again. I couldn't move.

How can this be happening to me?

My stomach was churning, and I could feel the blood drain from my face.

'Zara? Zara? Are you OK?' Raj asked, his laughter starting to fade.

I shook my head, and I could see him say something to Ashley, but I couldn't hear any of his words anymore.

I was going to vomit.

I was going to pass out.

I staggered off the chair, my legs weak, and stumbled into the bathroom, vomiting down the pan and collapsing onto my knees. My body was in a cold sweat.

Ashley rubbed my back; before then, I hadn't even noticed she was in the room with me.

'Babe, are you OK? Will I get Raj?' she asked, looking concerned.

'No. No. Don't get him,' I managed to say.

'You look as if you've seen a ghost!'

I swivelled onto my backside and faced my best friend. 'Ash?' I whispered, feeling sweat drip down my face.

She was crouched down beside me. 'Yeah, babe.'

'The priest from the pictures?'

Ashley couldn't help but giggle at the thought. 'Yeah?'

I glanced around the room, ensuring there were no hidden security cameras from Quinn's secret investigators.

'It was me!' I barely said the words, just over-articulated with my mouth, terrified I'd get caught.

'What?!' She stared at me in complete disbelief.

I pointed hard at my chest. 'It was fucking ME!'

Ashley's face fell, and I thought for one second she was about to whitey as well, but, for the first time in her life, she was speechless.

'No, no, no, it wasn't. You're at it! I don't believe you, Zara Smith,' she said after a few moments, looking concerned.

With a puff and pant of sheer effort, I crawled to the corner of the bathroom where a pile of dirty towels lay on the floor. I rummaged through them, eventually exposing the dark robe I'd stolen from the terrace the previous night, now stained an emerald green after an eventful evening with the Hulk.

Ashley gasped loudly, holding her hands to her face. 'The sacred robe!'

I nodded guiltily. 'I thought it was a spare costume! I had no idea! I went as a Death Eater, I went as Professor Snape.'

'Zara! *No. No.* What the fuck? OK. OK. We can fix this. Right, does anyone know?'

'I don't think so. Well, not apart from the Hulk, and, well, Tom.'

She let out an almighty gasp once more. 'TOM? THE HULK?'

'Oh my God, what if Tom tells Quinn? What if he explains the full thing to her?' I screeched.

Suddenly there was a loud knock at the door and both Ashley and I gawked at one another. 'Are you guys OK? Can I come in?' Raj called out.

I shook my head frantically towards Ashley. No one could know about the photo.

'We're fine. Give us five minutes. Zara has . . . erm . . . girl problems!' she called back and I darted her a dissatisfied look.

'Ah, right. Erm . . . well, OK. I'm just outside.'

'Ash!' I hissed.

'It's the only way he'll go. Tell me what happened!'

I explained the entire story in quick, guilty whispers, hoping to God Raj didn't overhear from the other room.

'What am I going to do?' I asked, bowing my head in defeat.

Ashley thought hard for a few seconds and then breathed. 'Right, well, first, you can't see it's your face from the photograph. Your head is tilted backwards clearly enjoying the moment. Was that the only photo that was taken?'

I raised my hands in the air, 'Well, considering I didn't know about this one. How the fuck should I know?' I felt the panic build in my bloodstream.

'OK, well, let's hope it is. And secondly, we have to ditch that fucking robe. Throw it in the water or something.'

'Like fake a suicide attempt?' I asked, getting carried away with the plan.

Ashley's face screwed up as much as it could, which wasn't much considering the large amount of Botox in her forehead. 'No, like getting rid of the evidence!'

'OK,' I agreed. 'But Ash, it's sacred. What if we get cursed or something?' My head was running on overdrive. My entire body was shaking with nerves.

She attempted a laugh. 'Cursed? Babe, I'd say you're fanny-deep in some sort of voodoo curse at the minute. It can't get much worse, Zara! We'll grab one of your fucking bags for life, fuck it in, and chuck it in the water!'

I took a deep breath, thankful for some sort of light at the end of the tunnel.

'OK, OK. Thanks. I'm sorry, Ash,' I mumbled, feeling completely overwhelmed.

'Oh, don't thank me yet. If we get caught, I'm singing like a budgie.' She attempted a laugh, still looking woozy. 'Right, let's go back out, I'm still starving. When Raj leaves we'll have time to plan this properly.'

'How can you seriously eat again? I could go to jail!' I whispered.

She smiled towards me and laughed a little into her hands.

I reached over, hugged my best friend. We stood up and returned to the suite with the knowledge of a new sex tape, a warrant for my arrest and half of Italy searching for me weighing heavily on my shoulders.

Chapter Twenty-Two

That night, as planned, Ashley and I set off for a stroll down to the water. We told Raj we needed an early night and he had made plans with some of his uni friends for dinner. So when the coast was clear, we entered the hotel lobby. I pressed down on Ashley's arm nervously. Crowds of reporters and cameramen were hounding the guests for stories. I wore a pair of Ashley's most enormous shades in case someone recognised my cum face from the photograph. Ashley was dressed all in black with her hair tied back into a little bun. We held our heads down and hurried past, trying to look incognito.

'Excuse me, ladies! Ladies! Did you attend Quinn Foxx's party last night?' a reporter called out in a lightly European accent.

Ashley and I looked at one another.

'Eh . . . eh . . . no speak English, sorry!' she said in a broad Glaswegian accent.

We bolted through the doors out into the clammy street, me clutching her arm tightly with one hand and the bag of evidence in the other. When no one was in sight, I let her go and pushed her shoulder.

'"No speak English, sorry"?' I hissed. 'You spoke in your own fucking accent!'

She seemed startled. 'I panicked! Don't fucking start on me, Zara! I'm trying to get you out of this mess!'

I sighed. 'I know. I'm sorry. Come on. I just want to get rid of this!' I shook the bag, and we began walking once more.

The town of Bellagio was completely surrounded by the stunning mountain views on the lake. There were hotels, restaurants and houses built around it, and, as we wandered, we quickly discovered how tough it would be to toss the bag away without anyone witnessing us. The tiny, cobbled streets were full of couples on romantic walks, and I couldn't help but think of Andy with a lump in my throat. I knew I had to talk to him, but what would I say? He would never understand, and, truthfully, I didn't know what I wanted anymore. But I didn't want him to hurt.

We continued our walk along the lake for at least another half hour, darting through the cobbled streets with Ashley's large stilettos clumsily getting stuck between them at times. We were trying our best to find hidden spots away from tourists and locals and as the night sky became darker the crowds thankfully began to dwindle. Eventually we came to a small, dark corner at the edge of the lake, Ashley halted.

'This is the place, Zara,' she whispered.

I glanced at her nervously, then round about us.

'Go!'

'What if someone comes? I can't, Ash! I was an altar girl growing up!'

Before I could say anything else, Ashley snatched the bag from my hands and tossed it straight into the lake below us. I gasped. Then, slowly, we peered over the railing, watching the bag bop around the dark water, slowly sinking until it disappeared completely.

A sense of relief washed through me.

I turned to Ashley, who had an evil grin slapped on her face. She cleared her throat and said, 'Now, it sleeps with the fishes,' in her best *Godfather* impression. I couldn't help but laugh loudly for the first time in what seemed like forever. I rested my head on her shoulder.

'I'm going to hell, aren't I?' I asked.

Ashley patted my head. 'It was a genuine mistake. You thought you were a dark wizard,' she said and erupted into laughter again.

'I'm so glad you're here, Ash.'

She wrapped her arm around my back and squeezed me. 'I'm glad I'm here too, kid,' she said in the same *Godfather* accent, and I pushed her away as she giggled. 'Let's get back to the room and get food.'

'OK,' I replied.

With the evidence gone, we headed back to the hotel for a night of room service and catch-ups.

Back in the room, Ashley gave me a pair of her pyjamas and we lay on top of my bed eating tagliatelle and cannelloni.

'You know,' Ashley began with her mouth full, 'this is easily the best food I have ever tasted in my life.'

I nodded back, devouring the fresh tagliatelle coated in rich tomato sauce.

'I didn't think Dave would let you come here, you know? After Dubai,' I replied, panting for cold air as it burned my mouth.

Ashley smirked. 'He didn't have a choice. I needed to find you. He knows I won't do anything, I suppose. We're perfect just now,' she said, beaming.

'I'm so glad. He's good for you, Ash.' I waited for a sarcastic comeback about how she was good for him more like, but it didn't come. My mind instantly returned to Andy. Was he good for me? He was kind, serious, trustworthy, but at times I wasn't sure if he understood me. The real me, flaws and all. I felt the fallout weigh heavily on my shoulders and I knew, now that I had ditched the robe, that it was time to apologise. 'When I didn't come to the party, was Andy mad?' I asked, feeling my nervous belly begin to play up.

Ashley looked up at me reluctantly. 'Honestly, he didn't seem mad. Just embarrassed. It was a riddy when you think of it. All your family was there, so it was kind of . . . awkward. Everyone looked at me like I knew something, but I just saw you leave in a taxi, I had no idea we'd be in Italy a few days later.'

I felt my heart sink to the bottom of my chest. 'I feel so bad,' I said, trying not to get upset again. 'Did you tell him where I was when you figured it out?'

Ashley nodded. 'I just said you must have gone out to see Raj and Tom. Like I genuinely thought you had. *Fuck me*, I didn't imagine this shit storm when I arrived.'

'I should phone him,' I said quietly.

Ashley gave me a warm smile of encouragement. 'I think that would be the right thing to do.'

I gulped down the rest of my plate, picked up my phone from the dressing table, and finally took it off flight mode.

Ping, ping, ping, ping, ping, ping . . .

Jesus Christ, I wasn't prepared for all the hate messages.

'Half of them will be from me calling you a nutcase – sorry in advance!' Ashley piped up from the bed, still munching her chips.

'From my mum, Mum, Emily, Jason, Andy, you! Raj, you again! I am not ready to tackle the texts or WhatsApps just now.' I felt anxiety begin to build inside me as I realised how many people I had let down.

Once my screen stopped flickering with alerts, I walked onto the terrace, closed the door and pressed on my phone to call Andy.

Every part of me was quivering. I could hear the international dialling tone, and my heart was pulsating, half hoping he wouldn't pick up and half wanting to get this over with.

'*Zara?*' he answered. His voice was faint and he sounded tired.

I looked at the time and realised it was just past midnight back home.

'I'm sorry. Were you asleep?' I replied, feeling my heart thunder through my ribcage.

'I've not slept for days,' he responded, and I immediately shut my eyes.

How could I have done this to someone?

'Are you OK?' he asked.

I felt water drip down my chin, unaware I was crying until then. 'I'm OK.' I sniffled, composing myself. 'I'm so sorry for bailing on you like that,' I said quietly.

I heard a puff down the phone. 'What the fuck happened? I don't get it?'

I shrugged my shoulders. 'I got scared, I think. It was all happening so fast, and I was . . . overwhelmed.' I could hear the faint laughter of strangers on their balcony above me and held the phone tighter to my ear.

'You could have said that then. You can't run away like that, Zara. I've been scared shitless that something happened to you.' He sounded so calm, considering the circumstances.

'I'm sorry. I know. I'm sorry.'

'Did something happen? I don't get any of this.'

With his question, I felt my heart rip open. He didn't deserve this – any of it.

'Andy, I was with someone else last night.'

The phone line was silent.

'Andy? I'm sorry.' I began sobbing. 'Say something, please.'

I could hear his voice crack down the phone.

'Who was it?'

'I honestly can't even remember his name. An Italian bouncer, it was nothing.'

'An Italian? A random? You left me at our house-warming to fuck a stranger?' I could hear the anger and hurt build down the phone.

'It was a mistake. We didn't even have sex. But, I did betray you. I got so drunk and really confused and I was hurting . . .'

Silence echoed down the line.

'Andy?'

'So, what now?' he asked.

'What do you mean? I've broken your trust. I've disgusted myself, and you don't deserve this.'

'And what do you deserve then, Zara?' he asked.

'I don't know. A fucking broken nose or to be called a fucking slut or something. Say something to get back at me!' My voice was getting louder as my crying got more intense.

'I . . . I . . . don't know what to say. I honestly think there's more to it, Zara. How can you be ready to move in with someone one day, then fuck off to Italy and shag someone else the next?'

'I know. I was hurting. I don't know what I was thinking.' I sobbed.

'You were hurting? Why were you hurting? You were ready to move in with your fucking boyfriend.'

'I'm sorry. I'm so, so sorry, Andy.' It was all I could say.

Andy tutted down the phone. 'Do you know something, Zara? If you called me to say you slept with someone else and it was a genuine drunken mistake, I'd probably have said we could try to move past it. But why do I get the feeling you've let someone else down rather than me? You're still not telling me the truth.'

He knew. My insides squeezed inside, and I felt sick. I couldn't say another word.

'You can't even be honest with me, can you?'

'I have been honest. I just . . . I don't know what you want me to say.'

'But why? Why would you do that if you didn't want us? And don't say some bullshit thing about being too overwhelmed to move in.'

'I honestly don't know, Andy. I was upset. I'm sorry.'

'Stop saying fucking sorry!' There was a brief pause down the phone and then Andy replied more calmly, 'Is there someone else? Is that it? And I don't mean the Italian.'

I paused, feeling my heart beat fast at his realisation.

Truthfully there was someone else. There had always been someone else throughout our entire relationship. Even if I was too scared to admit it. And as much as I knew Tom would never work, especially after everything, I knew even now that Andy would always be second best to him.

'I'm going to be home soon, can we talk then? Properly? I'll explain.'

'Pppppft. I think you've said enough to be honest, Zara. I don't want to speak to you. Just go . . . go enjoy Italy. Sounds like you're having a great time without me, hen.'

The line went dead.

I stumbled back towards the table and chairs and sat down in shock. It was over, but I couldn't take it in. I closed my eyes and felt the breeze hit off my face. I don't know how long I sat there, going over and over the conversation in my head.

What do I want?

I had no idea.

I don't even know who I am anymore.

Behind me, I heard the patio door open slowly with a little creak. Ashley was standing, holding a can of Coke.

'It's not Irn-Bru, but it's all they had.' She shrugged. 'Come on in, Zara.'

When I stood up again my legs felt numb. I made my way back into the room, sipped some juice and lay on the bed. Ashley turned off the lights and jumped in beside me.

'What did he say?' she asked.

I cleared my throat. 'I told him about the Hulk. But he knew there was more to it, and he ended it.' I was staring at the pitch-black ceiling above us.

She gasped. 'Fucking hell. Are you OK?'

'I don't know who I am anymore. I can't believe I've hurt him like that.'

Ashley sighed. 'Zara, look at what happened with Dave and me after I was giving out sookies in Dubai.' She laughed a little. 'If he's the one, the universe will bring him back to you.'

'That's the thing, though. I don't know if he is, Ash,' I replied, feeling laden with guilt for saying it out loud after everything I had done to him. 'He's like the perfect boyfriend to move on with and marry. He wants to plan, he gives me security, trust. But . . . there's something missing. Something that isn't Tom. I just . . . . I don't think he's the one for me right now.'

Ashley squeezed my hand and whispered, 'I don't either, babe.'

Chapter Twenty-Three

The following day I woke to Ashley's voice in the distance. My eyes narrowed as the bright Italian sun peered through the terrace doors. I rolled over to check my messages. A few more from my mother and Emily, but zero from Tom or Andy. *Great.* Ashley was on the phone outside; I could make out Lisa and Olivia's voices echoing through her FaceTime. It occurred to me I hadn't even thought about the clinic all this time. A feeling of guilt once again washed through me as I swung my legs out of bed and readied myself to put on my fakest smile to the girls holding the fort back home.

As I walked up to the door, I heard Olivia ask, 'Have you told her yet, Ash?'

I stopped. A feeling of dread went through me. *What now?*

'No, babe, not yet, but I told Raj!' Whatever it was, she sounded pleased.

Eventually I peered through the door. 'Morning!' I said to Ashley, who jumped unexpectedly.

'Oh, she's up! Morning!' She appeared flustered, pulling in her seat to let me squeeze by her. 'I'm catching up with the girls. Say hi.'

She turned the screen round to face me, and I waved to them, tugging down on my matted bedhead. The girls waved back. They were sitting huddled together at the Individualise desk.

'How's the holiday, Zara?' Olivia asked cheerily.

I laughed a little at how unaware she was of the commotion I had caused in Lake Como. 'It's been fab!' I lied. 'How're things back home?'

The girls bobbed their heads enthusiastically. 'Really good. We've been mobbed!'

Ashley held her shoulders high. 'They are killing it, Zara! We're so proud of you both!'

The pair looked happy with the compliments, and I smiled at their buzz and felt relieved at how well they'd managed without us.

'Right, girls, we better go! We'll see you tomorrow!' Ashley called out.

'Bye, bye.' The pair waved and blew kisses across the screen, and it cut out.

Ashley pivoted to me on her chair, looking sheepish.

'Tomorrow?' I huffed, placing my head on the table with dread.

'We have to check out of here by eleven, babe. There's a three o'clock flight back home I'm going to book us on. We need to get back to reality.'

'What time is it?' I asked, still not fully awake.

'Nine. Come on. Get washed, we have lives to live! And a fucking ferry to catch.'

I knew she was right. My credit card couldn't handle another night in Italy, and neither could my nerves.

At any given moment, I presumed Dog the Bounty Hunter would burst through the doors, and my secret muff dive would be broadcast on MTV.

'Did you get a decent sleep then?' Ashley asked.

'Yeah, pretty much,' I replied. 'Ash, have you heard anything from Tom?'

Ashley looked concerned. 'No, I haven't. Sorry babe.'

'It's OK. Just in case he had reached out.' I paused, 'Ash?'

'Zara,' she responded, sipping on a coffee.

'Is there something you're not telling me? I heard the girls say—'

Ashley puffed. 'I didn't want to say anything right now, OK? With all of this going on.' She looked nervous, and so was I. I didn't think I could take another blow this holiday.

'Oh God, have they found the robes?' I asked, feeling my stomach wrench. 'They'll be searching for DNA next.'

'No, no, Zara, calm it. It's me. I'm . . . I'm pregnant!' she said. She had the brightest smile on her face as she waited nervously for my reaction.

'What?' I could feel my bottom lip quiver.

She nodded. 'I'm preggers, up the duff, with child, however you wanna say it.'

I sat upright in complete shock. 'I don't know what to say!' My hands were stuck to my face in disbelief. I was shaking.

'Say congrats like a normal fucking person would for a start,' she said with a laugh.

I swung my arms around her neck. 'Congratulations! *What the fuck!* But oh my God!'

She laughed loudly at my reaction and hugged me back.

'How far on are you? When are you due?' I asked, finally finding my words.

She lifted her phone and turned the screen to a little scan picture.

'I'm thirteen weeks, babe. I wanted to tell you, Zara. I found out like two weeks ago. Me and Dave had a big reveal cookie for your house-warming gift at Andy's, but obviously you didn't show. So everyone else knew. But I had to tell you myself before I shoved the scan pics all over the Gram and shit.'

I felt my eyes tear up. 'I'm so sorry I missed your reveal, Ash!' I clutched her tightly.

'You had to do what you had to do, Zara. Besides, you didn't know!' She pulled back, unable to take the smile off her face. 'So that's why you didn't tan that Prosecco with me!' I twigged. 'Wait and why you're eating carbs!' I gasped.

'Why I'm eating everything more like!'

And I reached over and squeezed her again.

'You're going to be an auntie again, Zara Smith!' she screeched.

My heart felt warm as I looked proudly at my best friend. 'And you're going to be a mum, Ash!' I said the words out loud but still couldn't digest them.

We sat for an hour on the balcony discussing possible names, future careers and styling options for Ashley's little bun in the oven. It felt amazing to finally have something positive to look forward to after a weekend of turmoil and heartbreak. I couldn't believe Ashley had managed to hold back her news till my life was sorted out. Still, I wished I had known. I wished I could have been there for her and lived the first thirteen weeks with her and not been the total liability I had been recently.

Raj joined us on the balcony, and he immediately smiled when Ashley told him I knew about the baby.

'Wait, I can't believe you told him before me!' I exclaimed.

'I had to tell someone over here!' She giggled.

'And I think it will be the making of you, Ashley, I do!' Raj squeezed her shoulders kindly.

'We're going to head soon, Raj,' I replied, knowing he would be jetting back to Dubai soon and we would all be separated once more. 'Ashley's booked us on a flight at three.'

'That's why I'm here,' Raj responded. He crouched at the table beside us. 'I think I'll head home for a bit. Help you guys at the clinic and catch up with some Glasgow buddies. What do you think?' His smile turned into a grin as he looked at me.

'Seriously?' I laughed.

'Erm . . . YES!' Ashley leaned over and hugged him.

'Well.' He cleared his throat, 'I don't think Tom will be returning anytime soon. Thanks, Zara.' His eyes widened, and he began giggling. 'He texted me this morning asking to extend his break.'

I felt a wave of nausea sweep through me at the thought of Tom playing happily ever after without me.

I felt my eyes water and I immediately lowered my head to the ground. I didn't want today to be about me, again.

'What about your wife? Will she not be ragin'?' Ashley asked.

Raj shook his head. 'The in-laws are visiting Dubai for the next few weeks. They'll keep her busy, and it's a perfect excuse for me to boost.'

'It looks like the old team is back then!' Ashley beamed at us.

'Well . . . mostly.' I sighed. Not knowing if Tom would ever return to the clinic was painful.

'So, three o'clock flight?' Raj asked, pulling out his phone.

I nodded back. With a few silent clicks, he was done.

'Let's get back to fucking Scotland, eh? I'm done with the sun for a while!'

'I fuckin' hear you, boss!' Ashley screamed at the top of her voice.

A few hours later, Ashley, Raj and I were on a budget flight back home. I was straining hard to be optimistic as we journeyed back towards the grey skies of Glasgow. I knew everything was about to change. No Andy, no Tom, and perhaps I was losing a bit of Ashley too. Her priorities were changing and although I was overwhelmingly pleased for my best friend, I started to worry I was getting more alone by the second. My head was spiralling and running on overdrive. Finally, I was heading back to the city I knew and loved, but now, more than ever, I felt utterly lost.

Chapter Twenty-Four

I entered my cold, dark apartment around eight that night. Raj and Ashley offered to come up, but I declined, not wanting to upset their lives any more than I had already over the past few days. I felt like an utter liability. As I pushed my stiff door open, I saw boxes all over the floor. Andy had returned my life, my old unattached life, back to me, and my spare key lay on the floor where he had posted it back through the letterbox. I sighed. This felt real. I was single. *Single again*, having destroyed the only proper relationship I had ever had with someone who really cared about me. Tears and snot streamed down my face as I shut the door behind me.

As I switched on the light, I noticed the enormity of the upheaval. My entire living area was jam-packed with boxes and over-filled Ikea bags laden with clothes. My footsteps echoed around the bare apartment, and as I tried to pass the chaos with my weekend bag, I stumbled and tripped over the mess, making me sob louder.

What have I done? I was crying unbelievably loud now, but I didn't care. I couldn't bear the sight of the situation I'd landed myself in – the reality of being back to square one all over again. Eventually I reached my bedroom and lay down on the bare mattress, staring at the ceiling.

My phone started ringing in my pocket. Mum calling.

I sighed, pressing the silence button, not ready to listen to her lecture quite yet.

Ping. One new message.

Mother: *Are you alive?*

I tapped back immediately in case she took it upon herself to show up.

> *Yes. Just came home, and I am not ready to speak yet.*
> *Sorry xx*

Mother: *Glad you are home, Zara.*

I flicked onto Instagram and searched for Andy's page. User not found. *Great, I'm officially blocked.* I paused and swiped onto my call log – phone Andy. I held the phone cautiously to my ear, not knowing what I'd even say to him. Call failed. *Ideal, I was double blocked.*

I wanted to talk to him. It felt strange being back in Scotland without him. Being totally alone again. I wanted to say how sorry I was and that I'd made a massive mistake, but I knew I didn't deserve any forgiveness after everything I'd done.

I went onto Quinn's account. Her rant was still there and clocking up hundreds of thousands of views. My stomach twisted. Her video was reposted by her army of fans trying to find the muff-diving culprits. Poor Matteo, I thought. People knew he was dressed head to toe in green paint and was working at the party. Even Inspector Clouseau could solve that mystery. What if he was being held captive in some Vatican prison because of my broken heart and horny vagina?

Shit.

My head and heart raced more as I lay in bed with crippling anxiety soaring through my veins. I pulled the cold pillow over my head and prayed for my mind to finally fall asleep, and, eventually, in the early hours of the morning, it did.

The following day I woke to my alarm going off and a deep feeling of dread as I peeked at my phone. I still had over thirty unopened WhatsApps from my Dynamo disappearing act, but no new notifications from the night before. I wondered if Tom would ever reach out to me. I wondered when he'd return to the clinic and felt nervous at the thought. I walked through to the living room and ransacked a bundle of Ikea bags, eventually finding some suitable attire for work. I pulled on a pair of skinny black jeans and a plain black vest top, grabbed a claw clip and headed off to the clinic, make-up-less and puffy-eyed, looking like Marilyn Manson after a night on the gear.

As I walked through the clinic doors, I was greeted by a cheery Lisa and Olivia, who ran over and enveloped me in their arms. Raj and Ashley were grinning from behind the desk.

'How was Italy, Zara?' the girls asked.

I nodded, trying my best to put on a bright face. 'Yeah, lovely. So beautiful!' I replied, heading behind the desk. 'Well, I take it you guys finally met the big boss?'

'Yes, finally!' Olivia said.

'It's lovely to be back, girls,' Raj said happily.

'You two done a great job while we were away,' Ashley said to the girls, who looked delighted with themselves.

'You did. Thanks so much for everything,' I added, feeling guilty about my spontaneous, erratic departure to Europe.

'How are you feeling, Ash?' Lisa asked.

She flicked her hair back, rubbing her stomach through her leather mini skirt. 'We're great! Glad I can finally post about my little walnut now all the important people know!'

I smiled at my friend.

'Oh! We should host a wee event for the socials!' Olivia screamed.

Ashley's veneers glistened at the thought.

'Well, I can already see Ashley's taught you everything she knows, girls! Always an opportunity,' Raj said.

'Like a baby shower? Is that not like towards the end of the pregnancy?' I asked.

'No, like a party to share the good news to our clients. You are such a big part of Individualise, Ash. Glasgow will be buzzing!' Lisa said.

Ashley smirked sassily. 'Of course they will.'

'What about a gender reveal party?' Raj suggested. 'Do you want to find out the sex?'

Ashley looked excited at the prospect of an entire event centred around her. 'Of course I do! I need to know if this baby will be draped in Dior or Adidas.'

'OK, set it up!' Raj said. 'It'll be good for the company and a nice celebration while I'm back home. What about next Friday?'

Ashley screamed and stamped her six-inch heels on the tiled floor excitedly.

'Ash, I can't believe you're still wearing they bloody shoes.' I laughed, examining the thin, uncomfortable-looking heels. 'You need to be careful.'

'Oh, Zara, I'm not trading the Louboutins for anybody. These bad boys are staying! Right, OK, I'll text Dave and book one of they companies that arranges the reveal. And I suppose because it's a social media thing for the clinic, I'll book it all on the company card, right, Raj?'

Raj was walking away from the desk and darted her a look.

'Welcome back, boss!' she added, letting out a mischievous laugh. Raj raised his hands on his head and walked through to Tom's room to set up for his first client of the day.

'OK, guys, please tell me you have the inside scoop on the Quinn Foxx scandal?' Olivia said as soon as Raj shut the door.

Ashley's eyes shot up from her phone to gaze at me. I could feel my heart pound in my chest as my hands turned sweaty.

'*Hmm*, nope. We didn't see a thing!' Ash said when she realised I couldn't muster a reply. 'Of course, we saw the post Quinn did the following day and there were some news reporters lurking about the hotel, but that's about it.' She shrugged dismissively.

'Aw, no way, we've been dying to get the gossip! We thought you would know more!' Lisa replied.

I shook my head, still finding it hard to speak.

'Look how funny this is. My friend sent me it today.' Olivia retrieved her phone from her back pocket and clicked onto her messages, and there I was, legs wrapped around the neck of a giant green monster, bouncing my pussy up and down on his face while he munched on my ham sandwich, all set to the noise of a donkey neighing.

My mouth gaped wide open in shock as Ashley held her hand over hers, trying not to giggle. *Fabulous, I was now a meme!*

'Poor Tom, though!' Lisa replied softly.

'I thought he would see the funny side of it,' Olivia replied. 'He's normally got a wicked sense of humour with things like that.'

'Oh, trust me, he didn't! Sorry, girls, I better get changed.' I walked into my room, feeling the world's weight on my shoulders. I hadn't anticipated the questions. And now my clients would come in and no doubt ask some more. *What if one of them recognised me? What if the story broke and I was outed? What if Tom was still mad and told Quinn it was me?* Panic was starting to surge through me when Ashley walked into my room.

222

'Hey, you OK?' she asked.

'Everyone is going to ask questions!' I snapped under my breath, trying to speak quietly.

'Of course they are! It's all over the news, babe. We just need to keep our stories straight. We didn't see or hear anything.'

'I don't see what the big deal is! Two adults having an intimate moment is suddenly worthy of headlines worldwide?'

'Well, you were doing it during one of the biggest engagement parties of the year. *And* you were dressed as a fucking priest, mate!'

'A wizard! How many times – I was a fucking wizard!' I shot back.

The room turned silent for a moment before Ashley giggled. I looked at her and tried hard not to laugh at the entire situation.

'I'm sorry, Zara. But the whole thing is crazy!'

'I know. I just want to forget about it all and move on.'

Ashley came over and put a hand on my shoulder. 'Let's get today over with first, and each day after will get better with time, OK?'

I cooried into her and her tiny bloated belly. She rubbed my back.

'I hope so, Ash,' I replied, feeling comforted by my best friend.

'Come on. Your first client is here. Get organised.' She pulled away, briefly squeezing my chin before heading out of my room.

The rest of the day I was jam-packed with clients, and all of them bombarded me with questions. Everyone wanted to know how Tom was and how the trip went, and a few openly asked about Muffgate. I managed to swerve the gory details and remain as private as possible, reflecting the questions back to them and their own personal lives.

That night I headed home to an apartment full of cardboard and immediately sighed. There was no way I could sort through this tonight.

Ping.

One new message from Jason.

Hello???

I typed back a quick reply.

Hey yeah. So sorry. I know I've gone AWOL. So sorry! Andy and I broke up, and I'm in a downer. Ran away to Italy and switched my phone off. Hope you're OK xx

Italy? WTF! I thought something was going on with you and Andy when you didn't show up at your party. Don't be down for long, girl. You will find a better one x

Thanks, Jason. I'll phone you in a few days xxxxx

I put my phone down again and let out a bigger sigh.

Ping.

New notification from Tinder: *Check out your latest matches.*

God, Tinder. I thought. Here we go again, lurking through the heaps of creeps in Glasgow.

I clicked on the app feeling a slight hint of guilt that I was still on it, and had been even when Andy and I were together. Maybe I'd known deep down it wouldn't be forever after all. I began flicking through the mound of familiar faces. *Same old fuckboys wanting fucked*, I thought. *And still, here I am.* I was disheartened and not paying attention to anyone I was swiping past. *No, no, no, God no, no.*

My fingers abruptly halted as the last profile I expected to see popped up.

Andy? *My Andy.*

I felt sick as I stared into his eyes on the screen.

Then heart thundering, I swiped down the screen to read his bio.

Hi, my name is Andy. Relatively new to the dating scene. I am looking for a new dog mum for my fur baby. Stay city centre. Good job, nice car and needing a new Mrs. Apply within :-)

I suddenly felt a stab in the stomach. I wasn't sure if I was angry or sad or going to throw up.

A cold shiver ran down my back. Looking for a new mum to his fur baby? I thought of Tyson and felt queasy. I was his mum. I mean, the cunt nearly killed me. Andy should have added that to his bio: *The lucky lady will be required to purchase a truckload of aloe vera and a top-of-the-range Shark hoover as Ty casts like a fucking yeti*. I mean seriously, the hairy bastard would give Cesar Millan a dog allergy.

I stared at the screen, glaring at his photographs. One of him at the beach in Dubai, one candid professional photo at his friend's wedding last year, and one selfie at the gym. He looked good. He looked happy. I felt myself tear up.

I knew I had caused this and as much as I understood I wasn't right for Andy, I felt my insides tearing apart at the thought of him with someone else. Someone who could potentially give him everything he wanted. Everything I wanted for myself.

I screenshotted his profile and sent it to Ashley.

ALERT! Andy has Tinder!!!!!!

Typing . . .

Shitttt! U OK? What a wee dick! X

> *I feel like shit. Should I contact him? I feel sick xx*

No No No! Don't contact! What for? This will pass. Stay strong. Xx

Besides . . . You had Tinder, even when you were together! That speaks volumes xxx

Go match someone hotter and get your mind off him. Please don't text him.

Dave and I are going pram shopping in East Kilbride if you need to go out. Maybe next weekend? xxx

> *I'd rather have my lick out leaked on Pornhub than shop prams. I'll be OK. Thanks though ☹ xxxx*

I'd say that's probably already happened by now, babe. Phone me if you change your mind xxx

I lay back on the bed, still analysing Andy's profile. I knew I'd swipe for him if I saw his pictures and cute bio. So many other girls would be doing the same. I wondered who he was speaking to, and my chest felt unbelievably heavy. I missed him. His cute face, his kind manners, his silly jokes and cuddles. My finger hesitated on which way to swipe. What would he think when he saw my profile? Maybe he'd be mad? Or perhaps he didn't care? I wasn't sure if I should swipe out of general courtesy. Like a *'I'm sorry I fucked up'* swipe. Maybe it would act like an olive branch? I mean if he'd matched me too, maybe this would allow us to clear the air. Maybe with Tom out of the picture I could eventually see myself with Andy?

I paused for a split second and scrunched up my eyes. Swipe – left.

I closed my eyes, knowing I'd made the right decision for him. I wasn't ready to commit. He wasn't ready to forgive me.

I waited for a further minute contemplating my decision.

I loved him. I didn't know how to be alone without him anymore, but, truthfully, deep down, I still loved Tom more.

Chapter Twenty-Five

The week that followed went by in a blur, I spent my days painfully quiet, upset and tortured on social media by relentlessly stalking Quinn Foxx's page. Eventually I woke up one Saturday afternoon on my day off with fuck all to do. The sun was peering through my bedroom window, and my eyes squinted as they adjusted to the light. Finally, I stretched out, irritated at my body for waking up when I'd happily sleep the weekend away instead. Since coming home, I'd continued to ignore my sister and most of my friends, as I wasn't mentally equipped for any questions yet. But after a colossal sense of boredom set in, I glanced at my phone.

Tinder: *One new match.*

My heart quickened as I frantically clicked onto Tinder to see if Andy had managed to reach out somehow. I felt my shoulders sink back into my fake-tan-stained mattress. Instead, I had a new match and a message from Darren, whoever the fuck he was. I let out a small puff of despair.

Darren: *Hey Zara, how are you? Please tell me you are one of the girls who talk on this. I haven't had a conversation with a female in a long time.*

I smiled at my phone, flicking through Darren's pictures of hiking the Scottish hills and bar crawling through Glasgow. He was handsome. I typed back:

> *Hey Darren. I'm good, thanks. Yes, I can talk! Haha. This app is brutal, though. Where you from?*

The rest of the day, I chatted freely to Darren about Netflix, food and how lousy dating was in the twenty-first century. He seemed genuinely friendly and easy to talk to. He also kept my mind occupied and my stalking level of Quinn's Instagram page to an absolute minimum of maybe only five thousand clicks. The day flew by, and around 9 p.m., Darren upped the messaging ante after an entire day of whining about Tinder.

Darren: *OK, so crazy question. I don't suppose you fancy meeting up tomorrow? I'm free for a few hours in the afternoon and think it's always best to meet up quickly before my messages dry up. No pressure, but my chat is better in person.*

I screenshotted the entire day's chat immediately to Ashley, followed by *?????*.

No reply. *Come on.*

I started pacing my apartment. I had no intention of meeting anyone else after my sex life had blew-up the internet but part of me wanted to go and forget about Tom and Andy for a while. *God, Ash, tell me what to do!*

Darren: *OK, I take it that was too soon. Promise I'm not a serial killer just enjoy your chat!*

Me: *OK. Sorry I was hovering. Just got out a serious relationship and was in two minds but, yes. Sure. I suppose it would be good to get out for a bit. Where do you fancy?*

And just like that, as quickly and as easily as the chat had started, my first date was arranged.

The following morning, after *finally* getting a reply and seal of approval from Ashley, I began to get ready to meet Darren. It was the first time I had dated in almost a year, and the more I thought about the situation the more my stomach was twinging with nerves. But I knew I needed a distraction, something nice to happen that wasn't messy and destructive. The other option would be spending the entire day in bed with ten packets of Monster Munch, reliving the past few weeks in a cold sweat.

There was something about Darren, though. He seemed laidback, almost as though a friendship had flickered between us. Two like-minded, lonely people wanting to spend time with each other. *God, what a pair of sad fucking bastards.*

I decided on a pair of black jeans and a tight bodysuit, with a black blazer hanging casually off my shoulders. I put my hair into waves, and I had to use a generous amount of black root spray, not having had time to contact Bombshell, my local hairdresser, for an appointment to disguise my greys. I wore large gold hoop earrings and put on some make-up, and for the first time in weeks, I actually felt strangely excited to do something other than wallow in self-pity in a pair of curry-stained Eeyore pyjamas, which were now bobbling at the thighs from overuse.

We'd agreed to meet at The Dockyard Social for a couple of day drinks at two. He picked up his little boy at six on a Sunday, so I knew there was no ulterior motive – just casual drinks and getting to know one another. I headed out of my apartment following a quick spurt of my favourite Jo Malone perfume and hopped in a taxi to Finnieston to meet Darren.

The Dockyard Social was a lively, casual food court inside an old warehouse on the other side of the city. Pop-up street food venues and bars lined the perimeter, surrounding rows of tables and benches. There was live music, and people brought kids, dogs and families there too. I walked through the tunnelled entrance, snapping a few of the inspirational graffiti messages and posting them on my Insta story.

'Zara?'

As I entered the hall, a tall, muscular man called over from one of the benches. *Damn, Darren is hot!*

'Hey!' I walked over, waving. 'Nice to meet you!' I said, feeling nervous at soberly chatting to a man for the first time in a while. I quickly scanned the room to make sure no clients or friends were in the vicinity.

'I got you a mojito. I saw on your Instagram that you like them?' He blushed slightly as I sat down.

'Thank you so much! And ten out of ten for your stalking skills, Darren!' I giggled a little.

Darren had the most piercingly blue eyes and black hair, and with a pale complexion he was very striking. Tribal tattoos ran up his arms, ending at his neckline. *Ding-dong!* He wore a white shirt and denim jeans, which were slightly ripped at the knees.

'So . . . erm . . .' he said, looking nervous.

'So . . .' I replied, laughing a little awkwardly.

'Sorry, I'm the worst at this. I haven't dated in a while.' His voice was soft yet manly and robust.

'I'm the same. Don't worry. I've literally just split up with my ex. So have you been single for a while?' I asked, sipping on my mojito as he drank his pint of Tennent's in a very masculine way.

'Been single for three years now. I haven't so much as kissed anyone, dated or anything in that time.'

Jesus! No wonder his muscles were so big, I thought. He must be doing the one-handed shuffle every night, the poor cunt.

'Wow, that's a while!'

'It ended badly.' His lips pursed thoughtfully as he reminisced about his past. 'What happened with you and your ex, if you don't mind me asking?'

I gulped down more of my mojito. *Unfortunately, I'm far too sober to explain that situation.*

'*Well* . . . Everything was good with us until I found out my ex from before him was getting engaged, and things turned a little weird with my current boyfriend.'

232

I noticed the lines on Darren's forehead scrunch together in confusion. 'Why would that change your relationship?' he asked.

Because I ran away to Italy to try to get him back, Darren, that's why.

'Because . . . we all worked together and . . .' I hesitated, unable to find the right words to paint an honest picture without me looking like the biggest cheating arsehole that walked the planet.

'Because your man got jealous?' Darren asked.

I took another large sip and nodded. I could feel the blood rush to my face in panic. 'Yeah, so jealous! It was strange. He cast it up all the time as if I'd care, and of course, I didn't.' *Well, two minutes in, and there goes the honesty, Zara.*

'Aww, babe. He must have been insecure. I get that, though. A good-looking girl like yourself.'

I smiled at the compliment, feeling slightly guilty about my lies. 'Anyway . . . Tell me about you!' I said, changing the subject.

Darren spent the rest of the afternoon buying me minty mojitos and telling me all about his son, Junior. Darren worked for Sky in a call centre and played five-a-side with his friends in his spare time. He was charming, laddish, and the more pints he downed, the more he opened up to me. We laughed and told stories about our travels and past dates, easing any lingering tension. It was a great escape. I enjoyed painting myself as a happy-go-lucky gal, a far cry from the traumatic, depressive, self-destructive person I really was.

'Do you fancy something to eat?' Darren asked.

I shook my head. 'No, honestly, I'm fine, thanks.' I was trying hard to be mannerly even though I had been eyeing up the curried waffles since I arrived.

'Cool. I'll maybe get something in a bit. I've been eyeing the waffles on their Instagram page for weeks,' he said.

Oh, was this a sign? I thought. *Dun dun da dun . . .*

Darren and I continued to chat. The time flew by and three mojitos in, I was feeling tipsy and having the best time I'd had for a while. After a few hours, I noticed him glancing at his watch, and I remembered about his son.

'*Oh,* I take it you need to go and get Junior soon?' I asked.

Darren hesitated and smiled. 'Yeah, I should. But . . . I was thinking of asking my mum to collect him for me, and we could . . . I don't know . . . have a few drinks at mine. I mean . . . if you fancied?'

I hesitated slightly, feeling my head sway, not expecting this.

'It's just that I haven't enjoyed myself like this for ages, Zara. I don't want it to end just now,' he explained.

And truthfully, neither did I. It had been the first time in days I hadn't thought about Tom. Where he was or if he was coming back or even giving me a second thought.

'I'd love to spend more time with you too. But—'

'That's it settled then,' Darren interrupted, laughing cheekily.

'Darren!' I called out.

'Let me text the gaffer.' He brought out his phone and began typing. 'My mum, I mean, ha.'

I hesitated. Darren was lovely, kind, and handsome, but was I ready to bounce fanny-deep into another fling with someone? But hey, people do say you find the love of your life when you least expect it. Maybe it was Darren? Maybe he was *my* Quinn?

Shit. I suddenly had a flashback to the thick, wiry bush that was protruding halfway down my thighs. I wasn't prepared for anything to happen sexually. *A couple of drinks and maybe a cuddle, Zara. That is it.*

'OK, will we head?' Darren asked, smiling up at me with his ocean-blue eyes.

With one last slurp of my cocktail, I stood up and nodded.

'OK, a couple more drinks. Let's do it!' I replied.

Darren and I popped in a taxi and headed back to his house just outside the city centre in Cessnock. He insisted on paying. His home was a new build in a lovely private estate complete with new fixtures and fittings, but the inside was cluttered with small toys lying all over the place. There were plates piled up in the sink, and his washing was squeezed onto the radiators the way only a man would do. I felt very judgemental for someone whose home resembled the Amazon depot more than a city-centre pad.

There were cute pictures of him and his son hanging on the wall from professional shoots they had participated in.

'These are cute!' I said, pointing at the pictures, while I slipped my shoes off.

'Yeah, my mate is a photographer, and she said I had

to make this place a little more homely!' He shrugged and laughed a little.

She? I thought. *Hmmm* . . .

'So, a drink? I have white wine or . . .' He looked through his cupboard. 'Bottles of Bud?'

'Could I have wine, please?' I walked into his living room, which flowed nicely from the open-plan kitchen area, and sat on the sofa.

Behind me, I heard Darren pouring from the bottle, and I began to feel nervous.

'Here you go, gorgeous.' He handed me the glass, and I smiled back at him as he sat beside me.

'Thank you!' I was suddenly aware of how alone we were now, and felt my heart begin to quicken. I sipped my wine slowly.

'I'm going to be honest with you, Zara. I'm shocked I finally have a girl back here! It's been a while!' Darren was chuckling loudly at his accomplishment.

'Well, it's only for a glass of wine,' I reiterated.

Darren raised an eyebrow at me.

'What!' I gasped and slapped his arm.

'I'm just surprised. We get on well. We both like one another.' Darren sat his pint on the coffee table and leaned into my body. I could feel his hot weight press down on top of me and I tried to remain calm, but inside I could feel jungle drums blaring out a severe case of the minge twinge. Darren's lips came closer and closer to mine until finally, we kissed.

His lips were wet and soft. I could taste the bitterness of beer. In an instant, he grabbed the back of my head and pushed his tongue inside my mouth. *Oh, daddy!*

We snogged like teenagers for the next twenty minutes. It felt so good to be desired, to be caught up in this exciting moment with someone again. No strings attached. No guilt. And, most importantly, I wasn't thinking of Tom fuckin' Adams.

'Come upstairs with me?' Darren mumbled through the kissing.

I hesitated, pulling back, discreetly wiping his saliva off my lip.

'I shouldn't. No. I can't,' I replied, covering my face in sheer torture as my vagina barked aggressively from my jeans.

'Why can't you? We like one another. We're adults. When is it ever the perfect time?' he whispered, kissing my neck.

When my pubes aren't protruding out of the fabric of my underwear, that's when, Darren, I thought. This cunt would seriously need a pair of oven mitts to slip the hawn tonight unless he fancied a trip to The Royal with some severe finger abrasions.

'Let's go up to have a cuddle then? Just a lie down? Nothing has to happen,' he said.

I glanced at his warm, cheeky smile and nodded back.

'OK. But I should head soon,' I warned before getting led upstairs to his bedroom.

'Deal!' he said.

Everything was dark in his bedroom until he popped on the side light.

'Don't be shy!' he laughed, ushering me onto the bed. I watched him as he took off his top. His hairy, tattooed chest was entirely on display, and my mind was tortured. 'I'm just getting comfy, darling,' he said as he lifted the remote and popped Netflix on in the background.

I lay back in his bed, still fully dressed and shivering slightly.

'Come, I'll warm you up, Zara,' Darren said, pulling me towards him.

I could feel his warm breath on my cold skin, and I closed my eyes. Then, once again, we began kissing. Only this time, his hands caressed, rubbed, and squeezed my body. Slowly, he began touching my boobs and running his hands down my back, squeezing my arse. I was panting, enjoying being handled as I pushed my groin against Darren's big dick.

God, he felt so hard.

'I'm sorry, it's been years since I've been in this situation! I can't help myself,' he said, running his tongue up and down my chest. 'Take this off!' He slid off my bodysuit and I had a flashback to the last time I wore this top on a date when Mark began sucking the gusset like a lollipop. I smiled at the memory between the kissing, and was thankful when Darren did not do the same. Instead, he started squeezing and sucking my nipples.

Oh, Jesus Christ! I felt goosebumps travel from my head to my toes.

Why did I not shave?! I asked myself, over and over. *Why, oh why, oh why!*

Because, Zara, you've seen more helmets than Hitler this month! Stay strong.

But then he caressed me again, and the hotter I became, the more the little Catholic voice in my head got fainter and fainter.

Darren's hand wandered between my thighs, gently rubbing my clit in circular motions over my jeans while he bit my lip teasingly. I could feel my fanny beginning to expel large amounts of cum, and I was grateful for my fuzzy foliage keeping it contained. Finally, he parted my legs and gyrated his muscular body on top of me, and I decided there and then I couldn't wait any longer.

'Wait. Stop. Please, do you mind if I use your shower?' I asked.

'What? Right now?' He sounded confused as he stopped dead on top of me.

'Yeah. Sorry! I need a moment.'

'Do you want me to join?' He giggled.

'Darren!' I warned.

He gave a frustrated laugh, unmounted me and nodded his head. His strong arms led me to the bathroom with his penis pointing the way through his trousers. He turned the shower on for me and laughed as he left the room. I could hear his strong Glaswegian voice calling out, 'What are you doing to me, man?'

I couldn't help but have a sudden spring in my step. *No,* I thought, more like *what am I about to do to you, pal.* I searched the bathroom like Scooby Doo, looking for a razor or perhaps a pair of scissors to trim my pubes. Fuck, the backup option would be to raid his shed for some shears. I felt desperate, my clit was throbbing and I really needed to cum. Eventually, I found an old rusty Bic razor in the bottom of his toiletry bag. *This will have to do.* I jumped into the shower and began shaving as swiftly as possible. My heart was racing just in case he returned to the bathroom and found me with two legs over my head bent like a fucking croissant, fanny lips meeting him at the door. When I finished, the bath looked like someone had attempted to shave Chewbacca, so I grabbed a small heap of the thick black curlies and flushed them down the toilet. Then I used the showerhead, desperately attempting to rinse any evidence of excess shavings and blood loss from the shitty instrument I had to use. I patted my poontang dry, applying extra pressure to the new wounds I had obtained, and, *finally*, ten minutes later, I was as bald as an egg and ready to have a fanny-filled night of passionate sex and attention that would make me forget everything that happened in Italy.

I strutted confidently out of the bathroom wearing only a tiny towel to find Darren lying on his bed, smiling mischievously. I walked over and kissed him on the lips.

'*Mmmmm* . . . Feel how wet I am, baby,' I said as seductively as possible. I felt like Naomi fucking Campbell with my fresh puss, keen to pick things up where we had left them.

But Darren pecked me back unenthusiastically and said, 'No wonder you're wet, you're just out of the shower, hen! Here, listen, have you got another top to go home with?'

What? I was so confused. Here I was, wearing the smallest hand towel, waiting to be pounced on, and he was making small talk.

'Erm . . . What? No, why?'

'When you were in the shower, I got a little bit excited.' Darren giggled and held up my bodysuit with one finger.

I gasped. It was tarnished, well and truly destroyed. My cute little Urban Outfitters bodysuit was encrusted head to clip with slimy white spunk. *Is this cunt having a fucking laugh?* I felt so violated. Never mind that I had just shaved my full nan for nothing.

'Well . . . OK.' I paused, then said frostily, 'Thanks for that.'

I sat down on the opposite end of the bed, bewildered, whilst he became absorbed in his phone. The room fell silent as I tried to wrap my head around the situation. He was the one that hadn't had sex in ages. He invited *me* here.

Eventually he looked up from his phone. 'Aww, come on! Is someone in a wee huff?'

Huff doesn't cover it, ya fucking pervert! I thought.

'No, I'm fine. I'm going to get my clothes on and head, though. I have lots to sort at my place.'

'You sure, babe? Do you want me to phone a taxi?'

I stood up, heading back to the bathroom to collect my jeans. 'Nah, I'll walk, thanks.'

There was no way I was waiting here for thirty minutes with Sir Spunksalot. I had to get out of here.

When I was dressed, I headed back downstairs to find Darren perched on the arm of his sofa, lingering on me. He stood up as I walked in, and I buttoned my blazer to hide my naked chest.

'Here you go.' He handed me a Tesco carrier bag with my tarnished bodysuit inside.

'Great, a goodie bag,' I said sarcastically.

'And I'm not even charging 10p for the bag.' He winked.

'I think I should be charging you forty quid for a new bodysuit,' I snapped.

'Aw, lighten up. It's a wee bit of jizz, pal.'

My face screwed up in disgust. *Ewwww*. I would generally have pushed the matter, but truthfully I suspected he might need to phone a plumber for a pube blockage the next time he used his shower.

'See you, Darren,' I said, and left.

I started walking through the gloomy Glasgow streets, my arms wrapped tightly around my chest as the cold hit my unprotected nipples and my semen-stained top swung freely in a fucking carrier bag. I wondered how Andy's new dating life would be going. Some lucky burd would probably be getting wined and dined by him, not spunked and dumped like me. Had I blown my one shot of a normal life with Andy? All for that one guy I knew deep down was totally out of my league. That one guy who'd hurt me so much, but I still pined for him. My mind slipped back to Tom and Quinn. I couldn't get his face out of my mind, how angry he'd looked when I told him how I felt. I wondered if he'd ever speak to me again? If he'd ever forgive me? And just as I sighed deeply a huge double-decker bus flew past me and my carrier bag slipped out of my hands straight into a dark puddle. I bent down, carefully fishing out the bodysuit with one finger, and returned it back to the damp carrier bag, my face filled with sheer disgust. *Ewww.*

What a fucking night.

Welcome back to the dating world, Zara.

Chapter Twenty-Six

The next day I walked through the clinic doors to see Lisa and Olivia there already, gushing over Ashley's phone.

'So cute! I love it,' Olivia was saying as Ashley beamed.

'You need to get the Isofix for the car, too. It's a game changer, babe,' Lisa added.

No one seemed to have noticed me stepping through the door.

'Morning!' I called out.

I heard back a few distant '*Heys*', but they were all preoccupied with Ashley's phone. I hung my jacket on the stand and joined them at the desk.

'What's happening here?'

'Ashley's pram and accessories! How cute are they?' Lisa replied excitedly.

'I don't know. I haven't seen them. How cute are they?' I replied, feeling a little out of the loop.

Ashley briefly peeked up from her phone. 'Aw, I didn't send you them. I knew you wouldn't get it,' she said.

I felt my heart fall a little.

'Wanna see?'

'Yes, of course, I do!' I said and leaned towards her.

Ashley proceeded to show me photographs of a light grey pram, carrier, and car seat, all matching.

'What do you think?'

'Yeah, really nice colour. I like them!' I gave a thumbs up, not knowing how to compliment a pram. It had four wheels and was for a baby. That's all I could contribute.

'See, I knew you wouldn't get it,' Ashley puffed.

I raised my eyebrow a little at her hostility. 'It's a nice buggy, Ashley. What won't I get?'

'Oh, it's not a buggy. This is like the top-of-the-range, bespoke, *crème de la crème* of prams, Zara,' Lisa informed me cheerfully.

'Well, it's beautiful.' I shrugged. 'I better get organised.'

I headed into my treatment room while the three girls continued conversing about the features and fixtures of the pushchair. I wondered why Ashley hadn't sent me the photos the day before. We shared everything. I knew our lives were at different stages just now, but I still wanted to be involved. She hadn't even asked how my date with Darren had gone. Granted, it was awful, but normally I'd share my overview of the horrendous experience, and me and Ashley would have a laugh about it.

There was a knock on my door as my first client arrived.

'Hey, Maria, come on in!' I greeted her warmly.

Maria was a relatively new client. She had visited the clinic a few times over the past year. She was in her

245

mid-forties and worked at Glasgow University teaching medical students.

'How are you, Zara? I expected you to be more tanned after some time in Italy!' she said, hopping up on the bed.

I smiled as I sterilised my trolley. 'I could be in Hawaii for a month and come back whiter, Maria!' I laughed. 'OK, stay still, and I'll map out your face, missus.'

I held up a tiny white thread and pencil and carefully examined the symmetry of Maria's face. Her skin was flawless. I could tell she looked after herself well. Her lips had remained in excellent condition after her last lip-filling treatment.

'I'm thinking Botox and slightly more filler in the cheeks?' I replied.

'Zara, oh my God, the cheeks! I couldn't believe how much that changed my face. I'm addicted!' she replied.

I laughed. 'Total game changer! But we do subtle in here, so don't get too addicted!' I warned.

I set up the products while chatting with Maria, who told me all about her son starting high school and trying to keep him interested in his studies.

'You know Ashley's expecting?' I replied, gently piercing through her skin with my syringe.

'Yes! She just told me about the gender reveal on Friday night!'

Shit, I had forgotten about that.

'What have you got planned for her?' Maria asked.

'Well, I'm not sure. You know Ashley, she pretty much plans it all herself. I turn up, drink wine and leave with the hottest man at the bar. That's kind of my role just now.'

I finished the Botox and started on the filler in Maria's cheeks.

'Wait. What about Andy?' she said, sounding shocked.

I shrugged. 'We split!'

She gasped loudly.

'Oh, sorry, was that painful?' I asked, stopping her treatment briefly.

'No, I'm fine, I'm just shocked to hear you split up!'

'Ah. No, it's fine. It was all on me, I'm afraid. But I'm back on the dating train and struggling with it all, to be honest.'

I finished up and pressed a piece of the gauze into Maria's face.

She looked into my eyes sympathetically.

'Whatever happened, don't be too hard on yourself. It's OK to take some time on your own. It heals you and makes you realise what you want.'

'Thanks, Maria,' I replied, feeling a heaviness fall onto my chest.

'Just don't rush into anything with anyone. You need to get used to being yourself again at times.'

I smiled down at her warmly. 'Thanks.'

I had clients back to back the rest of the day. I enjoyed their company and hearing their stories of work, life and weekend plans. Listening to their lives almost made me forget about mine and I enjoyed the moments where my mind didn't run at one million miles per hour. When I'd finished with my last client, I walked back onto the clinic floor to find Ashley rubbing her feet on the sofa.

'Are the heels finally getting to you?' I asked.

She smiled. 'Never! They're just feeling tight today. Maybe I need a size up?'

I laughed and sat down beside her. 'Maybe you need sliders or something for work?'

Ashley rolled her eyes at me and carried on rubbing her feet.

'So my date with Darren was a nightmare!' I began.

'Oh my God! I completely forgot about that! What happened?'

I felt my shoulders relax, excited to divulge my latest dating disaster to my best friend, when Dave walked through the door.

'Hey, you ready?' he said to Ashley, waving across the room to me.

I waved back briefly as Ashley stood up.

'Yes!' she screeched. 'We're on our way to the gender scan for Friday's reveal!'

'Oh my God! Amazing!' I clasped my hands in excitement for them.

'Yip, going to see my boy's boaby on the screen, eh, Ash!' Dave laughed.

Ashley shook her head. 'Boy's? Well, as long as he's got a bigger one than his da!' She winked cheekily at Dave, then turned to me. 'You OK to lock up? Raj has just left; he was catching up with some hospital guys,' she said, putting on her long trench coat.

'Yeah, fine. Good luck!' I called out as the pair rushed out the clinic door.

Just before it shut, Ashley popped her head back in and said, 'Oh! And remember it's product day tomorrow.'

'*Ohhh*. OK,' I said, but she'd already left.

In the silence of the empty clinic, my heart began to beat heavily in my chest. Product day meant Andy. It meant a rundown on the past month. Italy would have to be acknowledged due to the sudden lack of staff. *Shit, shit, shit.*

I felt my head go dizzy with anxiety.

Should I call a sicky? Should I ask him for a chat?

I sank into the sofa.

Over a month had passed since the last product day and in that time, Tom and Andy had gone to Dubai, Tom met Quinn and got engaged, I did a runner to Italy and managed to ruin two of the most important relationships in my life, Ashley announced her pregnancy and I was suddenly single. *How can all of that have happened in one month?* I asked myself.

A stab of guilt flashed through me as I thought back to Tom, the Hulk, and even the little bit of wanky panky I'd had with Darren the night before. How would Andy act seeing me again? Would he pretend nothing had happened? Or blank me completely? My stomach twisted at how awkward it would be between all of us in the room. Everyone knowing but saying nothing.

I threw my hands over my face.

I don't think I can do it.

But part of me wanted to see him. I wanted to know he was OK and to be around him again.

Eventually, I stood up, took a deep breath, locked up the clinic and walked home to gather my thoughts. I knew I'd have to face Andy at one point and as much as it terrified me, I was prepared to do it. That night I raided my boxes, pulling out clothing options and beauty products. Clothes heaped over my sofa and coffee table as I tried to find the perfect outfit for the next day. Finally, I found an old bottle of Fake Bake and mixed it with an even older bottle of cheap tan and applied it all over my body. I had to look good. I went to sleep that night wondering what my life would be like if I hadn't found Tom's stupid note.

A smile came over my face on hearing my alarm go off the following morning, knowing today I'd maybe get a chance to apologise to Andy and perhaps get my life back on track. I wanted the last month to be erased. Tom didn't want me. I was crazy to think that he would. I'd pushed Andy away and betrayed his trust. And right now, my life, house, and mind were upside down. Today would be the day I asked for forgiveness and sorted all of it out.

I got up, showered and put on enough make-up to gain entry to the Oscars. I opted for a black smoky eye, red lipstick and a tight black dress with a belt at the waist.

I headed into the clinic with my head held high and my speech prepared.

When I walked through the doors, Raj and Ashley were standing at the desk.

'Oh, wow, Zara!' Raj said, slurping his morning coffee.

Ashley winked at me. 'You're looking amazing!'

I smiled at the pair.

'You guys are acting like I don't try this hard every day!' I laughed back.

Raj spat a little as he attempted to swallow his drink.

'Hey!' I gasped. He had found my joke a little too funny.

'I take it this effort isn't for our benefit?' he said, raising one brow.

I took a deep breath. 'No. It's not. Today is when I apologise to Andy, face to face, and go back to my old life.'

Ashley and Raj glanced at one another with a look of concern on their faces.

'What?' I asked.

Raj shrugged. 'Nothing!'

'No, not nothing. But is that what you want? You want to go back with Andy? I thought he wasn't the one?' Ashley asked.

'I want to forget everything that happened over the last month. I want to forget that stupid note Tom left me, that blew up my life completely. I just want to feel normal again. Like my life is following some path that resembles a thirty-one-year-old's, instead of meeting random guys and them spunking all over my clothes for fun.'

Raj spat a lot more of his coffee out this time. 'I'm out. She's all yours, Ashley!' He walked across the clinic floor towards his treatment room, shaking his head.

'I know things didn't go as planned in Italy, babe. But maybe it's because you and Andy aren't right for each other. You said so yourself. Just don't rush back into things with him to make yourself feel better,' she said.

I felt my shoulders fall.

'It's not fair to him or you,' she continued.

'I need to do this, Ashley,' I replied.

'OK, OK. But please think about what I'm saying,' Ashley urged, looking at me with apprehension.

'How did the scan go?' I asked, keen to change the subject.

In an instant she was smiling again. 'Good! We got to see the baby wriggle about. We don't find out the sex till Friday's party though.'

'That's so exciting, Ash,' I replied, feeling a surge of happiness for her.

She nodded back, still looking worried.

I spent the morning with two clients, providing consultations and treatment plans for their wedding days. Both brides were ecstatic and full of energy, but I found it difficult to match as I thought about the meeting. I caught myself sneaking glances at the clock, counting down the time. *One more hour and Andy will be here. Forty-five minutes. Half an hour.* I could feel my stomach twist.

I'd planned it all out in my head.

He'd host the meeting. First, I'd remain as quiet as possible. Then, at the end, I'd ask to speak to him alone. I'd start by telling him how I got scared and made a huge mistake, how I missed him and Tyson and that I would do anything for a second chance.

I meant it, too, with every ounce of my body.

The clock seemed to be moving slower than usual. Nerves pulsed through me and my breathing was becoming shallow as the time approached.

Finally, my last client left, and Raj gathered us on the sofas. Lisa and Olivia were chatting about how great my outfit looked, but as I smiled and nodded at the compliments, I couldn't concentrate. I was going over my speech in my mind. Answering what he might say in my head, so I was prepared for any reply. So many doubts were slamming into me. What if he had met someone else? He was on Tinder. What if he got angry? What if he asked me about Tom? The what ifs towered on top of me, and anxiety flooded my veins. This was my chance to put everything right that I had done wrong, I couldn't mess it up. I stared at my hands and watched them tremble as they rested on my knees while the rest of the group chatted casually, waiting for the meeting to begin.

Finally, around one, I heard the door open.

I closed my eyes. This was it.

'Good afternoon.' An English woman's voice filled the room, and my head swivelled instantly.

'I hope you don't mind the intrusion. I'm Linda, and I'm filling in for Andy today!' Her jolly, sincere voice made my heart plummet to the ground.

'Oh, not at all. Come in, Linda!' Raj stood up to greet her, and sweat descended on my body.

'But not to worry, I've studied your accounts and I know them inside out!' Linda said.

The group stood up to make introductions, but I sat there in a trance. He couldn't even face me.

'Zara, *psst*, Zara.' I heard a whisper from the other sofa. 'Zara, are you OK?' Ashley asked.

I shook my head. I felt like an idiot. All dressed up, and he didn't want to see me. He didn't want to see me so much he'd sent her.

'Raj, I'm sorry. I don't feel too good. I think I need to sit this one out,' I said, feeling my bottom lip begin to quiver.

'Erm . . . yes, yes, sure. OK,' he said after taking one look at my face. 'Do you need a lift home?'

I shook my head, not wanting to create any more interruptions to the meeting. 'I'll be OK, thanks.'

'Text me later. Let me know how you are,' he added.

I gathered my things quickly and headed straight outside. The fresh air was welcome on my skin as I felt cold tears stream down. I put my head down and walked home, where I bundled myself straight into bed.

I was alone for good.

My life was a mess. I was a mess and I didn't know how to fix any of it.

Chapter Twenty-Seven

The next few days were devoured in bed. Raj wasn't pleased that I took another couple of days off but I promised him late nights and weekends over the next few months to compromise. I didn't answer any calls and only replied to a few messages to let people know I was alive and to prevent potential visitors from checking up on me. My bed felt crumby, and it rustled as I woke, surrounded by empty bottles of Coke and wrappers from my four-day Just Eat binge. I wanted to bounce in an Uber and drive by Andy's apartment or check to see if Tom was home, but I knew there was no point. My mind was on overdrive, thinking of Andy dating again and Tom joyfully in love, planning a wedding while feasting on pasta with Quinn Foxx. I didn't want to be around anyone. I felt so unhappy that I didn't want to infect any of my friends with my loneliness. But before I knew it, it was the day of Ashley's gender reveal. And the day I'd have to vacate my house again.

I dragged myself upright just after noon and trekked over the growing mess. My muscles ached from days of inactivity, and my head hurt with potential questions I might get asked at the party. The thought of facing Emily and my mum after vamoosing for Italy tore me up inside. I'd once again be the let-down of the sisters ruining the only real relationship I had ever had. I could already feel the disappointment from halfway across the city and I was not looking forward to facing it head on. I walked through the kitchen and opened the fridge, starved after a week of snacking on random takeaways. Great. Not even a can of fucking Irn-Bru. My eyes skimmed over the fridge as it hummed in the background, landing on a bottle of cold rosé wine, gifted to me by a client for moving in with Andy. *Perfect.*

A few hours later, with newfound confidence swarming my veins after downing the bottle on an empty stomach, I was ready to face Goliath, never mind my mother and sister. I could hear the chatter coming from the clinic as I crossed over a drizzly George Square into the building. I was greeted by familiar faces, from clients to members of Ashley's family.

'Hey! Hi, how are you?' I asked as people smiled towards me.

I spotted my mum and sister across the room and headed straight to them.

'Zara!' Emily gushed, wrapping her arms around me.

'Nice of you to turn up, Zara. I almost thought you had done another runner!' my mother piped up. I rolled my eyes at Emily, who looked uncomfortable as I kissed my mum incredibly hard on the cheek.

'*Mwah.* Pleasure to see you, Mother,' I said and pivoted to greet the other guests.

'Have you been drinking?' she asked as I strolled away. 'Emily, she's drunk!'

I wandered up to Lisa and Olivia, standing with a group of young clients.

'Hey, biatches! How are my favourite girls?' I stretched my arms widely, slightly bashing into some of the guests.

'Oh, sorry!' Lisa said to them as they shifted from the bump, and we all giggled.

'How are you doing?' Olivia asked.

'Me? I'm great! I've had a bottle of wine, and I'm out for the night! How are *you* doing?'

She laughed loudly. 'I'm great! I'm glad you're feeling better.'

I smiled and scanned the room for Ashley. I finally spotted her tall, slim figure with a tiny bump across the floor, taking selfies effortlessly as she posed in front of her neutral balloon arch and teddy bear-backdrop. I stumbled across to see her.

'Zara!' she gasped happily.

'Hey babe, and . . .' I lowered my head to her stomach and whispered, 'Hey, baby!' I stood back up straight and said, 'You look fucking sensational, by the way. If Dave hadn't already done so, I'd impregnate you right here, right now, on the spot!' I winked at her as she laughed.

'Stop it!' She grinned a little, then lowered her voice. 'I was worried you wouldn't come. I pictured you in bed with either a Tinder date or a bottle of Whitley Neill at your side.'

'Nope, not the Tinder date . . . Not since my top was vandalised, which I don't even think I've told you about. All this baby talk has got in the way. But I have had a teeny tiny bit of wine!' I threw my hands up in the air and bumbled back a little.

'Shit, a little too much, I think. Sober up a bit, eh?'

'Oh, lighten up – just because you can't drink. Don't be a big spoilsport!' I said, jokingly pointing my finger towards her.

Before Ashley could respond, Emily came towards us with her phone, shouting, 'Picture time!'

Ashley assumed her pre-rehearsed bump photograph and beamed towards the phone. I stood beside her, placing both hands on her bump.

'Say cheese!' Emily called out.

'Cheeeeeese!' I screamed.

A couple of people in the crowd turned to stare. Emily looked slightly uncomfortable.

'Zara, *shhhh*,' she whispered, gesturing downward.

Jesus, why is everyone here so fucking serious?

'So when do we find out what you're having?' I asked Ashley.

She huffed. 'When Dave arrives. He's picking his mum up. She missed the train.' She rolled her eyes and checked her watch. 'He shouldn't be long, like half an hour or something.'

I laughed loudly. 'How inconsiderate of her!' I joked.

'There's a guest book over there, and you must write a message to the baby, Zara. Have you seen it?' Emily said.

'No! I have not!' I replied.

'Come, I'll show you.' She linked my arm and helped me feel a bit more steady walking across the clinic floor to a book filled with inspirational messages to Ashley's little bump.

I flicked through the rainbow-coloured book with Emily standing beside me.

'Isn't this cute! The idea is the baby reads them on their sixteenth birthday and knows how loved they've been since, well, before they were even here!' Emily gushed, and I knew instantly it was her idea.

I started to laugh.

'What?' she asked.

'Nothing,' I replied, shrugging my shoulders, attempting to hold in my giggles.

'Zara, what is it?' She laughed back a little, looking confused.

I sighed. 'I just don't know a sixteen-year-old that would care about some guest book. I mean sixteen-year-old me would much rather have a bottle of cider and a twenty deck rather than read a book!'

I could see from the expression on Emily's face that I had insulted her.

'What? Oh, Emily, what?' I asked. 'The book was your idea, wasn't it?'

She nodded.

'I'm sorry! Give me the pen. Here, I'll write!' I said, holding out my hand.

She passed me the pen, and I leaned over the page. My eyes skimmed past some of the earlier entries.

We don't know if you're a boy or a girl yet. But we do know how much you're loved! Auntie Tina x

Who the fuck was Auntie Tina? I giggled to myself. That had to be a client.

We're all here celebrating you, and you don't even know it! Happy sixteenth birthday, little one. Stick in at school and dream big. Laugh, love and live! Karen x

Wow. This was getting ridiculous.

Pen in hand, I flipped to a clean page as my vision blurred a little, and began writing.

You're almost old enough for me to fill you in on all the crazy stories about your mum! Remind me in two years to tell you about Dubai! Love always, Auntie Zara xxx

I smiled as I drew a heart around my entry. Funny and unique, I thought. A small queue had formed behind me, and I moved to the side, chatting with some clients.

'How was Italy, Zara?' one older woman asked.

'Traumatic! But the food was delicious!' I replied. She chuckled back.

'I take it this means you're back to work on Monday?'

I turned to see Raj standing in a smart suit behind me.

'Boss!' I wrapped my arms around him tightly. 'Yes. I'll be here! Pinky promise!'

'How are you?' he asked, pulling me away slightly from the clients.

'Good. Grand. I'll be fine! Have you booked your flight home yet?' I asked, keen to change the subject.

He smiled slightly. 'Yes, it's in a few weeks' time; I need the sun! And hey, I'm glad you're feeling better. You've had a tough few—'

'ZARA!' Ashley's voice cut through the noise of the party. I turned to see her storming over, her vast heels clattering across the floor.

Raj's eyes widened. 'Uh oh.'

'Why would you write that in my book?' she hissed.

'*What?* I thought it would make you laugh.'

Her face was bright red, and I could see how furious she was. 'Well, it won't make fucking Dave laugh, will it?'

Raj looked between us in confusion. I bit my lip, trying to hold an awkward laugh in.

'Seriously?' Ashley put her hand on her hip. 'You don't have anything to say?'

'Wooooow, calm down, Ashley. Zara, go have something to eat. Ash, calm down,' Raj said.

'Yeah, have something to eat and sober the fuck up!' Ashley snapped at me.

Jesus! That was not the reaction I was going for.

I stepped away from my friends, shaking my head, conscious of the atmosphere I was causing. I could see Emily's worried expression from across the room, and I shrugged back innocently, not knowing why Ashley had got so worked up. I headed to the buffet table and lifted a plate. The table was covered in colourful platters, filled with various types of meat, cheese, bread, and sliced fruit. In the centre was a giant white-iced cake with cute teddy bears. *Ohhh yes,* it looked like a Costco cake. My stomach rumbled loudly. I hadn't eaten anything substantial for days and hadn't realised how hungry I was until this moment. Standing here alone, tanning the buffet, perhaps wasn't a bad idea after all. I seemed to be offending people as soon as I opened my mouth.

I lifted some meat off one of the platters, some cheese and a handful of grapes, shoving a few in my mouth to make more room on my plate, I sliced a large mound of cake and began eating alone in the corner.

The music from Ashley's Taylor Swift playlist filled the room as everyone chattered, waiting patiently for Dave to arrive and the party games to get in full swing.

Buzz.

I brought out my phone to a new message from Jason.

Hey, have you got back to Anne about shifts yet? Next month's rota is made up and you're not on it? X

Instead of replying, I sat munching away and soaking up the alcohol, while swiping through potential matches I could maybe hook up with after the party.

Nope, too bald. Nope, too serious. Oh, yes. Yes.

Suddenly there was a mighty screech, and I raised my head.

'Oh my God. My cake!' Ashley screamed.

There was a collective gasp of horror in the room as I glanced around, wondering what I had missed.

'Someone's cut my cake!' She stood in shock with her hands over her face.

Oh, shit.

I glanced down at my large piece of cake and froze.

Stay still, Zara. Maybe no one will notice.

Ashley's eyes scanned the room, and I felt like everything was happening in slow motion until they rested on me.

'Zara?' she hissed. 'My reveal cake?'

What?

I paused as a wave of confusion ran through me. I glanced down at my plate and noticed the baby-pink sponge inside.

Oh, shit.

No, no, no.

'Erm . . . congratulations?' I replied, attempting a smile which was full of icing and pepperoni.

Ashley stormed towards me with Emily at her back.

'You've done this deliberately, haven't you?' she barked.

'Wait, what? I didn't know. I thought it was just a Costco cake, Ash. I thought you popped a balloon at these things? Baby reveal balloon or something?'

I felt attacked. It was a genuine accident. I would never ruin something like this for anyone, never mind my best friend.

'You thought it would be a *balloon*?' she repeated, her eyes fixed on me.

Emily put one hand on Ashley's shoulder. 'Wait, Ashley. A lot of people have balloons to reveal the sex, maybe Zara—'

'No. No. I'm sorry, Emily, I'm not having it. We always make excuses for her!' She shook Emily's hand off and turned to me. 'Maybe if you actually asked me one thing about this party, one thing about my pregnancy, you would know I was having a cake reveal, Zara! You are just so wrapped up in your little world that you don't stop to think about one other person. *It's Tom . . . no, Andy . . . no, Tom . . . no, Andy!* And look, you've lost them both! Get over it!'

The room had fallen deadly silent. I sat there in shock at Ashley's outburst.

'I'm sorry. I genuinely didn't know,' I replied.

'Aww, stop! We've heard it all before. This was the one day that I wanted. One fucking day and you've still managed to mess it up.'

I felt a hand on my back and turned to find Raj standing there.

'Come, I'll give you a lift home, Zara,' he said.

I looked around at the disappointment on everyone's faces, then nodded back to Raj.

'Yeah, good idea,' I replied, setting my plate down.

I tried to look at Ashley, to communicate how sorry I was, but she immediately looked away.

'I'm sorry, Ash,' I said, then walked through the crowd with my head down.

As I opened the door, Dave stepped in with his mum, smiling towards me.

'Congratulations, it's a girl! And I'm sorry. OK?' I walked by him, feeling my eyes flood with guilt and shame.

★

The car ride home with Raj was silent. I pressed my head against the cold glass window, wondering how I'd managed to mess up again. Then, finally, he pulled over just outside my apartment and cleared his throat.

'You going to be all right?' Raj asked.

I nodded as I fought back the tears, not wanting my voice to wobble if I spoke out loud.

'I know you didn't mean that, Zara. But, if you hadn't been so blottered, maybe you would have noticed.' He put his hands in the air in defence.

I attempted to smile, agreeing with him, and undid my seatbelt.

'Raj?' I asked, still hovering in the car.

'Yes.'

'Have you spoke to Tom since we got back?' I looked up to my friend, holding back the tears.

'I haven't, no.' He looked at me sympathetically knowing how much everything hurt.

'OK. Well, thanks for the lift. And I'm sorry about all of that.'

'I know you are. Hey, take it easy,' he replied, winking as I climbed down from his car.

I waved him off, headed upstairs, and climbed straight back into my crumby bed.

Chapter Twenty-Eight

The following day, barely awake, I held my head tightly and grumbled. *Why is a wine hangover worse than a regular hangover?* I pulled the covers above my achy head as I had a sudden flashback of munching Ashley's cake and ruining her party.

Buzz. Buzz.

I lifted my arm and began searching the bed for my phone as it rang. My eyes squinted at the screen.

Emily.

Great, here goes the first lecture of the day.

'Yeah, hello?'

'Jesus, Zara. I've been trying to get you all night. Did you go out?' she asked.

I turned to the small clock on my bedside – 8 a.m.

'It's eight in the morning. I'm in bed! I was escorted straight home after being thrown out of my clinic, remember?'

The line went silent for a second.

'Have you checked your messages?' she asked.

Suddenly I felt a stabbing pain of panic run through me. 'No, why? What's up?'

Emily was quiet.

'Emily, what's wrong?' I repeated.

She cleared her throat. 'Ashley fell at the party not long after you left. Went right over on her ankle and landed on her bump. Raj and Dave rushed her to the hospital.'

'What? How? Is she OK? Is the baby OK?' I sat up in bed. I felt sick.

'Yes. They are both fine, just shaken up. But she got kept in for observation overnight. She's getting another ultrasound this morning and if everything's still looking good she'll be discharged soon.'

I couldn't believe I wasn't there for her. She must have been terrified.

'It was so scary, though, Zara. Everyone was crying. Literally, the worst gender reveal in the world!' Emily exclaimed.

'Yeah, partly my fault,' I added.

'Well . . . I thought you should know to maybe . . . contact her? To put things right, or something?' she said.

'Thanks for phoning, Em. I'll call later, OK?'

'OK. Bye, Zara.'

I let go of my phone and held my head in my hands for a second.

Poor Ashley. Poor Dave.

I felt my hands shake with panic and dehydration.

I had to make it right with Ashley. *How the fuck did she manage to fall?* I asked myself. Then I realised exactly what I could do.

I jumped up, washed my face, downed a pint of tap water, brushed my teeth, got changed, and headed to the city centre. I knew exactly how to make it up to my best friend.

An hour later, after a brief trip to House of Fraser, I sat outside Ashley and Dave's flat, sipping on a hot chocolate from Costa. The street was fairly quiet for a Saturday morning. A few joggers passed by, and a couple of mums were on the way to the park with their kids. It made me smile, knowing that it would be Ashley and me in a few months, and I realised how much this baby girl was about to change all of our lives.

It was just past 10 a.m. I had texted Dave when I was leaving the shops so I knew they would be arriving back anytime. But I felt sick with nerves. *What if she doesn't want to speak to me?* I replayed my drunken antics over and over in my head. While I waited, I texted Raj, Lisa and Olivia an apology message for my behaviour. Hopefully they would all forgive me too.

Eventually, Dave's car drew up. Through the window, I saw Ashley's make-up-free, pale, tired-looking face. I walked down the steps to the kerb.

She opened the door slowly, and I felt my insides squeeze, not knowing if she'd tell me to bolt or give me the lecture of a century.

'Hey,' I said quietly.

I felt her arms wrap around my neck as she sobbed on my shoulder.

'I was so scared, Zara. I thought I'd lost her,' she whimpered.

I held my best friend tightly in the street for what felt like forever. I didn't ever want to let her go.

'It's OK. I know. I know. You're both going to be fine, Ashley,' I whispered.

'Come on, you two, let's get the kettle on,' Dave said gently.

I walked with Ashley into their living room. Lots of gifts and balloons surrounded the place from the party. Ashley lowered herself onto the sofa, and I sat beside her.

'Ash, I just want to say I'm so sorry about yesterday,' I blurted.

She puffed like it was the last thing on her mind. 'It's OK. I shouldn't have screamed like that in front of everyone,' she replied.

I shook my head. 'No, you absolutely should have. I deserved that. But I genuinely didn't know the cake was—'

'Zara, I know you didn't.' Through the sadness pulling at her face, she managed a smirk.

'You do?'

'Of course I do. It was such a Zara thing to do anyway. I don't know why I was so surprised,' she said.

I breathed a sigh of relief and smiled. 'So what did the doctors say?' I asked.

She smiled, stroking her bump. 'They said everything's OK. I've got to look for any bleeding or pain in the next few days, but the scans and things are fine.'

'Thank fuck!'

Ashley agreed as Dave came in and handed her a mug of tea.

'I've got a present for you – well, for you both!' I said. Ashley sat up, looking surprised.

'For us both?' Dave said, looking enthusiastic.

'Aye, the baby, Dave, don't get your hopes up!' I laughed.

I passed over the large bag from Fraser's. Ashley lifted out two shoeboxes, one large and one small. She raised an eyebrow curiously and began to pull on the lid of one box.

'So, I know you only have skyscraper heels, Ash. But . . . I thought . . . just until the baby's here, you could try these?'

She lifted out a pair of Vivienne Westwood pumps. They were black and pointed at the toe with the signature crown at the front. Her face broke into a smile as she opened the second box – a tiny pair of matching baby pumps.

'Aww, Zara, I love them!' she gushed. 'They must have cost you a fortune!' She held up both pairs to Dave and laughed loudly at the cuteness.

'Trust me. I owe you. I've been a mess lately.'

Ashley shrugged. 'You're my mess, babe,' she said, winking briefly at me and then returning to the shoes.

'No, I mean it. I know I haven't been there for you with everything that's gone on in Italy, but you're the most important person in my life, and I'm so sorry,' I continued, wanting to get everything off my chest.

Ashley put down the shoes and reached for my hand. 'Zara, I've got you. We've got you. You have been scatty, but you will find your way. You always do.' She squeezed my hand tightly, reassuringly, and I nodded back.

'I feel so out of the loop, like I'm missing this. I'm missing all of your pregnancy and I felt pushed out by the other girls,' I admitted.

Ashley's face twisted. 'I just didn't want to bother you. I feel like all I ever talk about now is this baby!'

'And so you should! I promise I'm here now and I want to know everything! OK?'

Ashley pursed her lips. 'Deal!' Then she reached over and hugged me again.

'Right, you two must be shattered,' I said, pulling back. 'I should go and let you sleep. If you need anything at all, just phone me, please!'

Ashley nodded. 'All I need is to know we're OK. I'll see you Monday?' She stood up to walk me out.

'Yes, Monday! You better be in your new pumps, hen!' I warned. 'No more slips or trips when my wee niece is in there.'

'Aye, for sure! I'm not doing that again!'

I walked to the front door and hugged my best friend once more.

'Love you, Ash.'

'Love you more.'

I headed back to my apartment to lie in bed with a grateful smile on my face. I had zero plans but to nurse my headache with paracetamol and orange Lucozade, and when the Chinese opened at four I'd order a chicken curry, fried rice and salt and chilli chips. *Bliss.*

Around two, my TikTok scroll was interrupted by the sound of the buzzer. My body froze as I wondered who it could be. My mind buzzed back over the last few days wondering if I had insulted anyone else I had to make amends with.

I walked to the door as it buzzed loudly again.

'Hello?' I said apprehensively.

'It's Mum, Zara.'

Shit, the flat was still boxed up, with piles upon piles of clothes and underwear lying around the floor. My kitchen worktop consisted of empty wine bottles and takeaway boxes. *Shit. Shit. Shit.*

I pushed the button to let her in and sat on the couch, defeated. I knew the thirty seconds it took her to walk up the steps wouldn't be near enough time to hide or disguise anything about my current living situation.

I heard the noise of her designer heels approaching and felt nervous as she walked through the door.

'Hello?' she called out, scanning the room.

'Hey, I'm down here.' I gave a brief wave from the sofa.

I could see how much she was holding back a revolted look on her face as she approached me and kissed my forehead.

'Well?' she asked, clearing her throat.

'Well?' I repeated.

'What is going on, Zara? You've had Emily and I worried sick.'

I let out a large puff. 'I've apologised to Ashley, and we're fine now. I know I fucked up.'

'Language.' She rolled her eyes, then grinned sympathetically. 'I'm not even talking about yesterday, Zara. That was just the cherry on top of the cake.'

'OK, well, what do you mean?'

'Italy? Andy? Day drinking? Where do I start? Tell me what the hell is going on, please?'

I sighed. 'Basically, I've fucked up my entire life, Mum. I know it already, so you don't have to tell me how much of a disappointment I am, OK?' I felt empty. I didn't have the energy to try to defend myself anymore.

'And how have you managed that then?' she asked, briefly wiping the Dorito crumbs from the sofa and then taking a seat.

'Trust me, you don't want to know.' I slumped back, hoping the sofa would swallow me whole so I could avoid this conversation with my mother.

'Because you left Andy? Or ran away to Italy?'

I smiled at her frankness. 'Both.'

'So your life is over because you're single?' She tutted at me.

'Well, I also declared my love for Tom, who is getting married to a fucking goddess.' I shrugged once more.

My mother sighed, still staring at me. 'And you think your life is over because of men? Have I not taught you better than that?' There was a brief silence in the room. When I didn't say anything else, she continued, 'Do you have a roof over your head? Money in the bank? A job? Family and friends?'

I nodded back.

273

'Well, you haven't fucked up your life quite yet. In fact, you have a long way to go.' She smiled at me warmly, and I felt a little surprised. My mum had always been tough on my sister and me to do well, and when I didn't live up to her expectations, she was never shy in telling me. 'You have, however,' she cleared her throat, 'fucked up my pension. Look at the state of this flat!'

I laughed a little. 'I know. Andy dropped off the boxes from his place. I don't feel like sorting it just now.'

'There will never be a time you feel like sorting it, Zara. But, when you do, you will slowly begin to get back on track.'

I remained silent.

'Have you spoken to Andrew?' she asked.

I immediately felt my eyes fill and shook my head, disguising the tears.

'Do you want to resolve things with him?'

'I don't know. I feel so bad for what I did.' I placed my head in my hands, thinking of how much easier life was with him.

'If you don't know, then the answer is *no*. But, Jesus, I have made mistakes when it comes to men, Zara. We all have. Look at your father, for example.'

I looked up from my hands, knowing she could never resist a dig at my dad.

'Right, stand up. Come on!' She shot up and gestured for me to do the same. 'Let's make this house a home again. Come on.'

'Mum, I don't feel up to this right now,' I mumbled.

'I know. But unfortunately, I'm your mother, and I am pulling rank.' She slipped off her Gucci shoes and headed over to the pile of boxes. 'I'll sort in here. You focus on the bedroom.'

Thank fuck, I thought, as I had no idea where my stack of lube was hiding in amongst the rubble.

Reluctantly, I got up and began pushing through boxes of clothes that needed to be put away to get to my bedroom.

The afternoon of sorting and tidying flew by as I hung and folded my clothes and arranged my bedroom. I felt relieved and comforted having someone to talk to and that I wasn't doing this alone. My mum called out from the next room as we chatted about Ashley and the baby, Emily and the kids, and she even filled me in on some of the neighbours' gossip around her street. She hoovered and washed while I sorted and organised.

My room was beginning to take shape as the wardrobes filled once more. Finally, I was down to the last box, the biggest and heaviest of them. My mum assisted me while we pushed it through to my room, and I began unpacking again.

My face lit up as I opened it. It was all my nursing diaries and assignments from university.

'I remember how stressed you were writing these!' My mum lifted a stack of papers I had written during my first year at university titled 'How to Care for the Palliative Patient'.

I smiled back. 'I know. It seems like a long time ago now.'

I was piling up the text books in order before moving them onto a shelf.

'Look at you now, running your own clinic!' She seemed impressed.

'You know I was going to go back to the wards. I really wanted to. Just before Italy,' I admitted, wiping the dust from my anatomy book.

'Oh?' My mum seemed surprised.

'Yeah, there was a bunch of jobs that came up. surgical advanced nursing practitioner post, and it sounded amazing. Like proper hands-on acute nursing.' I beamed at the thought.

'Well, why didn't you?' she asked, sitting on my fresh bedding.

'Andy thought it was a bad idea because I'd have to work less at the clinic, and financially there wouldn't be better money in it.' I shrugged.

'And what did you think?' she asked, raising an eyebrow.

'*Me?* Well . . . I still would have loved the job. But I didn't want to rock the boat with him. We were moving in, so, financially, I had to consider him.'

My mum was silent for a few seconds. 'Hmmm,' was all she said.

I turned back to face her. 'So you think I should have gone for it?'

My mother shrugged. 'If it made you happy and that's what you wanted then, yes.'

I paused. A brief silence filled the space between us again.

'I know I'm hard on you at times, Zara. But it's only because I want you to be happy above all. Yes, I want you to have a great career, a husband, and your own bloody home, but it's because I worked so goddamn hard all on my own. I built my career as a single woman when I had you and your sister to care for. So I don't want you to do it the hard way as I did.'

'I know you did, Mum.' I felt myself thinking back to the long hours my mum spent nursing when I was a child. How she would work constant nightshifts to make sure she never missed a sports day or parents' evening, all while I watched her fire up the ranks and become a lead nurse in Glasgow. 'The closing date has probably passed. And I was supposed to have taken on extra shifts to get an interview because I've been out the wards for so long now.'

'Why don't you check?'

'Check?'

'Why don't you punch into that phone of yours, you know, that thing that's never out of your hand, and find out when the closing date is? You may still have time. Or there may be something similar that catches your eye.'

'But I haven't done a hospital shift in almost a year!' I laughed, shaking my head.

'But you *have* worked with lead surgeons and run your own clinic. Assessed and practised treatments. Promoted health and well-being and provided dignity and respect. You follow the nurses code of conduct every day in that clinic. You may work as an aesthetics nurse, Zara, but you are still a nurse.'

She was right. I know I hadn't done any shifts in the hospital but I work as a nurse every day. I suppose I hadn't seen my clinic work as a form of nursing until now. I smiled at my mum, then lifted my phone and searched for the job application. I scrolled down to the bottom of the advertisement.

'It's still on!' I gasped excitedly, and continued to read. 'Closing date . . . *oh* . . . what date is it? Mum? What date is it today?'

'The twelfth.'

'Oh, no. It closes tonight at midnight.' I glanced up from my phone and looked at my mum.

She winked. 'Well, we better hurry up and finish this unpacking. Then we have an interview to get you, eh?'

Chapter Twenty-Nine

I woke the following morning feeling different to how I had for a while. I felt re-energised and well-rested and happily alone. I raised the sheets to my face and inhaled the fresh smell of *Lenor*. *Ahhhh*. *My* room was neatly organised, my closet bursting with clothes. No boxes, no chaos. It finally felt like home again. A smile spread across my cheeks as I sat up, admiring the unobstructed, clean floor with a weird sense of relief. I had been living in squalor in a crusty-underwear-and-pakora-sauce-smelling apartment. I hadn't realised the full nastiness at the time, but now it was gone I admired the freshness.

I looked forward to my day at the clinic, seeing Ashley, Raj and the girls, catching up with my patients and socialising again. Finally, I was feeling more like myself.

I checked my phone and saw it was 07.30 – just enough time to get ready and enjoy a coffee. There was one new message from my mother:

Remember to let me know if you hear anything from HR. Mum x

I felt a crunch of nerves recalling the application I'd submitted last night for the surgical advanced nursing practitioner post. My mum had stayed till late in the evening assisting me in writing the best application I had ever done. Even if I was utterly under-skilled for the position, I at least knew I couldn't have presented myself better. She'd helped me incorporate the essential buzzwords to land an interview and explained how I had a lot of transferable skills to offer from working at the clinic. We'd spent the night laughing as we reminisced about both our nursing days and spoke about how much we missed the wards.

I made my way to the kitchen and ran my hand over the shiny worktop that no longer consisted of dirty dishes or takeaway trays. I felt optimistic for the first time in months. There was a tiny bubble of hope that I could carry on again. Not for Andy, not for Tom, but for me. I boiled the kettle and replied to my mum.

I will do. Thanks for last night. I feel so much better today. Love you Mum x

The clinic was bustling with its usual morning rush. Ashley was creating social media reels of her baby reveal, pretending it wasn't a fuck-up and was the best day ever. Lisa and Olivia were working through the back, while Raj and I had back-to-back clients all morning. When the knock on my door came, I had just finished my second client of the day.

'Your ten o'clock is here,' Ashley called out. 'Will I send him in?'

I was wiping down the trolley and replied, 'Yeah, just send him through, please.'

A few seconds later, my clinic door opened, and Jason entered with his hands on his hips.

'So I literally have to make an appointment to speak to you now!' He tutted with a glint of humour in his eyes.

'Jason!' I gasped, happy to see my friend. 'You're my ten o'clock?'

'I am indeed. I need some Botox and a catch-up, and since you don't return any messages, I combined the two!' He laughed.

I hugged him tightly. 'I'm so sorry, I've been a shit pal,' I admitted. 'I'm so happy you're here, though!'

Jason nodded. 'Me too. I have frown lines. Please, take them away!' He dramatically held one hand off his forehead and sat on the bed.

'So, just Botox today?' I asked, gently marking his forehead with my pen.

He nodded back, allowing me to concentrate.

'So, what have you been up to? How was Italy?' he asked.

I immediately puffed air out of my mouth. 'A nightmare! A lot happened on that trip that I'm trying to forget,' I replied while washing my hands.

'Ouch. And you and Andy?' he probed.

I approached Jason with my syringe and shrugged. 'We're over.'

'Like over-over for good or taking-a-break kind of over?'

I began gently injecting his forehead. 'Honestly . . .' I paused, knowing it was the first time I'd say it out loud. I thought about the last few days and how my life was finally getting pieced back together again and smiled. 'Over-over. When I came back from Italy I was a bit of a mess, I missed him and his stupid dog so much, but, now, I think I'm over it. I feel a lot better being single.'

'Oh, thank the Lord!' Jason blurted.

'Jason!' I said. I had the feeling he'd been holding back so many opinions until now.

'I'm sorry, Zara. But the way he acted when you told him you were interested in that job just put me right off him. I mean, he made you not go for that. And that was bad energy right there. Pure controlling behaviour. Plus your skin has never looked so good getting away from that dog. You were so blotchy and eww.' He shivered as he recalled my allergy.

I giggled at his insult knowing it came from a good place really. Then I thought back to that period of feeling nervous even mentioning the job to Andy and how against the career change he seemed to be despite what I wanted.

'And if it's any consolation, I would have fucked off to Italy too!' he added.

I laughed and smirked, holding gauze against Jason's slightly bloody forehead. 'Well, if it's any consolation to *you*, I applied for one of the positions last night before the deadline.'

Jason shrieked. 'You didn't!'

'I did! I mean, not that I think I'll get accepted, but there's no harm in trying, is there?'

My friend's warm eyes looked up into mine, and he grinned. 'I'm proud of you, Zara! This is so exciting, you know! And hey, if they cunts at the hospital know their arse from their elbow, they'll give you an interview! You were my student, after all.'

I smiled at his kindness and laughed. 'Thank you! Just need to do around your eyes now.'

'Keep going, darling, I feel better already!'

'So should we study together? I was hoping to ask Anne for a reference. I need two and Raj can give me one obviously but I was hoping Anne could too.'

'Email her! And if not, I'll give you one. You were my best student after all.'

I squeezed my friends shoulder, 'Thanks, Jason.'

For the rest of his appointment, Jason and I caught up on his latest love dramas and once I'd completed his treatment I walked him back out to the desk. I hugged him tightly before navigating him towards Ashley, who was holding the card reader in her hand.

'Ash, this one is on me. I owe you, Jason. I'll call you tonight, OK?' I said.

'No, Zara, it's too much!' he blubbered but I insisted on paying. 'Promise me you won't go all weird and quiet again!' he said, returning his card to his wallet.

'I promise!' I replied, and turned back towards my room.

'Oh, and Zara?'

I turned back around to face him.

'We should hear something by the end of the day about interviews. I checked with HR when I submitted mine. I want updates!'

'Today?' I repeated, and he nodded back excitedly. 'I'll let you know.' I glanced at Ashley, who scrunched her nose up, looking utterly confused, and returned to my room.

I continued injecting clients that morning and eventually headed to Reception for lunch, where the girls sat around the desk.

'Are you organised for food? We are starving!' Ashley moaned impatiently.

'Yes! I have a piece and noodles in with me,' I replied smugly.

Ashley glanced at the other girls and laughed.

'What?'

'Nothing, just you're never normally organised enough to pack a lunch,' Olivia said, smiling and seeming impressed.

'Well, this is a new Zara, and I had a great sleep and made lunch. So what's up with that?' I laughed.

Ashley swung around in her chair as her long blonde hair swooped slowly at her waist. 'Nothing is up with it, babe. But we all decided to have a Greggs today and thought you'd be up for it. But since you are this organised, reformed person, we'll head without you then.' She grinned her biggest smile with her shiny veneers.

'I'll get my coat! The yum yums are calling!' I yelled.

We all laughed, popped on our jackets, and steered across George Square towards the bakery. The wind blew wildly in our faces, making my eyes water, although the ground was thankfully dry. I was clutching Ashley's bump tightly. 'You know this baby is going to be the most Instagrammable baby ever?' I said excitedly.

'Damn right! She's going to have her own Insta from day dot. Of course, closely monitored by her mum,' Ashley replied, giggling.

'Eh . . . and her auntie!' I laughed back. 'I'm so excited, Ash!' We were almost halfway across the square when Lisa stopped abruptly and interrupted us with a serious look on her face.

'Zara.' She gulped, grasping both my arms.

'Yeah?' I replied, unable to keep an uneasy smile from my face.

'Andy's there. Like right there. Outside Botox Boxx.'

I felt my stomach fall on the spot as my head couldn't help but slowly turn in that direction.

And there he was.

Andy was standing across the square, holding his phone in one hand, leaning on his car with the other while he spoke casually, oblivious to me.

I turned back to the girls feeling as if I had just seen a ghost.

'Come on, babe. He hasn't seen you.' Ashley tugged on my arm.

'Yeah, let's go. It's always hard seeing them for the first time, Zara,' Olivia said.

I walked a few steps with my friends and then paused.

Andy had been such a big part of my life for so long. I couldn't ignore him in the street. I had to say something, even if it was difficult.

'I need to go and speak to him, girls. I have to,' I said.

My three friends shared worried glances between them.

'You two head to Greggs. We will catch you up,' Ashley said, linking my arm for support.

I smiled at her. 'No, Ash. I need to do this alone. I need to sort this whole mess out.'

She hesitated slightly, hovering between the girls and me, but eventually agreed.

'I'll get your lunch. Meet you back at the clinic, OK?'

'OK,' I replied, feeling a swarm of nerves take over my body as my feet swivelled direction and headed towards Botox Boxx.

As I approached, my eyes continued to water, and I wasn't sure if it was because of the crisp weather or my nerves. His position remained the same. His back was to me, one hand resting on his car and the other holding his mobile at his ear. I could feel my heart quicken with anticipation. *What if he didn't want to speak to me? What if he started giving me abuse? What if he . . .*

'Zara?' He had turned around and I watched the smile slowly plunge from his face.

'I'll call you back, mate,' he said, pressing a button on his phone.

'Hi,' I said as I got closer.

'Hey,' he replied, lowering his head.

'How, *eh,* how have you been?' I asked.

I could feel my heart beating loudly in my chest. I knew him so well, but the conversation felt cold and forced.

'Aye, I'm doing good,' he said.

'OK. Good. I'm glad.' I nodded back, still smiling as I shivered in the nippy weather.

'I better get to work. Busy day,' he said.

I felt my brows raise at his dismissiveness.

'*Erm* . . . OK. Yeah, sure. Well, it was nice to see you,' I said, turning back towards Greggs. My breathing got shallower. I didn't want it to end like this. I wanted to clear the air, to apologise for my part. But I hated confrontation. *Maybe he wasn't ready to listen?* I thought.

I took a few more steps and turned back to Andy, who was shaking his head and staring back at his phone.

'Wait. Andy.' I cleared my throat and walked back towards him. 'I want to say sorry. I'm so, so sorry for hurting you. I'm sorry I left. I'm sorry I didn't call you, and I'm sorry I humiliated you in front of all of our friends.'

There was silence. I watched him rub his head in frustration, not knowing how to respond. He kept his eyes down and sighed.

'OK, well . . . that's all I wanted to say.' I tried to look into his eyes but they were so cut off from me. I waited on a reply, but the silence continued. I didn't know if he was broken or angry or if he didn't care at all.

When it was clear he wasn't going to say anything, I turned to walk away.

There was a grab at my wrist.

'Why?' Andy's deep voice echoed through my body, vibrating to my toes.

I turned to face him. He was still holding my arm gently.

'Why?' I repeated.

'Why ruin all of it, Zara? We were happy.' He let go of my arm then.

'I don't know. I'm sorry.' I felt my eyes fill and fought back the tears, knowing how much I had hurt him.

'We were moving in together, talking about starting a family . . .' he continued.

'No, you were, Andy,' I said quietly. 'You wanted all of that, and I loved you so I went along with it. I didn't want to have a family, not right now, maybe not ever. I wanted to nurse again, and you dismissed even the idea. I wanted to slow down but I felt pressured about my age and our relationship. But I loved you so much that I was doing everything to please you.'

He shook his head, not taking any criticism. 'If you wanted to please me, you wouldn't have fucked off to Italy and went with someone else.' I could see his face turn redder with anger.

'I know, and that's what I'm apologising for.' I could feel my bottom lip tremble.

'If you weren't ready for all of that stuff, moving in, having a family, Zara, you could have said to me?'

'I tried to tell you. I honestly tried. But, I knew that's what you wanted so I ended up shutting up and going along with it all.' I shrugged, overwhelming guilt flooding through me.

'If we were on different timelines you could have told me.' Andy sounded frustrated with me.

'I . . . I . . . did tell you, Andy, but at the same time I didn't want to lose you. I didn't want to disappoint

288

you. You constantly reminded me of what people my age should want. But I'm not ready for a family, Andy. I struggle to look after myself. But anytime I said that you would get angry. You'd judge me or pressure me, and I was scared you wouldn't want me.'

Andy puffed a slight laugh. 'And look what happened.' He held his hands up.

'I know. I should have said more. I should have sat you down and spoke about it properly.'

'So, you're on your own now?' he asked.

'Yeah.'

'And we both lose?' He laughed under his breath.

I came closer to him. 'No. We both win, Andy. I'm not your girl, and you deserve to find her.' I felt a tear roll down my face realising it was the first time I had been honest with myself.

'And what do you deserve?' he asked.

I took a step back and looked at the grey sky. *What did I deserve?* As I asked myself the question, I felt the world slow down around me, and I finally broke into a smile. 'I deserve another shot at life how I want it. I deserve to try again. To nurse in the wards if I want.' I shrugged. 'But mostly I need to try to forgive myself for causing this whole shit show in the first place.'

He took a deep breath in and attempted to match my smile. 'I love you, Zara. Maybe I always will.'

'I know, and that's what makes it so hard.' I paused, finally making eye contact with him and seeing a glimmer of the person I cared about so much.

'Zara?' he said.

'Yeah.'

'Was there someone else? Is that why you left?'

I closed my eyes, knowing how much the answer would hurt him. Then opened them back up again and nodded.

'Yeah.'

'And did you get him?'

I shook my head holding back the tears. 'He didn't want me.' I shrugged.

'Well, I'm sorry. I know how shit that feels.'

I attempted to hold my smile, trying to hold back tears.

'Yep, it is pretty shit, eh?' I stepped back again, feeling a pressure I hadn't known I was carrying lift off my heart. 'I'm so sorry, Andy.'

'I forgive you,' he said quietly. 'You're a decent person. Take care of yourself, OK?'

I scrunched my face to him, waved a brief goodbye, and walked away.

As I headed back towards the clinic I felt like I had been absolved from my deepest, darkest sins. My heart was racing, grateful and sad all at the same time. He deserved to know the truth and I felt awful about the hurt that I'd caused him, but at the same I felt released from the guilt I was carrying around with me.

My phone beeped, and I glanced down.

Check your email! I got an interview! Jason X

Oh no, oh no, this was it! My heart started pounding and my hands shook as I refreshed my inbox.

One new email from NHS Glasgow and Clyde Recruitment.

My eyes skimmed down the page.

Oh shit!

I galloped back into the clinic just as Ashley and the girls were taking off their coats in the staff room. Their faces were glum, and I could tell they were anticipating another Zara Smith meltdown. I called Raj into the room, and they all looked nervously in my direction.

'Zara, what's going on?' Ashley asked, her eyes wide with worry.

I cleared my throat. 'Last night, I applied for the surgical ANP job in the hospital,' I said, pacing the floor. 'Now, before you all say something, I know I'm underqualified and haven't got much acute experience lately, but I want it. I really want it. I've been thinking about it for a long time. And if I got it, I'd be able to work in both the hospital and here, like you did, Raj.' I took a deep breath before continuing. 'I just got an email calling me for the interview! I have an interview next Monday. I know I'm an excellent nurse, guys. I know I am. I deserve this!' I called out, shutting my eyes, finally rid of all my secrets. I knew Ashley wouldn't want me to work less at the clinic and would try to persuade me to stay. I was hoping for support but knew I'd be reined in. After a few moments, I opened my eyes and watched Raj gaze towards Ashley and smirk.

'Damn right, you deserve it!' he replied, clapping his hands together happily.

'Well . . .' Ashley said. 'What can we do to help?'

And just like that, I had all the people I needed in my corner. My mind was clear from men and drama, and I was focused. They believed in me, and, for the first time in a long time, I finally did too.

Chapter Thirty

Dear Miss Smith,

Thank you for your recent application for the post of Advanced Surgical Nurse Practitioner.

We are very pleased to invite you to the next stage of the process and welcome you for an interview on Monday, the 20th of September at 11 a.m. at the Glasgow Royal Infirmary Hospital.

Please see attached documents you will need to provide on the day of the interview.

On the date, we will ask you to take a seat in the foyer at level 3 management offices until called upon. As part of the interview, you will be given a scenario and asked how you would assess the patient discussed quickly to provide the correct diagnosis and appropriate treatment plan. We will then follow this with standard interview questions.

We look forward to meeting you.

Yours sincerely,

NHS Glasgow and Clyde Recruitment Team

A few days had passed since receiving my interview date, and I had memorised the email inside out, yet, at every given chance, I found myself reading it again just in case I was missing something. A clue or hint as to what I'd be asked on the day.

I sat on the sofa with Raj to revise after a busy evening at the clinic. Ashley had headed home to put her feet up, now feeling the exhaustion of pregnancy.

'You've got this, Zara!' he assured me, digging into his salad.

'Can you give me a scenario again?' I asked.

Raj huffed, having already spent almost two hours with me.

'Raj!' I pleaded.

'OK, OK. So, the patient arrives in the hospital vomiting. He has been struggling to walk for the last couple of days. He is in severe pain. What do you do?' he asked, scooping up his lettuce.

'I do his routine observations, take some blood, and do a full top-to-toe, A-to-E assessment,' I said confidently.

'OK, well, his blood pressure is low. He's tachycardic, and his temperature is thirty-eight point six. But his pain is very severe when you press on his right lower abdomen.'

I rolled my eyes. 'Come on!' Knowing already that it was a textbook case of appendicitis.

'Keep going!' He giggled.

'He's septic. So I'd put in a cannula, start him on IV fluids and a broad spectrum antibiotic, give him analgesia, an anti-emetic, start a fluid balance and book him in for a scan.'

'CT shows he has a ruptured appendix,' Raj continued.

'I'd page surgeons and get him prepped for surgery. Then, insert a catheter and continue with the antibiotics, regular observations, and fluids.'

'Perfect!' He began to get up.

'That was too easy!' I huffed. 'They won't ask me an easy one!'

Raj groaned and dived back onto the sofa in frustration. 'It's only easy because you know what to do. You got every scenario correct in the past two days, Zara.'

I sighed. 'My brain feels like it's going to explode,' I admitted.

'So does mine from listening to you!' Raj's phone rang, and he stood up to answer. 'No, no, the clinic's shut up for the day. It's just past six here. I'm helping Zara prep for an interview. But, yes, yes . . . uh huh . . . yes . . .'

While he was on the phone, I scrolled through my emails hoping Anne had replied to my request for interview reference, but there was no reply. I huffed slightly before texting Jason.

Hey, Anne still hasn't replied about reference. Can you send one for me ☹ *xx*

I was re-reading my book on minor surgical procedures while Raj continued his call.

Course. Has Raj helped you study tonight? I feel pretty confident x

I smiled back at my phone.

Lucky you! Yes but I feel overwhelmed! I'll call you when I'm home! And thank you so much for reference! You are the best! xxx

Finally, Raj returned to the sofa.

'OK, talk me through how I put in a central line again?' I smiled at my friend, who laughed and sighed.

'You get training for that! They don't expect you to put in a central line on your first day. It's not *Grey's Anatomy*, Zara!'

'God, I wish it was. Maybe I'd find my own McDreamy.' I smiled a sarcastically wide grin at my friend, who squeezed my cheeks.

'Well, that was your old McSteamy on the phone,' he said.

'What?' I felt my blood pressure drop, followed by my own spell of arrhythmias.

Raj shrugged as if he wasn't aware he had just shat all over me.

'What? It was Tom,' he said casually.

'*And?*' I pressed, feeling unbalanced.

'He asked how everyone was doing. He thinks he'll be home soon. I was telling him I head back to Dubai next week—'

'He *thinks?*' I repeated. 'Where is he? Where has he been?'

'Europe . . . travelling. He's been at a retreat, meditating and things. That's honestly all he's said.' Raj shrugged.

'Meditating? Tom?' I laughed. 'I guess Quinn Foxx has got her hippy claws into him, eh . . . he'll be vegan by next week!' I continued, full of pettiness.

'Zara!' Raj laughed loudly.

'So, does he call often? I can't believe you haven't mentioned this to me?' I said, having tried hard to box Tom on a shelf since Italy.

'He's called a couple of times. Short calls. Doesn't talk much, he just enquires how we all are, there is nothing to tell, honestly.'

'OK . . . OK . . .' I stood up, my books falling to the floor. 'Did he ask how anyone was in particular? Or just the group as a whole?' I probed, trying to be as subtle as Bigfoot's dick.

'In general. Zara! Jeez. Sit back down! Focus, we're studying!'

'No, we *were* studying. Now, it's all Tom Adams in my brain again. Did he say where he was? Like a country? Because Quinn hasn't updated her social media since the engagement party. *Oh,* did he happen to mention anything about the picture from the party? And what did he say when you told him about my interview? Wait, is he coming home for good? RAJ!' I had many questions, but Raj was as useless as a ham sandwich at a bar mitzvah. This cunt really needed to learn how to dig for information.

'He said he was still in Europe, and he'll be home soon. He didn't say how long for. I told him about your interview but again, he didn't say much,' Raj said, raising his hands in the air. 'I'm sorry, Zara. That was all. It was a quick conversation. I can't even remember most of it already.'

I flumped back on the sofa and groaned loudly in anguish. 'You can't *remember*? You are a world-class surgeon, and you can't remember a conversation that happened literally thirty seconds ago?'

'I'm exhausted, Zara. I'm sorry.'

I nodded in defeat and looked at the ceiling.

A brief silence filled the room and then Raj sat back up.

'OK, so . . . a patient comes through A and E. Massive leg injury, all gooey and lacerated from falling off a bike and getting it caught in some fencing. Also complaining of chest pain. What do you do?' Raj said.

I lifted my head and smiled towards my friend. 'You are getting better at these!' I laughed.

'I'm trying, I'm bloody trying!'

'You know, I'm glad he might be coming back. Even if it will be with Quinn Foxx. It's just not the same without him, you know?'

Raj smiled and rubbed my arm. 'I know. I know.'

We continued to revise for the rest of the night, and every night that followed leading up to my interview. My apartment was full of Post-it notes on assessing the unwell patient and how to spot triggers for the deteriorating patient, and although my mind occasionally returned to Tom, my friends quickly snapped me back to reality and what was necessary. Jason made up flashcards and emailed them over, and we spent most evenings on FaceTime quizzing one another. Ashley, Lisa and Olivia tested me throughout my working days, while Mum and Emily helped me revise the interview questions like *What attributes would you bring to this role?* and *Where do you see yourself in five years?* My mum's sternness reminded me of Anne, and she added a bit of pressure to the role, which was utterly terrifying, not to mention brutal when it came to feedback.

But I felt prepared. I felt supported. Despite not having the best start when applying for this job, I was making up for it now more than anything.

Chapter Thirty-One

It was the morning of the interview and my eyes opened with an optimistic glint; today was the day I could get my dream job! I took out my phone and messaged Jason, knowing he was up first.

Good luck! You can do this! Xxx

I was about to smile with confidence feeling prepared to tackle the day when I gasped all of a sudden as severe cramps ripped through my abdomen. *Oh God, no!* In a moment I was drenched in sweat. What was happening to me? *It will just be nerves, Zara. It's just nerves, calm doon!* I told myself as another cramping spell came over me. I sat up in bed and immediately doubled back over in discomfort. *No, this can't be happening, not today.* I glanced at the clock. It was 7 a.m.

OK, fine. I have a few hours to get it together.

I suddenly hit a brief spell of dizziness. *No, no, no.*

I shuffled out of bed, yanking at my pyjama shorts and bolted to the bathroom, just making it in time for the anal volcano exploding all over the toilet.

'Jesus Christ!' I called out, but the relief was momentary as the crampy wave came over me again. *Please, not again!*

But there it was, another episode of the squirts.

My stomach ached and my arse stung from overuse. I was still sweating profusely, and sank to the cold bathroom floor. As soon as the coast was clear I texted Ashley.

Ash, I'm dying! I don't think I can do this. I am shitting through the eye of a needle here, LITERALLY! SOS x.

The morning persisted like this. Anytime I attempted to get ready, I was running back to the bathroom and stripping down again. *What if this was a sign? What if this was the universe telling me the interview was a bad idea?* I lifted my phone not knowing what to do. Should I try to reschedule? I couldn't risk a bad bout of diarrhoea at my interview, but, hey, they were all nurses. Surely they would understand. My mind was in turmoil as my bum hole burned.

OMG, you're joking!!! We are mobbed at the clinic just now. I can try come over about 11 with some Imodium? X

I huffed frustratedly at my phone and began typing back.

My interview is at eleven! I can't do it. I'll have to cancel. X

Shut up and stop this! I will get Raj to drive me to the hospital before your interview. You can do this! You have studied so much. Get ready and I'll see you soon xxx

301

I breathed out a long sigh and sat up on the bathroom floor. She was right. I could do this. No bout of ring sting was holding me back.

Around ten I was finally all out of fluids, and my trips to the toilet slowed as what felt like my entire body was emptied. My mouth felt as dry as dust but I couldn't risk even a sip of water. *Was it just nerves?* I wondered. Or maybe the spicy chicken pizza I'd had the night before? Regardless, I had to go on. After cooling my arse with a bundle of cold, soaking-wet kitchen roll, I threw on my black knee-length funeral dress and a blazer and headed to the Royal Infirmary.

As I entered and walked through the doors of the hospital, Raj and Ashley stood waiting for me, looking concerned.

'You look like a ghost!' Ashley said.

'Thanks,' I replied.

'She's right. You are very peely-wally,' Raj said. 'Here, take these,' he continued, handing me the diarrhoea tablets.

I swallowed two immediately.

'Have some water,' he said, passing me a bottle.

'Can't risk it,' I replied, clutching my throat as the tablets worked their way down. I could see Raj bite his lip, holding back a grin.

As we made our way through the old Victorian building, I was revisited by the familiar hospital smell of bleach. It felt good to be back. Nerve-wracking but somewhat comforting. But as we continued towards the lifts, I felt my stomach gurgle. *Oh God, no.* I paused, holding my tummy tight, praying to make it through the interview with my dignity intact.

'Zara!' a voice called out, and I turned to see Jason looking pristine in a suit.

'Hi!' I said as he approached us.

'Wow, one of you smells AMAZING!'

'Well, it won't be Zara.' Ashley chuckled. 'Molton Brown,' she added.

'How did you get on?' I asked, interrupting the pleasantries.

He seemed ecstatic and full of energy. 'So freaking good! I got acute appendicitis! Buzzing! My friend was in just before me, and she got kidney stones, and her friend was in on Friday and got a bowel perf. Have you studied all of them?'

'She has!' Raj said reassuringly, rubbing my shoulder.

'OK. Let me know everything! Call me tonight and fill me in, OK? You will be fine, babe!' Jason said, winking.

'Thanks, Jason. I'll let you know,' I replied, feeling the intensity bear down on me.

'See you guys later.'

He waved us off, and we headed upstairs.

I was sitting outside the interview room at ten forty-five with Raj and Ashley by my side. My right leg was jumping up and down uncontrollably.

'Breathe, Zara. You know your stuff,' Raj said quietly into my ear.

I managed a brief smile back at him and faced the floor.

'Has your stomach settled, babe?' Ashley asked.

'I have nothing left inside me to shit out. I feel so drained.'

I noticed Raj and Ashley share a worried glance with one another, and I sat up.

'I'll be fine, though,' I said.

I heard the tapping of high heels walking across the floor and turned to see a woman dressed in a grey fitted suit.

'Joseph Fairly?' she called out.

A young man sitting opposite us stood up confidently and walked behind her.

'Do you know him?' I asked Raj.

Raj shrugged. 'I recognise him. Don't worry. Right now, you have just as much chance as anyone else, OK?'

'Yeah, thanks.' I smiled back at him but my stomach twinged once more. 'I think I need the toilet.' I moaned as another sweat attack loomed.

Raj winced sympathetically. 'There's one down the hall.'

I hurried towards the singular bathroom and sat down immediately.

I remained there for a few minutes, squeezing and sweating until the cramps passed, but nothing came. *Why is this happening today of all days?* Finally, I stood up, washed my hands and walked back to the waiting area just as Joseph, the other candidate, passed me in the corridor. He looked intense and upset as he marched out of the waiting area.

Raj was standing up as I re-entered. 'Everything OK?'

'False alarm.' I sighed, sitting back on my chair.

'Good, maybe the Imodium is working.'

'Did you see that guy leave, Zara? He was only in for like five minutes. I thought he was going to cry. This shit is fucking intense!' Ashley butted in, scrutinising the situation nervously.

I turned to her, ready to thank her for her encouragement, when I heard a woman's voice call out my name.

'Zara Smith?'

I stood up.

'Come this way.' She gave me a brief smile and began walking.

I turned to my friends. 'Here goes. Any last words of wisdom?'

'Stay calm, breathe and think logically. You know your scenarios. Go smash it!' Raj replied, briefly hugging me.

'*Emm* . . . I don't know. Good luck, obviously, and . . .' Ashley thought hard and gasped. 'Don't fart! They say never trust a fart. And today, of all days, you should NOT trust one.' Ashley burst out laughing as Raj joined in, and I shook my head at the pair of them.

I steered down the corridor, glanced back at my friends watching me and grimaced.

'You got this!' Ashley reassured me, giving me a thumbs up.

'Good luck,' Raj mouthed quietly, followed by a wink.

I walked quickly to catch up with the lady, who had paused outside the hospital's offices.

'I'm Isobel, Head of Recruitment here at the Royal. There will be three other interviewers on the panel, but don't worry. Take your time and try to relax,' she said.

'OK. Thanks.' I could hear my voice shake and immediately cleared my throat.

She smiled and turned the door handle to one of the rooms.

'After you,' she said as she opened the door, and I stepped in first.

Chapter Thirty-Two

The room was bright compared to the dark hallway. It had large old-fashioned windows and one long table in the centre. I noticed Anne sitting at the table immediately along with two others, and a single chair sat opposite them. Isobel shut the door behind me and joined the panel.

'Please, take a seat, Zara,' she said, ushering me to sit down.

I felt slightly dazed by the light and the interrogational way the room was laid out. My head was dizzy with nerves and dehydration.

'Yes, sure,' I replied, sitting down and facing the group.

'Last but not least, we have Miss Zara Smith,' Isobel started. 'Is that correct?'

'Yes.' I cleared my throat. I glanced up to Anne who remained incredibly stern-faced.

'And you are applying for the new advanced nurse practitioner post for surgery? Yes?'

As she said the words aloud, I felt my gut wrench. *Why the fuck am I here?* I felt out of my depth. But it was too late.

I cleared my throat again. 'That's correct.'

'OK, well, we will begin. As you know, I'm Isobel Reilly, Head of HR.'

I smiled back, acknowledging her.

'I'm Bill Bridges, Site Head of Surgery,' the man sitting next to Isobel said.

'Elise Cran, Accident and Emergency Consultant.' A pretty young doctor smiled warmly at me.

'And you know me already, Zara. Senior Charge Nurse to Surgical,' Anne said quickly.

'And I'm Zara Smith, Registered Nurse and Aesthetics Manager. Nice to meet you all.'

There was a brief silence in the room, and I noticed a stare between Bill and Anne.

They know who you are, Zara. Why did you say that?!

'Very well.' Isobel began. 'I'll explain how this interview will work, Zara. First, we'll give you a short scenario, and we'd like you to tell us how you would assess the patient, what examinations you would perform, what tests you may order, and, finally, what your professional diagnosis would be. And then we will ask you a few questions about this post.'

'OK, that's fine,' I replied nervously.

Please be appendicitis. Please be appendicitis.

'You are working a night shift and have been called to the surgical wing by one of the nurses. A patient is three days post hip replacement. She was being observed closely as she had hotness around the wound site travelling down her leg post-procedure. The patient had been reviewed that day and was getting treated for a wound infection with the appropriate antibiotics. But the nurses have alerted you tonight as she has dropped her oxygen saturation and is struggling to breathe.' Shit, I hadn't even thought about revising for post-op procedures. *Why hadn't I thought about post-op!* Anne finished and sat back in her chair, keeping intense eye contact. *Stop panicking, Zara. Just speak.*

I tried to gulp down but my throat felt incredibly dry.

'OK. Well, I would go to the ward . . .'

'I should think so.' Anne chuckled under her breath.

I shuffled in my seat, feeling my body stick to it underneath.

'Yes, I would look at the patient's medical notes from earlier that day. I'd examine the patient's observational chart and look for any changes from her earlier review.' I looked at Anne.

'The nurses have an emergency and are short staffed, so they haven't had time to do a full set of observations, but I have already told you she can't breathe.'

'OK, then I would introduce myself to the patient and carry out my own observations by doing a full NEWS on her,' I answered, knowing the patient would need to be scored on the National Early Warning Score to recognise how far she had deteriorated.

'You would do your own observations? As a senior nurse?' she questioned.

'Erm . . . no . . . *yes*. I'm not sure,' I admitted, feeling clammy and shaky.

Shit, shit, shit. I want to go home. I can't do this. I closed my eyes briefly as my head scrambled with insecurities.

309

'Come on, Zara. Just breathe. We all know interviews are horrible, but you were invited here because of your great application. You can do this.'

I opened my eyes to see Elise smiling towards me, nodding her head in encouragement. I took a long deep breath. *I can do this.*

'Yes, Anne,' I said, looking straight at her. 'I would do my own observations because I am a nurse, and that's what the patient needs. I would then do a full top-to-toe, A-to-E assessment. I'd listen to the patient's chest and order a chest X-ray.'

'What is your initial instinct regarding what's wrong with the patient?' Bill asked.

I felt flustered again. 'She could be septic, given they are treating her for a wound infection? But, she could also have a chest, urine, or wound infection. All common post-operative. I would take bloods and blood cultures and swab the wound if it hadn't been done already.'

Bill agreed.

'OK, so bloodwork is fine. Chest X-ray and urine dip all clear. All infection markers are stable, but she now has severe chest pains,' Anne said.

'I would give her analgesia, do an ECG, send a Trop-T and reread the medical notes to see if she had a doppler of her leg.'

'A doppler for a wound infection?' Anne laughed.

'It could be a pulmonary embolism. She could have had a DVT post-surgery, and the clot could have travelled to her lungs,' I replied, feeling exhausted.

'Therefore, the consultant and the numerous doctors who reviewed this lady would have missed this for what . . . three days?' Anne questioned me, raising one eyebrow to the sky.

'It's possible.' I shrugged, not knowing what else I could bring to the table.

'So, they haven't done a doppler of the leg, and her ECG looks normal. Her troponin level is normal. What test would you do, Zara?' Elise asked with a slight smirk.

'I would run a d-dimer and order a CTPA. I would also check the patient's blood gases as her oxygen requirement has increased and phone the consultant on call to discuss my plan.'

The four panellists shared glances with one another.

'We got there in the end. You're right. It *was* a pulmonary embolism. Well done, Zara. Correctly diagnosed,' Anne muttered.

'And how would you treat a PE out of interest, Zara?' Bill asked.

'Blood thinners. I am not a nurse prescriber, so I would consult with the on-call medics and ask them to prescribe it for me,' I replied, feeling slightly relieved the first part of my interrogation was over.

'Is that something you would be capable of? Prescribing medications?' Bill continued.

I laughed under my breath. 'Well, not just now. But, with the right training, I would be. That's what I'm hoping for.'

He briefly smiled back and took some notes.

'Moving on now, Zara. It's time for the non-medical section of the interview,' Isobel began. 'What brought you into nursing in the first place?'

'Erm, well, my mother is a nurse. I loved hearing her stories when me and my sister were growing up. How she helped people. I remember one day in particular when we were out in a restaurant, an elderly lady approached us and began chatting with my mum. My sister and I were oblivious and carried on with our meal, and when she left, my mum's eyes were watering. I asked if she was OK, and she said of course. She explained it was a patient's wife she once looked after who remembered her. So, when it came to paying the bill, the waiter said it was already taken care of. We were all so confused, and he said the lady paid for it because my mum held her hand during the worst moment of her life, and she'd never forget it. That really touched me. I wanted to have an impact like that. To help and care for people. Not just the patients but their families too. That's the first time I really thought that I wanted to be a nurse.'

I looked up, and the four interviewers were still.

'That's lovely, Zara. Good answer,' Isobel replied.

'I've never had a free meal,' Bill admitted as the others giggled, breaking the tension.

Anne sighed. 'I'm glad. It's not very ethical, is it?' she said.

I felt my body stiffen back on the chair.

'Moving on. Can you think of any negative sides of this job?' Isobel continued.

I sat up, guessing hard. This was my dream job. I'd wanted something like this for as long as I could remember. So what could I say that was negative despite having to work with torn-face Anne some more?

'Erm . . . no. I don't think so,' I replied, feeling hesitant.

'What about coping under pressure? As Elise said earlier, your application is excellent, but we have noticed you haven't worked in the acute setting for a while. Do you think you will be able to adjust to the pressure when you are responsible for calling the shots?'

The room felt very serious again. I paused, unsure how to explain.

'I hope I would. I mean, with the right training, I think . . .' I began, but Bill interrupted.

'Some of the candidates have acute, advanced training already, Zara, and it looks like you have just been injecting people's faces in a beauty salon for over a year, not having one single shift on record working in the hospital. So how would you feel in an emergency situation again? And I mean a real, life-threatening, emergency situation, not that one lip is slightly unsymmetrical as you're used to in your field.'

I felt the blood drain from my face. Why did I think I could do this?

Speak, Zara, speak!

But my mouth was dry, as that was precisely what I had been doing for the past year. I didn't know what to say. I wanted to put him straight and tell him exactly how I'd cope, but his mind seemed already made up.

'Yes, I understand if that's how you see it, Bill. But, I cope well under pressure and, for the record, I'd never leave a patient with unsymmetrical lips.'

Isobel closed her notebook. 'Very well. That's all we had to ask you, Zara. Thank you so much for coming today,' she said.

My head swivelled, observing a disappointed look on all four of their faces.

'You should hear by the end of the day if you are successful,' she added.

I stood up from my chair, noticing the sweaty silhouette I had left behind. 'Thank you for your time, all of you.' I smiled politely and headed out of the room.

Anne shook her head sternly as I pulled the door shut behind me.

What the fuck is her problem? I thought. Why did I let Bill speak to me like that? He had no idea how hard it was to run a clinic. I looked at my trembling hands. *I've blown it. I've blown all of it.*

I panted for breath in the corridor, still feeling furious at Anne's unwarranted frostiness towards me. *I am a good nurse and I don't want that woman to belittle me anymore.*

I paced the floor, reliving the interrogation.

How dare she speak to me the way she had, as if I was some silly wee lassie with no clue.

I felt a surge of rage build from my feet, thinking how hard I had worked to make Individualise grow and succeed. How I'd coped under the pressure of rebranding that place and putting it on the map worldwide. Then, without thinking, I marched back up the hallway and burst open the door.

The four of them were huddled together in some form of discussion.

'Zara.' Isobel gasped at the intrusion.

'I'm sorry. I'm sorry I've just burst in like this, but I need to defend myself, Bill. *Yes*, I haven't worked in the hospital for a while now, but I haven't been fannying around doing cosmetics. I have been running and managing the best aesthetics clinic in Scotland. I have learned and perfected intricate procedures that most doctors can't perform. I know every vein, nerve and artery that runs via the face and neck. Do you?'

There was a brief silence in the room. I could feel my face burn with bravery.

'I have learned from two of the top NHS surgeons in the field and work alongside them daily. As do you.' I stopped as my rant was coming to an end and pulled down my blazer. 'I know you may not consider aesthetics real nursing, but I can assure you all that I have studied incredibly hard, followed my code of conduct, and helped so many people this year. My boss is an incredibly gifted surgeon, and he chose *me* out of all the other doctors and surgeons to run his clinic because he knew I was the best. I am hard-working and caring, and I want to learn more.' I let out a huge sigh, feeling short of breath with defending myself. 'I know the other candidates have more experience, but I am good. I really am. And I'd work so hard making sure I was a success. I study, I practise. I am really hard-working.'

Finally, I stopped. The room was silent. Elise smiled towards me.

'I knew you as soon as you walked in, Zara,' she said. 'I recognised you from Instagram and TikTok promoting self-confidence and dealing with body issues, not to mention your work. It's pristine.' She turned to her colleagues. 'She's right. Zara is the best in her field.'

I felt a genuine smile appear for the first time that day.

'Can I see her recommendations?' Bill turned to Isobel and sat back in his seat as she shuffled through a folder and handed him a few bits of paper.

His eyes skimmed down the page.

'Your boss thinks you're the best practitioner he's worked with,' he said, raising an eyebrow. 'And I've worked many times with Raj.'

I found myself turning red at the unexpected compliment.

'And another candidate running for the same post has said you were his prodigy. Caring, compassionate, kind and his best student yet,' he continued reading as I blushed at Jason's reference.

'And this one got faxed through late last night, Bill.' Isobel handed him another page.

As Bill skimmed whatever was written there, his eyes widened.

Oh no, had Anne completed her recommendation after all? *Or my mum?*

Bill cleared his throat. 'I have known Miss Smith for many years and had the pleasure of working alongside her on the surgical wing a few years back.'

It must be Anne.

'Staff Nurse Smith is not only a kind, bubbly, caring and enthusiastic nurse. In addition, she is a quick learner and highly advanced in her current field. Miss Smith may be less practised in the acute division, but she has been pioneering the most pristine needle aesthetic work, going far beyond the expertise of any practitioner I know.'

I examined Anne's severe face. It couldn't be her. She had no idea about my aesthetics.

'With patient care driving her passion to keep learning and an overwhelming urge to help others, Zara Smith is far superior to all other candidates. Her most genuine trait is her kindness and natural, infectious way of lighting up a room. Miss Smith's desire to be the best person she can be separates her from all other candidates.

'But what Miss Smith doesn't yet recognise is that she is not only the best candidate for this job, not only the best nurse for the future of healthcare, but she is undoubtedly the best person I know. So, you'd be mad not to take her.'

I stepped back, full of confusion. *Who has written this?* Suddenly, my legs hit the back of the chair, and I fell onto it. I was overwhelmed.

Isobel, Elise and Bill looked at one another and laughed happily at my reaction. Even Anne smirked ever so slightly.

'Well, that was undoubtedly the best reference we've ever had, Zara,' Isobel said, breaking the silence.

Anne remained perfectly still, facing the floor.

'And the best arse-whipping. You certainly handed it to me, Zara. I'm sorry if I overlooked your specific field of nursing,' Bill said.

I nodded politely, not entirely taking it all in. I cleared my throat.

'Thank you all for letting me explain. And I'm sorry for coming back like that. I should go then.' I stood back up, feeling wobbly.

'I suppose you should thank Dr Adams for that glowing reference when you get out of here,' Isobel said, filing the paperwork away once more.

'Tom?' I blurted out before I could think twice.

'Sorry. Yes. Thomas Adams.'

My heart began to beat heavily in my chest.

Elise nodded happily towards me. 'Thanks, Zara.'

I turned slowly towards the door, feeling nauseous. *Why would Tom do this for me? I was the best person he knew? Why would he do this for me after Italy?*

I closed the door once more and held my face in my hands. My head was spinning.

I had so many questions. So much to say. From behind the door, I heard chairs being pushed back and quickly began walking back to the foyer.

'Zara! Wait, Zara!' I turned to see Anne walking towards me in her scrubs.

I held my hands up immediately. 'I know. I'm sorry for coming back like—'

'Why are you sorry?' she said. 'That's exactly what I would have done. It's difficult to speak up for yourself in front of superior ranks. It took guts. We want nurses who fight for their patients, and you fought for yourself in there.' Her words were kind, yet her face remained stern.

'Thank you,' I replied, somewhat speechless.

She turned back, ready to walk away.

'Anne, I'm sorry if you're angry that I didn't do shifts before this interview. I know you were trying to help me, and I noticed you were kind of . . . abrupt in there. I don't know if . . .'

Anne held her hands up, 'Oh, I'm abrupt with everyone, Zara. I didn't give you a reference because I haven't worked with you in a long time and if I was overly abrupt I apologise. It's just . . .' She considered her next words carefully. 'You frustrate the hell out of me, Zara Smith.'

I felt my mouth drop with shock.

'Oh. I didn't realise . . .' I replied back hesitatingly.

'Yes. Well, perhaps it's not something you can help. It's just that you are very good, Zara. Since you were a here as a student, you have this radiance that people warm to. You are kind, compassionate and a very good nurse. With good instincts. I could have moulded you to be a great nurse, yet you finished your training and shot straight back into aesthetics. Your head is in the clouds at times and it's somewhat frustrating.'

There was a brief silence between us.

'I had no idea you wanted me to stay on your ward, but I love aesthetics too, I love working with my friends.' I shrugged. 'But, I should have stayed here. This is where I want to work and I'm sorry it's taken me this long to realise, Anne.'

319

'Yes, well, just don't let me down this time, eh?' She pointed towards me. 'Welcome to the surgical team.'

'What? I got it?' Anne turned to walk away. 'Wait, Anne, *I got it*?' I screeched.

'You got it, Zara! You got it!' She turned back and winked at me, laughing.

'Because of Tom's letter? I got it because of his recommendation, right?'

Anne stopped and let out a frustrated sigh. She walked back, placed both hands on my shoulders and smiled.

'No. You got it because you had a great interview. You coped well under pressure, diagnosing and getting scrutinised for your decision-making. You stuck to your guns regardless. You showed great resilience coming back in, and the letter of recommendation just proved what we all agreed on. You are the right nurse for the job, Zara. *You* got yourself the job today. No one else. Now, please, don't let me down.'

I could feel my smile lift my cheeks with ecstasy.

'I won't, I won't. I promise,' I replied.

Chapter Thirty-Three

I ran back towards the waiting area, where Raj and Ashley were sitting in silence. Ashley's leg rattled, and her long acrylic nails tapped off the chair.

'Oh, for fuck sake, you were ages!' she yelled out when she saw me.

'How did it go?' Raj asked, standing up to greet me.

I was speechless. Not quite knowing where to begin.

'I . . . I . . . got the job!' I started to laugh as it sank in, and I felt my friends catapult towards me, wrapping their arms around me tightly.

'I knew you could do it, Zara! I knew you could.' Raj squeezed, and my feet lifted from the ground. 'How was everything? What did they ask?' he questioned excitedly, lowering me back down and finally composing himself.

'I got a post-op PE,' I replied, still gazing into space in disbelief.

'We didn't revise that one! Shit, I should have thought about complications.'

'Awk, who cares. She got it!' Ashley beamed. 'And everyone hates anything to do with PE anyway,' she added sassily. 'Auntie Zara got the job, baby!' She smiled to her bump.

Raj and I shared a humorous look at Ashley's reply, and we all began to laugh together.

'So, are we celebrating tonight? Drinks when Raj and I finish work?' Ashley looked keen.

'Yes, we should celebrate!' Raj replied.

'Well, you two can't drink, and my stomach or arse would not be able to handle a night on the town right now!' I laughed, gently rubbing my tummy.

'No! Zara!' Ashley moaned. 'We need to celebrate.'

I puffed, exhausted. 'Honestly, I could do with a night in to recover.'

'That settles it, then. We will come to you. But, first, I'll nab a takeaway from La Vita,' Raj suggested.

'We'll make it a Zara gets a new job and Raj's leaving us all over again and fucking off to Dubai type thing?' Ashley giggled.

'Sounds perfect!' I smiled. 'But I'm buying after that reference you gave me, boss!'

'Ahh! Did you read it? It's all true. No one could beat that one, Zara. It took me ages googling "*how to write the best reference*". I used all the buzzwords, you know.'

Ashley and I chuckled at his innocently kind comment.

'I can't even begin to tell you about the reference part of that interview. Let's save that for dinner?' I said. I'd need the rest of the day to digest Tom's letter.

'Deal! We better head, Ash. We have a busy afternoon at the clinic. And you look like you need to recover,' Raj added, putting his hand around my shoulder.

I nodded in agreement, and we began walking through the hospital and heading to the front door.

'I'm going to walk home. I need the fresh air,' I said as they steered towards the car park.

'OK, but keep your arse clenched just in case of an emergency!' Ashley joked before hugging me.

'I'll see you both tonight, around six?'

'If Raj talks a little less with his clients, we should be finished before then,' Ashley said, nudging his arm.

'See you tonight, Zara Smith ANP! Woo!' Raj winked, and I waved him and Ashley off.

As I made the short journey downhill to my apartment, I thought about Tom's reference over and over in my head. *Why would he do that?* Was he planning on returning and saving any awkwardness between us? Was this his olive branch so we could all move on? I'd watch him happily tie the knot and not care because I have a super new job? Maybe he wanted me to get the job so I'd work less with him at the clinic? I had no idea what his intentions were. I knew Raj had told him about it on the phone, but my head was whirling. I took a long, deep breath and shrugged, trying to let go of the tension in my muscles. I guessed I'd never know. I lifted my phone from my bag and decided to call my mum and Emily instead. I'd spent years analysing that man and his actions, and today I was happy to park him in my mind and just enjoy my accomplishment.

That evening after congratulating Jason on getting one of the posts as well, I watched *Grey's Anatomy* in my fluffy Primark pyjamas, hair tied up tightly in some sort of bun, and my hot-water bottle resting on my stomach. Finally, my gut had settled, and I managed to keep some toast inside me for longer than three seconds. I was tired, but I felt amazing. Here I was, lying in my clean city apartment, just washed and comfortable, knowing I had landed my dream job. I was sobbing, getting caught up with the ever-evolving emotional drama of *Grey's* while mentally taking notes, wondering when I'd be carrying out emergency procedures like Meredith and Christina.

Just after five, my buzzer rang. I leapt up, looking forward to a night in with my best friends.

'I knew you would get away early!' I giggled through the intercom, opened the door, and walked back to the sofa.

As the footsteps grew closer, I called out, 'Hurry up. You're letting the heat out!'

I heard a laugh and then a deep voice.

'I am strangely enjoying the coolness of Scotland again.'

My heart pounded in my chest.

I darted to the door and saw a tall, dark figure in the hallway.

'Hello, Zara,' Tom said.

I tried to speak, but nothing came out.

'Eh . . . hel . . . hell . . . Tom?' I mumbled.

'Can I come in?'

I felt my head bopping up and down without even thinking about it. He entered the apartment and shut the door.

'What are you . . . why are you here?' I asked, immediately self-conscious about my fluffy PJs and pale face. I walked back to the sofa and sat down, feeling my legs wobble with panic.

'I wanted to see you.' He shrugged his shoulders and walked towards me. He wore a smart black shirt, trousers, and a dark trench coat. I watched it glisten with rain as he came closer.

I tried to remain calm.

'Well, how did the interview go?' he asked, pulling his coat in as he joined me on the sofa.

My eyes widened. '*Erm* . . . yeah . . . good. I got the job.'

'Congratulations.' His perfectly symmetrical smile lit up the room.

'Thanks, and thank you for the reference, by the way. That was . . . unexpected but really . . . *emm* . . .'

'It was nothing,' he said.

The space between us turned quiet, and I could only hear the sirens from the major trauma happening on the TV echo between us.

'How have you been?' Tom asked.

I laughed slightly, thinking of how awful my life had been recently, and the last time we'd seen each other.

'I'm fine now,' I said, not ready to delve into it all. 'And you?'

'I'm fine now,' he replied, attempting to keep eye contact. I looked down, flustered, avoiding it at all costs. 'Great news about Ashley, eh?' he said.

'Tom, look, you don't have to do this. All this small talk. It's not like you, and I'm OK now, honestly. No hard feelings and all that. I'm so sorry for everything, but can we draw a line under it all? I should never have turned up to your party like that. And I can't even put into words how sorry I am about that picture. But I had no idea. I was drunk and hurting.' I sighed, not prepared to look back on the past few weeks after finally getting myself better, 'Can we just forget the past few months?' I felt my heart rate begin to pick up again.

'Oh. Yes, I see.' He smirked slightly, raising his brow.

'Are you back now?'

'Yes.'

'OK.' I was processing the information slowly. 'That's OK.'

Tom smiled. 'Zara?'

I was looking at the floor again.

'Zara?'

The way he said my name made goosebumps run up my spine. Slowly, I glanced up at his dark brown eyes.

'I'm back for you,' he said softly.

I paused for a second, waiting on something else. I wasn't sure what. But I remained still.

'I'm back for you,' he repeated, so calmly.

'You are taking the piss, right?' I laughed, stunned at his words.

'I'm not. No.' He seemed slightly taken aback as he adjusted himself on the sofa.

'After Italy? After me making a complete fool out of myself? Out of you. You're back for me. *Now?* Tom, do you realise how crazy this is?' I couldn't comprehend his words. I was shaking my head, not wanting to listen to any more bullshit.

'Zara, I know . . .' He reached over for my hand, but I stood up.

'No, don't touch me. You can't do this. You told me you didn't want me in Italy, and I've been a fucking mess, but now I've finally got myself better and you decide you want me again?'

Tom placed both his hands on his head.

'This must be a joke. You are engaged!' I felt my voice rise as I got angrier at his presence.

'I've always wanted you, Zara! Do you not see that? You chose Andy, then came to Italy and fucked my head entirely. That night after the party, I told Quinn I couldn't do it. I told her I wanted you. But it wasn't that easy. The media were hounding us after that picture, and it all got so chaotic.' He stopped and pulled down his shirt as I could see him get more frustrated. 'I was fucking enraged by you telling me you wanted me, then half an hour later shacking up with the security guard! Do you know how that felt?'

'You were engaged and basically told me to bolt!' My voice grew even louder as I defended myself.

'I finished it with Quinn the same night!' He called back, matching my tone.

'Wait . . . No, wait. You're trying to tell me you broke things off with Quinn the night of your engagement party?' I screwed my face up in disbelief. 'Well, why has it taken you a fucking month to come back? Or even contact me? I have been ill.'

'I needed time, Zara. Quinn deserved time too,' he said, sighing heavily. 'When I picked Harriette, I saw how much it hurt you, and I wasn't going to do that to someone else. We went on some holiday retreat afterwards and I sorted myself out. We also had some financial things to get in order, but we were over from that night.' Tom raised his hands in the air. 'I had no idea what to do,' he continued, his voice soft. 'I thought about moving down south, starting all over again. But everything came back to not wanting to lose you.'

'I won't. I can't,' I replied, feeling tears stream down my face.

'You can't?' He looked up at me with blurry eyes.

'I can't lose *myself* again, Tom. I've just got me back.' I felt my chest drop.

'I spent weeks analysing the mistakes we've made, Zara. We have never given ourselves a fair chance at this. There were always so many obstacles. So many people involved. Raj, Ashley, Harriette, Andy, Quinn, a fucking green Martian guy. But we always come back to one another.'

I felt my bottom lip tremble. 'You broke my heart, Tom.' I began crying loudly and shut my eyes. I felt his warm body press against mine as he wrapped his arms around me.

'I'm sorry,' he whispered.

'I'm sorry too,' I replied.

'No, I'm sincerely sorry about Harriette. I'm sorry I didn't fight for you with Andy. I'm sorry I didn't leave Italy with you. But, Zara,' he paused, 'everything I wrote in that note was true, I can promise you I am not going anywhere.' I could hear his heart beating loudly in his chest as I lay my head against it.

I broke away from his embrace, not allowing myself to be sucked in all over again.

'I've spent the past few weeks in a retreat learning about myself, and Zara, our timing has been off! I struggle to communicate what I really want with you because I'm afraid to lose you. I don't tell you in case you leave me again, and I can't bear to not have you in my life. I stayed quiet with Andy because, well, at least I still had part of you every day at the clinic. When I wrote you that note I meant every word, and I thought you read it that same night, and that's why you came to my apartment after dinner. But, you still chose Andy and I tried to move on.' He paused for a second, catching his breath.

'When you came to Italy to tell me how you felt I dismissed it because I was scared. That's what I do, Zara. I walk away or give a cocky, smart-arse answer when anyone puts me a serious situation, but I don't want to do it anymore. Being away from you has been the worst time of my life, constantly wondering if you had reconciled with Andy or if you bloody hated me. But, I had to heal and learn. I had to understand why I do the things I do to be the best man I can for you. And now I'm here and I truly believe this is it. If you still want it?'

I shook my head.

'You can't go on a retreat and change overnight, Tom. I'm sorry. We had a good time but we can never make it work. It plays out the same way in the end. I'm glad you've healed, or whatever, but maybe you just—'

'Zara, every time I closed my eyes on that beach I thought of you. I pictured your face walking into the clinic with your hair blown all over the place, or you slurping your food and spilling it down yourself. I thought of your sparkle, how anyone who meets you immediately wants to become your friend because everyone feels better being around you. I thought of you being a student in the hospital and texting your colleagues each morning on your day off to find out how the patients were. You are the kindest person I know. I thought about how we spent the nights turning Individualise around and seeing you so passionate and excited that it gave me butterflies and made me do better. You make me a better person, and I've thought about no one else since I left, because there is no one else for me.'

My heart felt like lead hearing the words I had hoped for since the moment I had met Tom Adams years before, but I still couldn't let go. There was always going to be a wall when it came to him.

'I can survive without you, Tom. I have a great job and friends. I can survive fine without you,' I said, unwilling to re-enter the darkest stage of my life, questioning his every intent and wondering if he would feel the same way a few months down the line.

'Why settle for surviving when you can live? Really live with someone who adores you.'

I shook my head.

'We'll find a way to fuck it up. We always do,' I said, walking backwards.

'Not this time. Let's go all in, Zara. No fucking around this time. We need to let go of the past and try this properly this time. You and me?' He came closer. His dark brown eyes were filled with tears. 'I love you.' His voice was soft and tender.

I felt my body quiver, and I stopped moving.

'I love you too,' I replied quietly.

He approached me, raised my chin to face him, and I looked at him properly for the first time since he'd got here.

I shut my eyes as he kissed me.

A soft, caring kiss. I leaned into it, and it felt like the world had stopped.

I had lost all control.

'You have no idea how much I've thought about your lips,' he replied.

I wiped the snot and tears from my face as he smiled, watching.

'Please say yes. Please tell me you still want me, Zara?' Tom's deep voice asked with uncertainty.

I looked at the man I had fallen in love with years before. Our journey flashed before my eyes. My first day encountering him, back when I was the scruffy student nurse with unironed shirts and last night's make-up on, how perfect and accomplished he'd seemed. Our flirty conversations at work. I thought about our first date having a picnic at his clinic and how magical it was – then seeing him in the hospital, caring for his patients and sharing fleeting, stomach-curling smiles across the desk. It was all so light and exciting. I adored him. I remembered how he spent hours with me turning Raj's clinic around together, championing my ideas and encouraging me every step of the way. *How when he encourages me, even when the task seems too much, he talks about it, and makes anything seem possible with his support. I smiled thinking of how much we laugh together, like properly laugh at the most inappropriate jokes and humour, but ultimately how he understands me. With no added pressure. How he knows me, the real me, scruffy hair, and messy Zara, yet doesn't judge. He doesn't want to change me. He loves my imperfections. He loves me. And then I realised, I wanted this. I want him.*

'Tom, I have wanted you every second of every day since the moment we met,' I said.

A look of relief washed over his face. He held me tightly in his arms.

'And are you all in, Zara? No fucking around this time. To really try this?'

I paused for a second, realising I had never been all-in before. I wanted to leap, but I was afraid. I'd always had my safety net. My *what ifs* planned out just in case. I took a little step backwards, trying to take it all in.

'Zara?' He sounded confused as I distanced myself.

'Wait, just wait,' I replied, completely overwhelmed. He watched me pace the floor.

'Tom, I don't know what I want in life. I don't know if I want kids or marriage or anything that normal people should want. I wake up in the morning and eat crisps or fucking Ferrero Rocher for breakfast, and I don't go to the gym or wash my clothes anywhere near as much as I should.'

He stood still, looking unfazed.

'I just really don't think I want kids, probably not ever. I want a good job and friends and a nice life,' I admitted guiltily.

'I don't know if I want them, Zara. And that's OK, to not know.' He paused. 'But, I know I want you. And if that means we have no babies or one hundred then we deal with that at the time, together. But, I'm standing here for you, not your bloody womb.'

I laughed a little as he smirked at me.

'I want to trust you. I want to trust myself. But what if it doesn't work?' I asked.

'But what if it does?' he said, and a fleeting smile passed over my face. 'Could you live with the regret of not trying?'

In that moment, I knew: I couldn't. I really couldn't.

I walked over to the coffee table and reached for my phone.

'Zara?'

'Just one second.'

No more second guessing. No more scrutinising every fucking situation. I needed to give this a shot. I scrolled through my apps with determination until I reached Tinder.

Name: Zara Smith
Age: 31
Location: Glasgow
Interested in: Males
Zodiac sign: Leo
  Biography: Hi, I'm Zara! Manager of an aesthetics clinic in the centre of town. Laidback and up for a laugh. Hit me up if you like cocktail dates and aren't looking for anything serious!

I continued to scroll until I reached the bottom of the screen and took a deep breath.

Account – deactivated.

I looked up towards Tom Adams and smiled.

'Now I'm all in. Let's do this properly, Tom.'

That night Raj and Ashley joined us for my celebration as planned. They shrieked and screamed, surprised to see Tom sitting on my sofa as they walked in. When we explained how we would try this whole romance again properly this time, my friends cried with happiness and exhilaration for Tom and me. Finally, we laughed together, enjoying each other's company as a group for the first time in what seemed like forever.

We sat around my living room sharing the best Italian food in the city, giggling hard, fighting over garlic bread and reminiscing about the best few years of our lives together – four entirely dissimilar people who had battled their own journeys of love, humiliation, motherhood, travel, and friendship.

As we debated and dramatised recent events while catching up with one another, we all shared an under-lying realisation that our group dynamics were about to change forever. Ashley was approaching maternity leave and embracing her own wee family unit. Raj was about to leave and return to his in Dubai, and my new dream job was starting in a few weeks, just as Tom had returned; refreshed, reliable, and for good this time.

I smiled more than ever before, appreciating my friends that night. Over the years, we'd developed an unwavering bond of pure love and admiration for one another. We'd cried together in the darkest moments but ultimately fought harder for each one of us to succeed, and we had.

So, it seemed only fitting that we all got our happily ever after in the end, right? And, hey, even if things didn't go to plan, I knew we'd always have each other.

Acknowledgements

I want to thank my fantastic publishing company Orion for encouraging me to continue to write this third and final book on Zara's escapades. An enormous special thanks to the lovely Rhea Kurien, who has filled me with confidence throughout the process. I know I sing your praises a lot, but I'm really not going to stop! I'm so pleased you found me as a self-published author and took a chance to sign my raunchy Scottish novels! You are a huge part of the success of this trilogy. You have provided me with unique ideas for this novel, helped with my one hundred questions per week, and enabled me to navigate the crazy book world, and I will be eternally grateful for it. Also, a special thank you to Sanah Ahmed for all your assistance over the past few years, Yadira Da Trindade and Frankie Banks for your excellent work and ideas behind promoting my books, and the rest of the team at Orion. You are all superstars, and I'm so appreciative of your work.

I'd also like to thank Elliott Fillingham for his support and guidance throughout the year. You go out of your way to help in every aspect of this journey, and it doesn't go unnoticed. Since we met, I can honestly say I feel much more supported and no longer feel like I am doing this alone. Thank you for all your input, business brains and continuous reassuring late-night texts when I'm having a moment. Even when others said my writing was 'too erotic', you still seemed to stick around. Ha! You have taken an enormous weight off my shoulders this year, and I will be forever grateful to you. And also, a sincere thanks to John Kerr for introducing us. Thanks, John, for buying my books, sending them to your pals, and finding me the best people to work with! You're one in a million.

To the fabulous Rosie McCafferty for proofreading my third book! What a journey we have had! I honestly don't think I could even contemplate writing a book without your advice and incredible ideas that add so much to these novels! Thank you for always being on hand, and I can't wait to continue our work together. You have a fantastic talent, and I will be forever thankful for your contributions towards my books.

A special thanks to all the Waterstone staff, in particular the Glasgow branches, who promote the hell out of these books! I am so fortunate to have you fighting my corner. Special thanks to the fantastic staff at the Glasgow Fort branch, who have smashed the sales for my previous books! I still get goosebumps walking past and seeing my work on the window display; it is genuinely a dream come true, and I'm not naive to how much this has helped contribute to the success of my writing.

To my mum and dad for your continued support. For promoting and boasting about your best-selling author daughter (even when you're not allowed to read my books). I appreciate all your endless love and support. To Andy, Arlene, Les and Joyce. Thank you for helping my girls (including Wrinkles) and me while writing this book. I would never have the time to work in the hospital and write if it wasn't for all of you. Thank you for always being on hand with babysitting, dance runs, late-night dinners, doggy sitting, and even attending last-minute book events. Between all of your dedication to my family, I know this wouldn't be possible, and I am so thankful for your endless love and support.

To all my fantastic work colleagues and friends in Ward One, thank you for always promoting and bigging me up to the patients! When I see the eighty-years-olds reading my books, I know it's down to you guys! I am so grateful to be part of such a fantastic team, from nurses to porters, to clinical support workers to domestics and medics. You guys are so supportive of my writing, and if it weren't for the positivity and endless hours of banter throughout our long-ass shifts, I wouldn't have found it possible. Special thanks to Maggie Donnelly, my work bestie, who is my biggest fangirl and biggest supporter! I know I put you through a traumatic experience in Benidorm, but I promise it was all in the name of author research!

To my very best friends, Emma Mcauley, Lisa Scott, Sarah Scott, Lisa Murphy and Michelle Patterson. Thank you for your dodgy dating stories/anecdotes that keep me in this job! I couldn't have gotten through the past year without your daily encouragement and motivational reminders. You are the first to know any news, and I value your painfully honest opinions, from Tinder swipes to contract reviews! You guys are the Ashley to my Zara and the true soulmates of my life. I love you all from the bottom of my heart.

And finally, to my two favourite people. The most enormous thanks to my smart, patient, kind daughters, Olivia and Grace. Thank you for setting aside the time in your lives to let me finish another book! We work as an incredible team, and I appreciate all the help you have given me during this time. I know it's been not easy when you asked for sleepovers or playdays with your friends, but many things went on hold because Mummy had to write. You don't seem to moan but accept all of this, and I am so lucky to have you.

This is our journey, and I couldn't ask for two better people to share it with. I love you to infinity and beyond, my gorgeous girls.

With love and eternal gratitude,
Sophie xx

Credits

Sophie Gravia and Orion Fiction would like to thank everyone at Orion who worked on the publication of *Meet Me in Milan* in the UK.

Editorial
Rhea Kurien
Sanah Ahmed

Copy editor
Jade Craddock

Proofreader
Suzanne Clarke

Audio
Paul Stark
Jake Alderson

Contracts
Anne Goddard
Dan Herron
Ellie Bowker

Design
Rachael Lancaster
Nick Shah

Editorial Management
Charlie Panayiotou
Jane Hughes
Bartley Shaw

Finance
Jasdip Nandra
Sue Baker

Production
Ruth Sharvell

Marketing
Yadira Da Trindade

Publicity
Frankie Banks

Sales
Jen Wilson
Esther Waters
Victoria Laws

Toluwalope Ayo-Ajala
Rachael Hum
Ellie Kyrke-Smith
Frances Doyle
Georgina Cutler

Operations
Jo Jacobs
Sharon Willis

Don't miss Sophie Gravia's filthy, hilarious and painfully relatable debut, *A Glasgow Kiss* . . .

A Glasgow Kiss [n.]

A headbutt or a strike with the head to someone's sensitive area

Meet Zara Smith: 29, single and muddling her way through life as a trainee nurse in Glasgow. With 30 fast approaching, she's determined to do whatever it takes to find love – or at least someone to sext! Cheered on by best friends Ashley and Raj, Zara embarks on a string of dating escapades that are as hilarious as they are disastrous. From online dating to blind dates, hometown hook-ups to flirty bartenders, nothing is off limits.

But when Dr Tom Adams, aka Sugar Daddy, shows interest, it's a game-changing moment. Zara has had a crush on Tom since her very first day at the aesthetics clinic she works at part time. As things heat up between them, Zara can't help but wonder: is this it? Or is it another disaster waiting to happen?

And follow up with the laugh-out-loud
What Happens in Dubai . . .

Everyone's favourite Glaswegian girl is back!

After having her heart well and truly broken, Zara Smith is more interested in fun than forever. But she's starting to wonder if she's slept with every (somewhat) eligible bachelor in Glasgow... and if there's such a thing as too much fun?!

With competition ramping up in Glasgow, Zara and her friends at Individualise can't pass up an opportunity to promote their aesthetics clinic - especially not when it involves an all-expenses-paid quick getaway to Dubai! It's THE summer destination for the sexy, rich and famous. Cue sun, sand and disastrous flirtations for everyone. But it's okay because once they get back to Glasgow, what happens in Dubai stays in Dubai, right?

Warning: this is NOT a romcom. It's dating in the 21st century and Sophie Gravia is about to give you all the toe-curling, cringe-worthy, laugh-out-loud details.